The
Jewish Ninja

By
Allegra Coleman

ISBN: 1499776845
ISBN-13: 9781499776843

Published by TPDS Inc.
Cover by Dolores Browne

Acknowledgements

While I was home recuperating from an illness, I discovered an excitement like no other. Most of my days were spent in bed, exhausted. The only way to keep from boredom was to drift into a wonderland by writing. When my fingers hit the keyboard, energy soared through my body, and though the doctors had limited my expectation of life to three months, vibrancy tingled from the souls of my feet to the top of my baldhead.

At the time of recuperation, the doctor's diagnosis had not been revealed to me. As I healed, my father proposed that I use one of his countless ideas to write a book or play. A story about a boy who joined forces with his rabbi to save the neighborhood by using his martial arts stimulated my curiosity.

Before I became ill, I was delving into a career as an actress in Los Angeles. My *Tae Kwon Do hyungs* (Korean martial arts techniques - see glossary for foreign words) also known as *katas* (the Japanese version) were a vital part of my warm-ups. That, coupled with my Jewish heritage and life long fantasy of heroically saving the world, made my father's idea perfect. The only problem was I wasn't a boy, nor did I ever imagine that I would think like one.

"May I make the protagonist a girl?" I asked my father.

"Do what you want," my father responded, and so I did.

It was a divine blessing that the doctors miscalculated my demise, because it only took me over twenty years to write this book. Granted, I have written many stories, plays, and articles during that time, but this novel was a never-ending delight that I couldn't seem to finish. Immersions into a myriad of excerpts, rewriting, continuous research, and life experiences took their toll. Acting, playwriting, illnesses, law school, law employment, creating and running an event business, later focusing on my amazing children and family, being hit by a car, a diagnosis of MS and more seemed to take precedence.

I have Patricia D. Netzley and the Longridge Writing Group to thank for giving me the encouragement I needed to finish this novel. Jennifer Burke helped me with typos that writers inevitably miss and Marlene Begg has been a blessing in helping with my final edit. Also, Master Paul J. Fasbinder from Pro Martial Arts was extremely helpful in fine-tuning my martial arts movements and terminology. I cannot thank him enough for taking the time to explain why specific gestures and motions made more sense than others.

Being Jewish did not help with my knowledge about Judaism. After all, decorating a Christmas tree, exchanging presents on the twenty-fifth of December, and running to Rittenhouse Square for Easter egg hunts were family traditions. The only reason I had a *Bat Mitzvah* was because it was the *in thing* to do. Thus, I crammed twelve years of Hebrew school into four months and forgot everything I learned after my big party. In fact, my Judaic knowledge didn't really begin until I was 26 and started scouring the Internet as research for this book.

It was my father who I must thank for sparking an idea and inadvertently giving me the opportunity to delve into a history I never knew. I also want to thank my mother who was my number one fan. She encouraged me and believed I had talent. Together, they gave me the ability that was necessary to strengthen the heart of my story, along with appreciating the unique, wonderful qualities people sometimes misinterpret. Without them, I don't know if the characters would have reached their depth.

It is through the love of my children, William IV and Amadeus that I was able to persevere. For it is their love and life that gave me strength through the harsh times that existence had to offer. Also, a quaint Judaic group on 17th Street in Philadelphia blessed me with enjoyable meetings about the Torah, and it is their guidance that began my quest for knowledge. Unfortunately, after over twenty years when I tried to find the group, they were no longer meeting. I cannot thank them enough for all of the information and kindness I received. My friends, Marnie and Moshe Narboni, have gone beyond what any friend could ask for in their teachings of conservative and *Hassidic* Judaism. These two people I hold dear to my heart. It is because of their *Shabbats,* holidays, and hospitality that a true sense of an *Hassidic* kosher home was revealed to me.

After I created the storyline that included *Turn a Cheek and Never Lose,* I found a web site called *Tora Dojo.* I give many thanks to the originator of this web site, Mr. Michael Andron PhD, for widening my thoughts in combining the martial arts and the Torah.

Also, I want to thank Rodeph Shalom for my ongoing education, and especially Jaime Murley for enhancing the *fun* in Judaism. My children now attend Hebrew School, and I join them in synagogue services. Rabbi Eli Friedman was a gem for helping me fine-tune the Yiddish and Hebrew words and phrases. It is through this divinely warm and trusting environment that my knowledge has grown and continues to blossom.

Last but not least, Fred Kogos's *A Dictionary Of Yiddish Slang & Idioms* and Yetta Emmes' *Drek,* along with my grandparents who are no longer with us, Lilly and Alexander Slakoff—they were essential guides for finding the perfect Yiddish word or phrase.

All whom I have listed above and those friends who have believed in me (you know whom you are), I cannot thank you enough for your encouragement.

From deep within my heart,

Note To The Reader

I've placed a small glossary at the end of this story that might help with some of the foreign lingo. There are various spellings depending on the source, so please bear with the selections I have chosen.

CHAPTER I

The Skunk

In our garage, I stood on the rims of my Reeboks, wiggling my head through a bunch of boxes, so I could get a glimpse at my dad's latest invention. My belly felt like a hip-hopper flip-flopping out of control. Finding out what new invention my dad was creating from that pile of junk next to his worktable was my objective. He had been hiding his latest gem for weeks and it wasn't fair that he wouldn't tell me what it was. Would it be anything like that robotic talking telescope he called Timmy? It stood slumped like a lifeless marionette lumped over in the corner. Its long skinny nose touched the cement ground, and the flat screen it wore for a hat flapped over its forehead covering its bulging iron eyes. The balls of my feet kept fidgeting in anticipation. As if he was reading my mind, his herculean body, sauntered toward the telescope. He plugged Timmy into one of the numerous outlets. Some sparks rocketed across the room and sizzled a big box filled with nuts, bolts and metal scraps. Our garage was suddenly celebrating July 4th. The robotic masterpiece danced the *Jerky* for a moment and then it hovered back into a lump.

I scanned the garage searching for Dad's newest contraption. There was a knitted blanket made up of bright ruby and yellow lilies. Lilies? He knew I loved lilies. Was that it?

"Don't think I can't see you spying on me through those boxes," he said still covering his head from the sizzling wires and smoke.

"I didn't want to disturb you," I answered as I tried to figure out how he could see me.

"You've got to be kidding. Alexia Bonet, you are a conniving little snoop; you just want a scoop for the school newspaper." He tussled my hair. "You've got it. It's here. And, you and Mom are going to be the first to witness its finesse." He picked me up and twirled me around. "Your bouncing curls are going to bound into knots when you see this one. Let's get Mom."

"You mean it works and you haven't shown us?"

"I was waiting for the perfect moment. You and Mom now get to witness my mechanical expertise at its heyday, and then I will give you the privilege of consuming my culinary creations." He straightened his back, lifted his chin, and brushed his lips against his fingers like a French chef.

I felt as though I was hurled into the middle of a sitcom. My dad's overdramatic flair always kept my brain level on high.

"Watch out! You're going to tangle your hair in that fan." I pushed him away from the rotating paddles.

"Man, can't I even bask a little in the triumph of my hard work." Then he looked up.

"That's what happens when you become overconfident," I said remembering a time when he had said those exact words to me.

"Touché," he said with a grin.

"You better tie your bushy mane over your head so Mom doesn't have a tizzy fit when she sips her soup and gets a strand stuck between her teeth." Then with a huge smile, I stuck out my tongue.

"Right back at you." He stuck out his tongue.

As I tossed my head from side to side, removing the hair from my face, my Dad mimicked me after he pulled his headband over long grey curls. His hairs swelled and curved like giant waves crashing on a beach. Everyone told me I looked like my mom, but my bushy bulk of curls were identical to Dad's. Mine were not silver though.

He grabbed his new project, concealed by a flowered quilt, and we sprinted through the garage door and called for Mom. When she appeared, he lifted his new device like a Greek God presenting an award on Mount Olympus.

"Abracadabra c-c-caboom, this will make our flowers bloom," he said as he lifted the blanket. A clump of colorful feathers rested motionless in the center of a birdcage. "Follow me."

We chased him as he rushed out into the cold brittle air. He unhooked the door to the cage. Still, there was no movement inside. Beeps began to chirp and a contraption crawled up his

2

arm. He pushed some knobs under its feathers, and like an eagle the mechanism lifted its wings and soared across our snow-covered fields—sandy dust floating from its butt.

"Fertilizer for the spring," he said, standing straight with his head held high. His cowboy lizard boots made him look even bigger than he was.

"As long as it doesn't fall on my head, Mr. Jelly Belly Genius," Mom said to Dad as she snapped some pictures, and then turned toward me.

"Alexia, better set the table for dinner. We've got a dinner guest - José. Oh Jelly, you might want to make sure your soup doesn't overflow."

Mom called Dad Jelly because when they started dating he brought her a grape filled doughnut every day after their 101 English classes. One time he forgot to give her the doughnut and she asked him where her "Jelly" was. He lifted the powdered cake from a paper bag. "It's been here for your taking." After that, she called him "Jelly" and they became an item.

"José? We don't know any Josés, and you never told me you were inviting a dinner guest during family time."

Uh oh, Dad hated when Mom invited guests during family time, except when his best friend Bill visited, sometimes with a date. I mean my mom did a lot of idiotic things, but I never got why Dad acted like a chimpanzee gorging on chili peppers when Mom asked someone over, especially men. Maybe he was jealous. This time he blamed it on her not discussing the issue with him. But, I think that was an excuse. He blew fire every time she invited a guy over, even when it was work related: maybe, because of that incident when Mom's old boss took advantage of Dad being out of town. You'll learn more about that later in the story, but the point here is that it was kind of sweet when Dad fawned all over Mom, but sometimes he went overboard.

"My Bonet Butternut Supreme is on simmer and I didn't plan on anyone joining us – certainly not any unknown named José. You could have at least asked me. We agreed weekends are only for family and *close* friends." Dad complained as he grabbed the mechanical bird and gave it a delicate shove into the cage. "That's been our agreement since Alexia was born."

"Calm down. You're going to break your bird." You don't need to get so hyper sensitive. José is Bill's partner and I just wanted to make sure your soup didn't burn. After all, your 'Supreme' needs to be savored not sizzled." Mom licked her forefinger, pointed it upward, and made an "s" sound while she twitched her hip to the side.

How she could flirt and smile in the middle of a fight with Dad was on the far side of lunacy. He was six feet four inches tall and bulky like a bull. His face swelled and eyes widened and he looked like he was going to charge. My gulp froze in the middle of my throat as I halted, expecting his steam to scald her. But, some how, some way, at five feet four inches, she chilled his fury. To her, his roar was a mere purr, and her cloak of words tamed him.

"You said, *'Any friend of Bill's is a friend of mine.'* Bill's out of town and he wants me to meet with his partner to go over my designs for an important meeting on Monday. Bill said José's a little eccentric, but a fun guy once you get to know him."

"Bill? My best buddy Bill Sanchez?"

My mom nodded her head.

"His partner's name is Bob."

"I know, but when I spoke to José on the telephone he explained that his real name is Roberto, and many people call him Bob, but José is his middle name and that's what he prefers to be called."

My parents were goofballs. Bob? Roberto? José? Who cared?

"Even if he says he's Bill's cousin, you never met the guy and you're inviting him into our home on family night."

"Cool it, Jelly. Tonight was the only time we could meet. You think some international spy is going to know Bill's cousin is supposed to call me?"

She had a point. Dad was neurotic when it came to his inventions. If Mom or I talked about his projects to anyone, he'd go berserk. When we went for strolls in town, someone would always give him a double take, and he'd start murmuring about spies and undercover agents like a crazy person. He had no clue that glances became stares because he was so tall and good-looking and when we tried to calm his angst by explaining this, he wouldn't listen.

I should've told him about all the girls in school who had crushes on him. Even my best friend, Tutti, said that he reminded her of the Greek God, Zeus. His big broad shoulders were accented by his sculptured face, which outlined his mass of hair that flopped all over the place. You couldn't help but be awe-struck. Why he focused on someone swindling his inventions was absurd.

On the other hand, he never had any questions about Bill's hourglass girlfriends visiting on our special night. Maybe he was a little sexist or really jealous because, Mom had a Miss America figure, heart-shaped lips, and entrancing sapphire eyes. When most men met her they couldn't stop looking at her. I'm not kidding. When Dad wasn't around, guys were always trying to talk to her and help her get things. They were like gnats gathering around an overripe plum. "Excuse me, can I help you carry that?" Or, they'd try and starts up a conversation about something stupid like, "Is that your sister?" But, for my dad to be jealous made no sense because Mom always softened like play-dough when she was with him.

I could never understand why he was so possessive. I mean did he actually think someone was going to kidnap Bill's cousin, impersonate him, and come up with a radical story about what he wanted to be called? His neurosis was crazy, but with his intense jade eyes, arched eyebrows, and fun personality, it was easy to ignore his idiosyncrasies. Plus, whenever he had an argument, it always seemed logical.

"Bob is supposed to be Bill's cousin. Isn't it weird that Bill doesn't call his cousin and partner by his preferred name? Plus, how long have we known him, and he never mentioned any José whatsoever?" His eyeballs darted upward and he scrunched his mouth. We headed for the garage where he dropped off his invention and went to the kitchen.

I wanted to pull my hair out. Why couldn't my parents compromise? They were so immature. Didn't Dad know that there was such a thing as a nickname? Why couldn't my parents compromise? Thank God, their squabbles never lasted or I'd have to be locked in an insane asylem.

"Jelly, it's just a short meeting and dinner. Bill begged me and there was no other time. Monday, when I meet with Bill, I'll ask him about José ...okay?"

"You could've told me. I don't want to waste this butternut squash soup on just anybody," Dad said with just enough time for him to bend down and spoon Mom a taste.

"Mmmmm... did you put some honey in that?" Mom's face relaxed and she let her lids dance.

One moment my parents were throwing spears and ramming horns and the next they were feeding each other s'mores. I never knew whether to hide behind a bush or try to find a stick to toast marshmellows.

The bell rang, and a sunken-cheeked man with greased-back black hair popped up on our security screen. The limp bouquet of flowers he held left a trail as he entered our house.

"Alexia, tuck in your shirt, and you've got some dirt on your face." She tried wiping the smudge off but I nudged her hand away and looked at my reflection. An inch from the looking glass, all I could find was a spec of dirt that I whisked away.

"Mrs. Bonet, eat ees goot to meet you. For a bootiful, taleented woman," he said with a thick Mexican accent as he wiped his nose with a handkerchief and handed Mom the wilted flowers. "Sorry about the rosees, but dee heat in dee car moost hab gotten too dem."

This guy's quick movements and exaggerated speech made me think of that cartoon mouse Speedy Gonzales. I imagined Dad being his nemesis, Sylvester the cat.

Mom took his coat, led him into our home, and filled a vase with water for the lifeless bulbs.

A booger bounced around his nostril. The pressure inside my cheeks made my curls coil because I had to conceal my laugh in order not to embarrass my mom.

"She's all yours," Dad said as he shifted Mom toward José and guided them towards her studio. "Come on, Alexia. We've got a feast to prepare." He pulled me, presenting all the fresh produce he had bought.

After I finished helping him place the final touches of his raspberry dressing on his goat cheese savory salad, and parsley on the seafood pasta à la Bonét, and Mom showed José her studio, we sat down for dinner.

"The washroom is behind that wall if you want to wash up," Dad said.

"I'm fieene, tank you berry much."

"Where did it go?" my dad mouthed to me as he crouched down, pointing his finger up his nose behind José's back.

I held my breath so I wouldn't giggle.

A scowl bolted from Mom over to us, with a quick smile back to José as she showed him his seat.

"Bill's going to be pissed if he finds out you were rude to his cousin," Mom whispered as she passed by Dad.

"So, ju are defeenatly a masteermine at createen stup. Maybee eet is a goot thin Beel mensioned ju to create someteen pour our mall," José said, sniffling into his hand and smearing his mucus on his shirt.

That's when this guy's endearing character came to a halt. He could've asked for a tissue or something. Totally gross.

"After all the scammers I've run into, this guy has got to be the worst. Your mom always falls for it. There is no way this guy is related to Bill," Dad whispered to me. "Even the magnificent aroma from my sauce doesn't cover the stink from this goon's cheap cologne."

"Excuse me, *Bob*. Could you pass some grated Parmesan?" Dad asked. José was too busy trying to gather his food on his fork with his knife. "Bob...Bob? Yo, José, could you please pass the cheese?"

"Oh escuse me. I eem so sorry. My ears are clogged from these terreeble allergees. Here ju go."

Towards the end of our meal, José excused himself so that he could go to the bathroom. He blew his nose in his hankie and wiggled his hips while walking away in his tight velvet pants. Dad and I looked at Mom with our eyebrows raised.

"If you look at the brand, they are Armani's." Mom's spine was taut.

"Most likely knock-offs." Dad shoved some pie in his mouth.

Get a grip. That's Bill's partner, and he knows a lot about architecture. Plus, I think he's kind of got an awkward cuteness," Mom said.

Mom was trying to sting Dad's attack, but he didn't flinch.

"Come on. Bill's got class. The closest this guy has come to any type of sophistication is wiping snot in his hanky, which I might add, he forgot to use."

I think Dad was the victor of this round, but his body began to slump when he noticed Mom's frown. For such a big guy, he was a major wimp. Then again, that's why he was so loveable.

"Whatever, honey. But, I'll make sure he didn't make a wrong turn. I'm still pissed at that tree trimmer who stole my patents for the Weed Dancer. He cost me a lot of money." Dad got up and looped around the corner.

I heard the rolling door to the bathroom bang against the wall and my father's boots pounding down the steps to the garage. The ruckus Dad created made my ears pop.

"What the hell do you think you're doing? Get your grubby paws off my things, you mucus-nosed moron!" Dad screamed.

Mom and I froze, and then we sprinted to the garage. We arrived just in time to see Dad pick José up by his collar.

"I joost was atmiring djoor tings."

Dad threw him to the ground. José tried to get up, but he placed his heel on José's chest. Mom started yelling for him to stop.

"You're lucky my wife has compassion, or I would ram this boot right through your snooping snout." He wiggled his foot in front of José's nose. "Don't ever forget about these crocodile skins, because they are going to chomp right through you if you come anywhere near my things again." Dad's contorted face turned blood red as he drove his cowboy boot through a pile of metal scraps, causing a thunderous crash. "Now get out of my house, you lying, good-for-nothing slime."

José ran out so fast that I doubt he realized his jacket caught on the switch that shut the garage. As it began to close, he banged his big, greasy head against it. He fell and rolled into the driveway before the door met the ground. Lifting the Canon camera from her belt loop, Mom snapped some pictures, then held her hands on her hips and glared at Dad.

"He had his dingy hands all over my stuff," Dad pleaded.

"That was Bill's partner and cousin."

"No way—he was an impostor," he protested.

"If you're wrong, you've got a lot of explaining to do on Monday."

"I'll take all the blame. Come on, let's not spoil our weekend." Dad grabbed Mom.

Her eyes threw daggers at his grasp, and he released his hand.

"How do you know he wasn't just admiring your inventions?" she asked.

"Because he was supposed to be taking a pee."

She was silent for a while. It seemed like she was contemplating what he had said. Then the side of her mouth shifted in agreement. "You better be right."

"Come on, let's finish dinner and have some pie on your new fancy furniture," Dad said.

We made our way towards Mom's stark, white, cardboard table set located in front of our sliding glass door—no kidding—actual cardboard. There was no way I could tell she had designed it for poor people. She had put some kind of finish on the material so it glistened in the moonlight like it was on the cover of some high-fashion magazine. Dad weighed over 200 pounds and none of the slats fell apart when he leaned on the table. The chairs didn't even wobble.

I went to bed early that night in order to be at my peak for my martial arts session with Master Luna.

***

At the end of my private tutoring class, we bowed and I turned toward the dressing room. Without warning, Master Luna placed his leg in front of my body and grabbed my arm. I spun around and jumped into a double kick with a loud yell, called a *kiyap*, causing him to fall flat on his face.

"You're ready," he said after he gained his composure, threw me a sly grin, and bowed.

"Ready for what, sir?" I asked as I bowed back.

"The Ming Black Belt Championship."

"But sir, isn't that the tournament where only champion black belts compete? I'm just a kid, a student. My Dad told me that only the best professionals participate."

"You're right, only the best black belts, from all over the world, are allowed to enter into Ming. You are one of them." Master Luna motioned me to relax. "It is the unparalleled that are and remain the best students and when a master enters a recommendation to the Ming Committee and the endorsement is accepted, that person, whether he or she is young, old or otherwise, is considered a professional and may compete at Ming. If you are under eighteen, and your application is acknowledged, all you need is permission from a guardian. My request for your admission has been approved, and your parents have given consent. You are now deemed an adult and ready to contend with the best."

I couldn't talk or move or do anything but bow, bow again, and then swallow some air.

"How would you like to do *Yeong-Wonhan Pyong Ahn* as your required *hyung* and we'll liven-up your free form pattern?"

"Yes sir," I said as I pictured a front flip into an axe kick, lifting my foot over my head, and ramming my heel down for a new move in my karate routine.

"We're finished for today. Now hurry up and get dressed. Your parents will be here any second."

As I changed my clothes I remembered my first day of karate with Master Luna.

"When you enter the *dojang* you should bow. It expresses respect for the studio," Master Luna said.

"My daddy says the place where you learn karate is called a *dojo*." I said.

"Sir," he commanded, raising his eyebrows with a smile.

"Ooops," I put my hands over my mouth.

Master Luna was staring at me with his eyebrows still arching upward.

"Ooops..." I said again as I straightened up and stood at attention. "Sir."

"That's better." Master Luna smiled.

"Sorry, Sir. I just don't know why Daddy called it a *dojo* and you didn't."

"Your daddy knows a lot and you are pretty smart for a four-year-old. *Dojo* is Japanese and *dojang* is Korean. In our school we mix the martial arts so either word is appropriate."

"Yes, sir." I said. "Sir, may I ask another question?"

He nodded for me to continue.

"Why does your *gi* snap so loudly when you chop and do your karate stuff? Mine doesn't do that, see." I kicked and punched hoping my uniform would make the same sound as Master Luna's. I looked up with a pout.

"Some people may say it is because my movements are swift and precise, but I'll tell you a small secret."

I smiled, nodding my head up and down with quick repetitions, and he bent beside my ear. "A lot of it has to do with the thickness of the material that my *dobohk* is made from," he whispered as he motioned me to feel the bulky material.

"And *dobohk* is Korean for *gi*," I stated straightening my back, a grin from ear-to-ear.

"Brainy and talented, we're going to have fun training together."

When I left the locker room and drifted to the front of the *dojo*, my eyes were glued to Master Luna as he glided across the floor. With the swiftness of a peregrine falcon he leapt over a sparring bag, ducked under a pile of boards that were lifted by mats, then punched and jumped into a spinning back kick. His crisp strokes sped through the air, springing each with a snap as though striking targets. Moving toward a bunch of thick boards stacked high and held between two blocks, he raised a muscular arm towards the ceiling. The resonating sound of a *ki-i-i-ya-a-ap* reverberated through the room, and his hand sliced through the stack as though he was splitting a Popsicle stick.

My parents honked their horn; I bowed and rushed to the door. When I passed the display of Master Luna's awards from all over the world, I peeked at the flyer that was posted on one of the windows. It had the information about the Ming Championship, and I saw that it was going to be held in two weeks—one day after my twelfth birthday.

***

For the next two weeks, if I wasn't doing pushups in our basement or in snow-covered fields, hitting and kicking the bag that hung from one of our trees behind our house, or karate-chopping any target I could find, I was at the *dojang* with Master Luna. Tutti, hung out with me and helped me train by holding the sparring bags and pretending to be my opponent—we were sure to mix intermittent snowball fights into the training. I thanked my lucky stars that it was winter vacation and I could train non-stop.

"A little break won't hurt you. Why don't you take a day off and Dad will take you and Tutti to see a movie—your muscles need a little rest," my mom said, interrupting while I was focusing on a new move.

"Mom, Tutti and I play in the snow and do other things, but there is no way I am taking that much time off my training. This will be the biggest day in my life. You just don't get it."

"It was just a suggestion. Your birthday's the day before the tournament. Don't you at least want to have a party?" Mom asked.

"Can you stop pestering me?"

"Sorry, I asked." She stepped backward.

I didn't mean to be bratty, but her pestering was getting on my nerves. She was clueless. I mean, this was an opportunity of a lifetime and instead of encouraging me, nothing I did was good enough. Master Luna expected me to be in topnotch shape and messing up was not an option. All I got from her was a sulky face that made me feel guilty.

"Why don't we do a small party with you, Dad, me, and Tutti and her parents? We can do a big celebration next year," I said.

"That's fine. I just wanted you to enjoy your winter break. I was going to have the Dancing Duo be the DJs and my mom and dad were excited about creating a new cake, in honor of you, from their bakery."

Tutti's eyes widened when Mom mentioned the hottest DJ's in our school. My lips tightened and I glared at Tutti, who then turned her head in a different direction.

"I'd love it if Bubbe sent a cake, and the Dancing Duo can come next year. I just don't want to be distracted right now."

"Whatever you want. It's your birthday," Mom said as she turned away.

"Alexia!" Tutti yelled as soon as my mom was out of sight.

"How many times have I bugged my mom to have the Dancing Duo DJs at one of our parties? Did she ever hire them? No. So, she waited until right before the Ming Tournament—she grates my nerves."

"Why didn't you ask her to have a belated party after your tournament? Your mom was just trying to be nice. I mean, the Dancing Duo are amazing."

"Yeah, I know. You're right. She just has such bad timing. I'll talk to her. My focus has got to be on my training until Ming. Master Luna has entrusted a huge responsibility on me, and I can't be distracted."

"Fair enough, but you really should give your mom a break. After all, she is the one who signed the agreement for Ming. And, Billy Bob actually sang at your last party and he's ten billion times better than the Dancing Duo. You're being a brat."

"Okay. I get it. I'll say something." My heart was racing as if I were on Highway 99 with no speed limit.

"Why don't you do your *heejungs*?"

I held back my laugh.

"You know, your routine where your chops and blows go into each other. The one that you made up for the competition is totally off the wall."

"Yeah, you're right. My *hyungs* always make me feel better." I tucked my body, flipping forward, and my right knee bent and shot out smashing the ball of my foot into an imaginary nose while my left leg drove backward shattering another opponent's ribs.

"At least getting mad at your mom inspires you," Tutti remarked.

"Yeah, just the aspirin I need to stop her from driving me loony."

***

Tutti and her parents came over on my birthday. While our parents chatted in the living room, Tutti handed me a huge black shiny package with a glowing green bow. Carefully, saving the ribbon, I then ripped the wrapping paper off the tightly bound present. The tape kept splintering, so Tutti zoomed in to help, and we tore the box apart. After clearing away all the bubble wrap and paper, I found something that I had desperately needed, headgear. Mine was beginning to wear. As I widened the head protection so it wouldn't squeeze my ears, I noticed *Alexia the Ninja* written in fancy embroidery.

"Your mom told me that this is what you wanted. I figured I'd add a personal touch. Happy Birthday!" Tutti said.

My red-haired, freckled-faced, alter ego held her arms out and dashed toward me, and we gave each other bear hugs. Then we continued to gossip and karate chop. Later, I blew out the candles and forked a teeny taste of the cake with a glass of milk. Everyone, except for me, enjoyed healthy helpings as we sat on Mom's cardboard furniture. Why my parents hadn't given me a present yet had passed my mind, but I was so preoccupied with Tutti and the Ming Championship that I forgot to say something.

"Come on, I've never seen you turn down Bubbe's Baron Booming Caramel Confection Apple Cake before. It's the best I've ever had," Tutti said as she fingered some icing into her mouth.

"You know I need to be in tip-top shape for tomorrow. Plus, we've never had Bubbe's Baron Booming Caramel Confection Apple Cake before, anyhow. Bubbe just created it." I elbowed Tutti. "I'll have some after the competition. You're going to be there, right?"

"I wouldn't miss it for the world."

***

The next day, my heart thumped as we searched for the gate where the contestants were supposed to enter and sign in. The stadium appeared to be endless. We made continuous wrong turns, and though it seemed as though every guard was giving us directions, I got nervous that we'd never find our way. I felt my heart beat in my temples. At last, we reached a sign that read *Contestants Only.*

"Are you sure you don't want us to stay with you?" Mom asked. "I'm sure they'd make an exception."

"Mom," I said, "It says 'Contestants Only.' Plus, I'm supposed to be an adult; otherwise they wouldn't have let me into the competition. You don't want me to be disqualified, do you?"

"She'll be fine." Dad waved as they left to find their seats.

I couldn't stop my feet from tapping in the long line as the man behind the desk checked IDs. Searching for Master Luna, I took many deep breaths and prayed for him to appear. He didn't.

"You must be Alexia Bonet, Master Luna's prodigy," a voice said. Looking up, the man at the front desk smiled at me. I nodded.

"Just sign here, keep going straight to your right, then go about ten feet and make a sharp left. Your *dojo* is number fifteen. You'll see them warming up on the field as you go through the big green door."

Bumping into various contestants as I made my way through the hectic crowd, a big bleached-blond, yellow-eyed woman crushed me against a cement wall. "Excuse me," she said. Her eyes turned into tiny slits while she sneered at me like a massive shark hunting for her feast.

Backing up, I forced a smile and bowed. I continued my pursuit for Master Luna. The woman's beady eyes haunted me. My pulse calmed when I saw my mentor and the other students from my *dojang*.

Master Luna's white tresses were intertwined with his jet-black hair, twisted neatly in a ponytail with the *yin/yang* symbol. I maneuvered with speed through an overpowering crowd.

Surrounded by men and women punching bags, warming their limbs, bending their bodies in all sorts of directions, and yelling *ki- yaps* throughout the halls that were hidden from the audience, I halted and bowed when I reached my mentor. An anxious feeling whizzed through my body.

"Bear with me for a moment while I say hello to some friends, and then we'll do our preparation."

As I listened to Master Luna speak in Chinese, French, and whatever foreign lingo to different contestants, excitement rocketed from my toes to my head. When Master Luna told Teddy, his assistant, to limber up the other contestants from our studio because he wanted to focus on me, I was flabbergasted. What an honor.

Master Luna guided me through various stretches and warm-ups. Then he took me aside and suggested that I take deep breaths and focus on my third eye so that I could picture my *hyungs*.

I closed my lids and envisioned a giant aqua eye in the middle of my forehead floating in a dark abyss. The green-blue color began to mix with the black pupil and swirl like a waterspout. I saw myself step through the middle of the spiral, stand at attention and bow. My highlighted figure illuminated in the vast darkness.

My chest lifted as I slid my left foot up my shin until it touched my right knee. At the same time I raised my hands to the front of my face. The inside of my right palm covered the outside of my left palm facing inward, and my fingers pointed toward the sky. Exhaling, light began to filter through the pitch black as my left foot slid down and met my right foot. The base of my body was planted securely on the ground. With care, my hands remained clasped as I lowered them. Then, with a snap, my hands still together, pointed toward the ground.

A golden shine replaced the pitch-black surroundings. I observed as my body was guided by a power I didn't under-stand. It was being controlled by my mind—however, it felt as if my movements were gliding with a mastery that was in someone else's care.

I placed my left foot in front of my right. My head turned sharply to my right. I made sure my hands were aligned with my arm and my shoulder. Visualizing an opponent on my right side, as if she were going to pummel me with a pipe, I elbowed right between her ribs. Then I envisioned a silhouette of a man about to bash me with his fist. I locked my arm downward and blocked his punch. My limbs obstructed the shadows of assailants trying to slug and wallop me from different directions.

I paid back one imaginary scumbag with a punch and a chop to the neck. Then I grabbed his head and pounded it to my knee. I released him; following with a roundhouse kick to the side and slammed the top of my foot into his ribs. A natural *kiyap* released from my lungs as I finished each section of my *hyung*. In my final round, as I blocked two assailants simultaneously, my right arm jammed the attacker's low kick and my left forearm lifted upward and knocked away a punch. Then I turned and intercepted another blast and ended my *hyung* with a loud *kiyap* as I launched my fist forward with a final thrust and heard a crisp tone click from my *dobohk*. When my meditation was over, and I felt as though I could conquer the world, I crossed my legs and waited to perform for the judges.

My focus was jarred when I glanced upward. The people on the top rows looked like ants searching for food.

As my eyes were drawn downward to the front row, I saw Tutti by my parents' side with her mom and dad. She signaled two fingers over her eyes, our secret gesture for ninja. I thanked God that they were near; otherwise, they'd be a part of the unrecognizable colony way up in the boondocks. Then, Tutti placed her forefinger toward me and lifted it, signing number one.

My name was called. Master Luna guided me in and out of the innumerable mats toward a section with three judges who stared at me with stern faces. I bowed to the judges, hoping they would be impressed with my *hyung*. They nodded for me to begin.

"*Yeong-Wonhan Pyong Ahn*," I bellowed from my gut.

The judges nodded their heads. The two men had placid faces—though I noticed the corner of one of their mouths lifted—but the woman furrowed her eyebrows as if she were a panther stalking prey.

A strong breath in and a major release gave me the strength to take my stance and focus on the force that the swirling eye gave me.

As I raised my clapped-hands in front of my face and my right leg lifted, a glare veiled the images in the bleachers. My mind captured each make-believe challenger as if I were back in my meditation.

My legs straightened, and I planted my feet firmly on the mat. As before, my hands stayed together as they sharply pointed downward.

Then with an abrupt turn of my head to the right, my body followed with a knife hand chop. Picturing the ghost assailants from my earlier mental warm-up, I blocked, elbowed and punched with snaps sounding from my crisp motions. A *kiyap* from my gut ended each segment energizing me for the next. The six-foot muggers I envisioned ensured that my front kicks reached high above my head and my back kicks soared to splits.

In a flash I was finished. Did I forget something? My nerves began to twitch.

I heard clapping from the audience, bringing me back to reality. Some people were standing. I bowed. The judges nodded. It had all happened too fast. Thinking about mistakes I might have made was not an option. My free-form *hyung* was next. I needed to go back to my third eye.

The judges told me to wait for a moment and then nodded. I bowed and pictured my spinning eye. Conjuring up the shadow of a man carrying an axe on one side of me, and a bug-eyed woman on the other, I flipped over the swinging axe and deterred the woman's punch with my forearm. As the shadows bombarded me, I obstructed their every move, flipping over weapons and using my body to jam their attempted brutality.

First, a flying front kick to the head, then a hurdling round-house kick, the forefront of my foot knocking my assassin's temple and ending with a spinning aerial into a back kick as if I were breaking my opponent's jaw; it felt as though a cool breeze was guiding me through an exhilarating obstacle course.

In my next section I was being bullied non-stop, so I rolled backwards as I obstructed every move. Then, I did my new move— a forward flip allowing my heel to plunge downward landing on the swindler's head. This caused me to propel into a side flip, streamlining me into a double back kick. The whole auditorium roared and clapped.

The one judge who'd seemed to be holding back a smile before, allowed his cheeks to dimple and the sides of his mouth to rise. The woman's wrinkled eyebrows smoothed, though she remained otherwise expressionless, and the other evaluator remained calm and tranquil as if he were watching a sunflower bloom from his window. I bowed and found my way back to Master Luna.

"You were amazing." He tapped me on the back. "Now, no more make-believe opponents where you have rehearsed the moves to defend the blows." He placed both hands on my shoulders. "I know I've said this before, but remember, these are not your normal contestants. Top ranking martial artists have been chosen from all over the world. You must be aware of every movement, behind, in front and around you. Some of their wallops can be brutal, so use your speed to avoid them."

"Yes sir," I said keeping that third eye in the forefront of my mind.

Master Luna sat me down and clued me in on every weakness and strength of each opponent.

"You have the advantage here because, though you are being judged as an adult, your opponents will still look at your young face and lithe body as a child's. You may be tall, but many of the contestants know who and how young you are."

"How do they know that?"

"Word travels fast. When I submitted you as a contestant, there was chaos. Many of the masters said that you couldn't have the maturity to compete." Master Luna pointed to the judge with the serene smile. "See the Judge sitting in the middle? That is Master Ming and he was my mentor when I began martial arts at age six."

"Ming? You mean Master Ming? This tournament's Ming?" He nodded.

"When I was your age he asked me to enter *The Kimyoto*, a competition much like this one."

"Did you win?"

"It doesn't matter. I enjoyed the challenge and made him, and the people that mattered, proud. That is all you need to do. Enjoy this opportunity. Take advantage of your youth. But, don't take it for granted." His voice was firm. "Don't get arrogant, but *do* keep your confidence."

"I understand, sir."

The first contestant I was up against plunged forward with non-stop attacks, but she didn't block very well and my first two points were obtained in a flash. The next few rounds seemed to breeze by like a swift autumn wind. Many opponents differed in style and technique, but Master Luna trained me to expect the unexpected. And, he was right about my age being an asset. Some of my challengers gawked at me like I was an insect waiting to be swatted. When I buzzed in with a sting, they were rudely awakened.

It was difficult not to be a little puffed-up. I mean, I was a kid and outwitting all these professionals. Most of them were at least ten years older than me. But, I heeded Master Luna's words.

Anticipating the unforeseen was a focus not to hold lightly. This became a highlight in my mind when the heavyset blond who had knocked me against the cement earlier stood across the mat. She was my next opponent.

"She was a pearl many years ago, a young prodigy like you. I don't know what happened, but she has forgotten about the art and lost her soul," Master Luna said. "Don't ever lose what is in your heart—your spirit."

The woman's beady, evil eyes were vicious as they gazed at me, and once in a while she would growl as she passed. Our scores were tied, and she continued to lash out, but I conserved my energy by avoiding her blows. I looked for the opening, and as she jumped to kick my side, I darted a hit to her stomach, earning my last and final point.

I had many more matches before a winner would be announced, but the fact that I'd won this one made me feel as though sugar was pumping through my veins. I had moved up the ladder and wouldn't have to fight that spooky-eyed animal again. However, my energetic surge didn't last. Each match got tougher, and I began to tire. Toward the final matches, the wind got knocked out of me and my ankle was turning black and blue.

"Don't you think you've had enough, sweetie?" Mom was headed in my direction and Dad was chasing her.

I couldn't let my mom discourage me. Maybe if she saw me trying to focus, she'd go away; so I let my neck tip back and shut my eyes. As I inhaled, a trickle of sweat dribbled down my cheek and a taste of salt surprised my tongue. My body began to calm. Then, all of a sudden, Mom was in my face with a bag of ice cubes. How embarrassing, they must've told the guys at the gate that they were my parents.

"No way am I quitting," I insisted as I pushed the pack of ice away and got ready for my last round. Mom glanced at Master Luna, who nodded his head as if he knew I would be okay. She paused, but lifted her hands and said that she was just checking to see if I was all right.

"Your mom just cares," Master Luna whispered to me.

"Yes, sir."

"That woman looks like the Hulk," I heard Mom say to Dad.

"It's okay. Look how far she's come." He wrapped his arm around her.

"I know. But, why has she been so snappy lately? I can't do anything right. I was just trying to ease some of the pain she might be feeling."

Their voices were swept away as they moved into the distance. I didn't mean to lash out at my mom. It's just that sometimes I felt as though she was trapping me in a corner with nowhere to go.

Though all my opponents were women, the next competitor had the muscles of a monster-man. She was even bigger than that ogre I'd beaten before. In the ring, she tried stomping on my foot and backing me off the mat, but I was too quick. After she turned while I did a side flip, my heel landed in her rib to win my first point. When she punched, I automatically blocked, but my effort seemed useless. Her strength was so powerful that I was thrown off balance and tumbled out of the boundary line. Our scores were tied.

No way was I going to let this Titan bully me off the mat. She kicked my ankle and curled her hand to finish me off, but I rolled on the ground and jerked my good leg up into her belly. My strike didn't faze her, but it was the last and final point of the tournament. With grace, this female hulk bowed and shook my hand. I was pleasantly shocked and bowed back.

Mom was on top of her chair taking pictures with her camera as the elderly Asian master of all masters handed me three trophies for both my routine and individual forms, along with fighting. Dad placed two fingers from each hand in his mouth and whistled louder than the ear-deafening sound from a passing train. Tutti was jumping up and down with her hands clenched high in the air. Meanwhile, my stomach was doing the hula while my head spun. Master Luna was called to the podium.

"I'm very proud of you, Alexia," Master Luna said as he bowed toward me and I bowed back. "Though you are the youngest to have ever won the Ming Black Belt title, this is only the beginning, not only in your never-ending education in the martial arts, but in life. You have been given a talent to use wisely."

My heart began to flitter. As I listened to his Zen-like voice, my feet felt like they had wings on them and were flying me to another planet.

Master Luna invited me to go with a couple of his buddies to a party, and I was psyched. Dad didn't see a problem, but Mom wouldn't have it.

"I don't care if we're going to accompany her. She just turned twelve and is still a kid. They are men – ten, twenty years older than her. She's still our baby. Plus, it's late." Then Mom whispered to Dad, as if I couldn't hear, "Don't forget I've got to prep the present." Then she grabbed us. "Come on. Let's go to Noodles Galore, order up a feast and watch a movie."

They must've been talking about my birthday present. I was so wrapped-up in the tournament that I had forgotten. They usually gave the best. However, Mom sure knew how to pop my bubble. I mean, shouldn't I get some kind of kudos, not only for my birthday, but also for winning the biggest karate championship on this side of the nation? Wasn't I supposed to be an adult – an adult who beat all the other adults? Plus, not only was Master Luna awesome, but most of his buddies were karate champions visiting from all over the world. Each one was an Adonis. And, two of his women buddies, I actually beat in the tournament. Mom was the biggest party pooper I'd ever met.

Dad argued my case a little, but ended up agreeing with Mom, totally lame like always.

***

We went to Noodles Galore, which was Mom's favorite Chinese restaurant, and ordered enough food to feed an army. The sweet and sour chicken tickled my tongue, but it peeved me that Mom always got her way and that Dad was a wimp for letting her get it.

After we stuffed ourselves and I made sure a huge piece of Bubbe's Baron Booming Caramel Confection Apple Cake covered my tongue, we sunk into our plush lime-green sofa. Mom pushed the button on the DVD, and we all became captivated as Bruce Lee used his karate techniques to avenge the death of his sister and to infiltrate the group of bad guys, making the world a better place. When it was over, I lay back and stared out our sliding glass doors into our backyard, fantasizing about robbers

22

surrounding our house and how I pushed my parents away and karate-chopped the bandits into oblivion.

A shower of sparks flew across the sky, bringing me back to reality. I slid the door open. One shooting star flashed after another. As the fresh winter air tingled my skin, I heard Mom's irritating voice.

"Alexia, shut that door. Bugs are going to get in. I'm going to finish up some things in my studio. Why don't you and Dad check out the twinkles in the sky?"

Mom knew how to irritate me. I mean, whenever I was having a good time, she flushed my fun down the toilet. And *twinkles in the sky?* Give me a break. Why didn't she just say stars? But no, convoluted lingo was a better way to get me out of her hair. As far as I was concerned, all she cared about was her next project. For someone who called herself spiritual, she lost out on the cool things Dad and I did. You'd think she would have wanted to celebrate with us. Plus, it was no shock that she'd forgotten about my birthday present.

I was about to confront my parents about their thoughtlessness, but Dad swept me up off my feet and carried me to the pasture behind our house.

"These are the glorious illuminations of the sky," Dad said as he twirled me around and placed me on a stool by the heater. He kept it by our fence so brisk cool winds wouldn't interfere with our jaunts. Opening his arms wide to the universe he announced, "It's named after that scrumptious treat."

"What treat?" I searched high and wide for something. I even checked his pockets.

"Ah, the world is so sweet and incomprehensible." He chuckled as he wiggled his clothes. "There's nothing to find," then he spun around and magically extracted a giant Milky Way bar from my ear, "except right here."

I still can't figure out how he did that. I mean, no kidding, the chocolate bar was gigantic and came from nowhere. Then he threw the bar upward and it landed in his hand with a remote control next to it. He pushed a tab that began to blink.

"Hello, I'm Timmy." A pointy-nosed robot appeared from behind a tree.

"You fixed the telescope. It works!"

Dad pushed more buttons. The screen on the robot's head lit up, and a kooky kind of staccato theatrical voice came from Timmy's mouth. He was like a cute magical movie character and made fun beeping noises. He jerked around and then squeaked, "Excuse Me!"

"Why should I do that?" I said not expecting an answer.

"Isn't that what you say when you bur-ur-urp?" Timmy said.

"Dad, how did you do that?"

"Well, isn't it?" Timmy repeated.

"Um, yes," was all I could say.

Then Timmy did a staccato dance. "Did you know that this is not only a star, but an incredible gem?" Timmy lifted its elbow and pointed its metal finger to the screen. "Eeeep, it's a spiral gal-ax-ax-x-y called the Milky-y Way Sys-s-s-tem, eeep." A myriad of stars filled the screen. "With 400 bill-ill-ill-ion stars that go way past Mar-ar-ars." Mars appeared. "With gas and dust not turn-ing to char-ar-ar-coal, but enhancing the sky with lots of spar-ar-ar-kle." Then a whole bunch of gaseous clouds floated across Timmy's screen and turned into a myriad of glittering lights. "And holding the oldest star in the gal-al-al-axy, is that awesome halo making it the max-ax-ax-y. Eeeep." A brilliant close-up picture of the Milky Way materialized on the screen as Timmy pointed his metal thumbs upward.

"I'm meeting the head executives next week. It's a small firm, but I think Timmy is ready for the market," Dad said as he handed me some chocolate.

We laughed, and boy, did we enjoy consuming the milky dark sugar.

"Uh oh, I think the electric warmer cooked some of this chocolate," I said as I handed Dad a concoction of syrupy brown goop.

"YOUR mom's going to kill me when she sees this chunky gunk smothered all over our clothes," Dad said. He gave my gooey face a great big kiss. "Oh well, what can you do? Enjoy what you've got when you've got it." He licked his fingers.

Wiping the smudged mucky candy from my hands and clothes was useless. Our coats looked like they had been smeared in mud.

My Dad tossed a hunk of chocolate high in the air and caught it in his mouth. We snuggled, and I got whipped candy all over his face. My mom would have had a hissy fit searching for sterilizer. But Dad just smiled, kissed my nose and wrapped my sticky body in his arms. While holding me, he leaned down behind the stool and grabbed his art deco box embroidered with lime-colored circles and purple-painted squares. The box was filled with rich dark Godiva and a variety of Hershey candies.

"We ate the last Milky Way, so we are going to have to replenish it tomorrow." Dad crept in front of a window in Mom's studio, hiding my view inside. "Shhhh, never tell her that I hide the box under my shirts. I keep them neatly folded so she won't mess with them." Dad pointed to the stars. "Now, let's focus on the facts out there." He pulled me away towards the field. "We just don't quite understand everything about them." A shower of shooting stars zoomed across the sky. "Close your eyes and make a wish. And do it fast or the funny bunnies will eat you alive." He tickled me so hard I couldn't stop giggling.

A glimpse of my mom's work window came into view before my lids closed. Huddling closer to my Dad helped me forget the fact that she was always engrossed in her designs. It was my birthday, but instead of hanging out with Dad and me, she chose to lock herself in her studio. Her persnickety attitude about cleanliness might have ruined our fun anyway, so I blocked what I thought was her callousness out of my mind.

While my dad rubbed my back as he held me, I must have fallen asleep, because I didn't remember going to bed—just Mom prying me out of my pleasant dream world.

***

"Alexia, Alexia! It's time to get up." My mom jiggled me. Flashes glared as she snapped pictures on her camera.

I covered my body. My mom shook me again, ripping off my covers.

"Mom, you're not fair. It's Sunday. I was up late last night looking at the stars with Dad. I need sleep." I covered my head with the only things left, my pillows.

"Your dad's already hammering away in his tool shed. Go look. It's so sunny and gorgeous even though there's still some snow on the ground."

My eyes peeked from under the downy pillows. Then I lifted my body upward so that I could see my dad out of the window. It must not have been too cold, because he was in our backyard without a coat. He placed the back of his hand across his forehead as if he was wiping sweat away.

"He's working on another idea—some kind of hand-held blood molecular gadget of some sort," Mom said. She grabbed my arm. "It's warm enough for a picnic, and your grandparents sent extra goodies. They're sorry they couldn't come to your tournament, but they wanted you to know they were thinking of you. Our Sunday spread is outside. Come on, you don't want to sleep through the day."

I tried to convince Mom that I'd meet her downstairs. Instead she began dressing me like I was a kid. Pushing her away didn't help. She yelled out the window to Dad and yanked me through the door.

As I stumbled down the stairs, Dad whizzed into the living room, karate-chopping the air. *Kung Fu Fighting* was playing in the background. Dancing and kicking, Mom followed Dad as they led me around the house. They didn't forget. This must've been the surprise. I couldn't wait to find out what scheme my parents had cooked up this time. As we entered Mom's art studio, a lump thickened in my throat. I hoped that this wasn't about mom's art project.

The last time she took me into her studio, she was supposed to help me with my science final. When we reached the center of the room, the phone rang and she talked with her finger held up as if she was only going to be a moment. After an hour, I left and had to finish my project without her help. My mom was a busy woman and I was used to her having to work extra hours, but I was floating high because of the tournament and this wasn't a time for disappointment.

Then I saw it. A sign was strung across the ceiling: CONGRATULATIONS TO OUR FLYING BLACK BELT NINJA. A framed picture of Bruce Lee performing a flying crescent kick hung underneath the lavender ceiling, and rose petals covered the floor.

"Oh, my God—I've wanted that for centuries. That's the collector's piece that's on display at the antique store next to the *dojo*. I never mentioned it because it cost a mint. How did you know?"

"We've got our ways," Mom said. "Wait until you see Sunday brunch." Mom snatched Dad's elbow. "First, it's about time for yoga, and second, it's warm enough to enjoy the sun outside."

I called Tutti to tell her the great news. She was whooping and cheering on the other end of the phone.

"You're the only one who knew how much I wanted that picture," I said.

"Your mom pried the info from me."

When I hung up the phone, Dad seized my elbow and he and Mom twirled me around and about, looping me through the tables, and eventually guided me over to the big field where we were about to enjoy our Sunday yoga class. As Dad wobbled, Mom began my favorite pose, the Salutation to the Sun.

"I only do this for you two." Dad heaved, crossed his eyes, and stumbled. "Why don't we break for our post-birthday picnic?" He then moaned, grasped for a breath, and rushed into the house.

Out of the doorway flew three jackets.

"In case it cools down." Dad popped his head through the doorway.

Where did all the cocoa smudges go?

Behind Mom, I motioned to Dad as if I was wiping gunk off my clothes.

He winked at me.

Our gourmet meal of goat cheese, honey crisp apples, wild berries, veggies with guacamole dip, and hot raspberry cider was beautifully set on top of our Mickey Mouse blanket. In the center, strudels, cookies and baked specialties, shipped from Bubbe and Zeyde, were positioned into a glorious sculpture of a ninja jumping into a sidekick, holding what was left of my birthday cake.

The way Mom positioned those baked goods to look like a ninja was totally cool. I was going to say something to her, but a doe hopping behind a buck as they passed through our yard, caught my attention. Any sound or movement would have ruined the portrait. After they pranced out of sight, our focus was food. The doughy goodies seemed endless. Dad put his dilapidated portable radio onto his beloved classical station, and we relaxed beside an electrical heater as we soaked up the rays.

"Who wants to split the last Danish? It's a Baron Cherry Cheese," Dad called out.

"I'm full," Mom answered.

"My tummy's going to burst." I held my belly.

"It's your final chance." Dad displayed the prized pleasure.

"If you insist. It's all yours," Mom said as she glanced at me and then shrugged her shoulders.

"Okay." I sighed as I stuck out my stomach and held out my hand.

After the final crumb was consumed, I inhaled and was about to spread out and relax on the blanket when my dad stood above me waiting.

"Oh, I forgot, it's Sunday," I said.

"That's okay. I think yesterday made up for today," my mom said. "Plus, digesting your food wouldn't be a bad idea."

"But it's Sunday tradition," I said. "Hit it, Dad."

After Dad motioned to Mom a questioning look, my mom motioned an approval. My father turned up the music, and I performed my award-winning *hyung* to Prokofiev's *Peter and the Wolf.* The music motivated my karate movements as I glided through the meadow.

"That whets my appetite for some of Paulie's homemade ice cream," Dad announced after he ran up and awarded me with a bear hug.

"Ugh," I muttered. "We better not," I said, pushing myself away. Dad feigned a fall towards Mom, grabbed her from behind and pretended that he was eating something. He licked his fingers. That sparked my memory that we had to replenish the Milky Ways. Paulie's kept them in stock just for us. "Well, on a second note, ice cream would top off a perfect morning."

My dad's mouth formed a big "Yes."

"You two have no shame."

We all bundled up and got into our fiery red convertible, then rocketed down the road, twisting and turning and singing as we headed for town. I knew that the cows and horses were snuggled in the barns keeping warm; otherwise, they'd be grazing in the pastures. Sculptured branches reached out from the barren trees, and spots of glittering snow decorated the hills.

"I love this time of year," I announced. "Wouldn't it be cool if it never ended?"

"You are so right. Floating white flurries are spectacular when they drift in the sky," Mom said, wandering into her own dramatic world. In the convertible, she lifted herself to her knees, one hand on the seat and one reaching for the sky. Why she did that and unhooked her seatbelt, I do not know? She was a security hound when it came to safety. "And the way they shimmer as they fall to the ground—or when the snowflakes are untouched and sparkle. Look at those dunes glistening in the sun. The decorations during the holidays are amazing. Look at that." Mom spread her arms in the direction of our neighbors.

Dad turned his head.

"Dad, look out for that skunk!" I screamed.

The bright sky turned black.

CHAPTER II

Tumbling Down
The Corridor

Was I dreaming or did this really happen? I saw the skunk again. It was smack in the middle of the road and Dad swerved so he wouldn't hit it. We bumped into the side of the mountain, and then the car began to spin. Then the skunk appeared once more, jumping up and down. I kept on calling out for Dad to turn. Dad angled the wheel to the far right and Mom pivoted toward the door. The shining sun burned my eyes. I blinked.

"You were very lucky," a voice said. "We were a little worried, but you are going to be just fine. You suffered a concussion and have been dozing in and out of consciousness for quite a few days."

Standing in front of me was a woman in a green doctor's outfit. Behind her I saw Bubbe and Zeyde. They had tears in their eyes.

My head was pulsating. As I rubbed my temples, I searched the room. My parents—where were my parents? "Mom? Dad? Where are you? Mom—Mom, are you okay? Dad? We don't really have to go to Paulie's. Hold me, Dad. Mom?"

A whole bunch of nurses and doctors surrounded me, trying to pin me down. I kept on thwarting their holds and kicked one male doctor right between the legs. A pang pricked my side, and I noticed a nurse holding a needle in her hand. Her face began to warp as her nose became elongated. No sound came from her mouth as it opened and closed. My eyelids became heavy as the room filled with a dark mist.

In the background Bubbe and Zeyde were praying for my mom and dad, hoping that they would survive.

When I woke, still groggy, Bubbe and Zeyde were discussing how another day had passed; then they started arguing about who should tell me.

"Tell me what?" I moaned.

"This is a time when we have to be strong for Alexia's sake," he whispered to Bubbe.

"Why do you have to be strong for me? I'm okay," I said.

Turning toward me their faces drooped.

They approached me as if I were a scared puppy, stumbling on words, and bumping into each other. Then Zeyde took my hands, and both, with solemn voices, explained to me how my parents couldn't hold on any longer.

"Dad?" Bubbe and Zeyde nodded. "Mom?" In a daze, I wondered if I was staring at bobble heads.

My throat filled with pain. I couldn't move. Tears poured from my eyes as I searched the room. It couldn't be true. Mom and Dad would never leave me. Bubbe held me, and Zeyde smoothed my hair.

"You know, Dad's got his big meeting, oh my God, it's this week. Did he miss it? And, I haven't told Mom how great her surprise was."

"It will be okay," Bubbe said as she lifted her delicate white hanky and snorted real hard. She offered it to me. I just stared at it, wiped my slippery face, and moved my head from side to side.

"No, thank you."

The thought of Dad taking that hanky and giving it to José crossed my mind. My cheeks began to dry. Poking fun was my dad's main agenda in life. He couldn't be gone. Then I imagined Mom glancing at Dad, chiding him like a child. My concussion must've confused my understanding of what Bubbe and Zeyde were talking about.

"Mom and Dad always made me click my seatbelt. I don't know why Mom didn't click hers. She could have really gotten hurt. I was scared that you said my parents had passed away."

Bubbe's hand gripped mine. The intensity traveled through my body and water trickled down my neck.

"She never did that before. If I did that she would've gone berserk."

My grandparents held me while I sobbed.

"Why did she do that?"

As I collected my composure, they began to talk about their bakery. I guess they were trying to distract me, you know, from thinking about my parents. The more they chatted, the heavier their Jewish accents became and the more they spoke what I thought was Yiddish. Bubbe began to flail her arms. Her mannerisms mimicked my mom's. It sort of made me chuckle, but then I thought about never seeing my mom again.

"We just fixed up the attic as an extra guest room," Bubbe said.

"And strolling through Steinbeck Park is exhilarating. You remember the square a couple of blocks from our bakery? It's got that cute little pond," Zeyde continued.

"And you can help us out in the bakery. Oh, my *shaineh maidel*, you are going to meet remarkable people and learn my baking secrets. *Hashem* must've known you were coming."

"Who's *Hashem*?" I asked. I thought I had heard my grandparents say that name before, but I hadn't met anyone named *Hashem*.

"*Hashem* is the Hebrew word for God. Most Jewish people don't like to say God or *Yahweh* because He is too important. Or, in prayer you might hear Him referred to as *Adonai* or *Elohim*. It seems complicated."

"Well, if *Hashem* and those other words mean God, then aren't they saying God anyway?"

"It's just the Jewish way. You'll learn more when you come and live with us," Zeyde said.

The nurse came in to take my blood pressure and pulse and all that vital statistic stuff. It wouldn't be so bad, but it seemed like the doctors and nurses were coming in all of the time and repeating the same mind-numbing questions over and over again, and all I could think about was my parents.

"Now, young lady, here are some prescribed exercises to do at least once if not twice a day," the nurse said.

"Okay," I answered.

Actually, a little physical activity rejuvenated me; movement calmed my nerves and took my mind off everything else. The following day I must've repeated the exercises six times. There was nothing else to do. I needed to get out of that dull depressing place. It smelled like medicine, and all the patients were sick and gloomy. I felt bad for them, but when I strolled through the halls all I saw were parents holding and cuddling their kids and rooms filled with flowers and presents, and I didn't want to be reminded that my parents couldn't visit me. Besides, there was nothing to do but watch boring TV shows.

Specific medicinal directions were handed to me, and my grandparents filled out paperwork so that I could be released. A nurse in a blue outfit told me I was ready to go and asked me if I wanted to sit in the wheelchair he placed beside my bed. He didn't even let me respond. He just bent down, placed his gloved hands on my legs, trying to position them.

"No, thank you," I said as I pushed him away. "I'm as healthy as Hercules."

"It's the hospital policy that I take you to the front lobby by wheelchair," he said.

"Then why didn't you say so?" I didn't mean to be rude, but the nurse gave me such a snooty look and he could've just asked me kindly to sit in the chair. I couldn't help myself.

I hopped out of my bed and ran to the corridor where I per-formed multiple handsprings. However, when I landed, I teetered a bit.

"*Oy vey*," Bubbe said as she clasped her hands and Zeyde chuckled.

"Whoa, young lady," the nurse said while he chased after me. "We're just following procedures. Once you're out of here, you're free to flip-flop wherever."

I saw Bubbe raise one eyebrow, and then Zeyde stroked my hair.

"Come on, Zeyde needs to get the car," Bubbe said. "And we need to stop by your house and pick up your belongings before we get back to our house and get ready for *shiva*."

"What's *shiva*?" I asked, wondering why they would plan any-thing at such a time.

"In the Jewish religion, after a funeral, for the following seven days, family and friends meet in a loved one's home and celebrate the life of the deceased. Rabbi Goodblatt has offered his assistance in the preparations so we can focus on our mourning."

At least I'd be able to see my home one more time before I went to Bubbe and Zeyde's. Mom and Dad had always told me that I was destined to grow up in *my* house. When Mom was eight months plus pregnant, she didn't have time to rush to the hospital because I had no patience. Dad said that I dove out of her belly. Sometimes he said I somersaulted out of her stomach and other times he made up crazy acrobatic moves representing my popping out of her womb. Though he switched his scenario thousands of times, he always ended his spiel saying that his little superhero was meant to live in this home. Him and Mom were bundled up, enjoying some new-fallen snow in the middle of our pasture. Then her eyes bugged out for an instant and she just plunked herself down in the snow. He tried to get her to hobble to the car. He even tried to carry her. But, she wouldn't budge. Then she sprawled out in the snow and ordered my dad to get some blankets. She said that her baby wasn't going to wait.

Even if it made me feel a little dizzy, tumbling in our meadow one more time was a keepsake—a way to hold on to my home— to my mom and dad.

I sat myself down in the wheelchair and allowed the attendant to roll me to the exit, but I refused to allow my feet to touch the footrest in order to emphasize that I was not crippled. Bubbe stayed by my side while Zeyde departed for the garage elevator, and we waited in the lobby.

"Thank you for you assistance, but you can go now," I said to the nurse as he stood, not budging.

The nurse eyed my grandmother, who nodded her approval, so he left.

I sprung to my feet. Whatever ache I might've felt didn't matter because the fact that I didn't have to be surrounded by misery anymore made my adrenaline fly. However, Zeyde was taking way too long. Tapping my toes on the rug didn't ease my angst, and the forlorn faces pasted on the slumped bodies in the waiting area reminded me of depressed kids sitting hopelessly in the back seat of a car during rush hour. It was either let myself get caught up in this traffic jam, or find an alternate route.

I heard a boom box outside as the doors opened and closed. Letting the music move me might place some smiles on those dreary faces.

Bubbe's furrowed eyebrows were disapproving. She always did that when she was irritated. Usually, I mellowed when she did that, but I was too overwhelmed with excitement to stop myself. I mean, Bubbe was always upset about something. Plus, this wasn't such a big deal. Who knows what she was thinking, but her shoulders went limp, she sighed, and disgruntled, returned to her *Bon Appetit* magazine.

"This is not a place for gallivanting around and disrupting everyone, young lady," a cranky old lady with a huge bandage on her cheek scolded me.

Thank God Bubbe was too absorbed in her cooking magazine to notice the little confrontation. I wanted to be accommodating so I stopped bee-bopping and fashioned some figure eights around the furniture in a graceful but calm manner.

"Remember we are mourning. Why don't you have a seat, *bubeleh,* and take a rest?" Bubbe said as I passed by her.

What mourning had to do with my being fidgety, I didn't know. Zeyde was taking forever, and I had no other way to release this nervous energy. Sitting down wouldn't help. So I continued on as if I didn't hear her. However, I noticed a bunch of evil eyes, and then sharp pains pierced the insides of my back. There was no choice, so I plopped myself down in exhaustion and shut my eyes.

My eyes bolted open when I heard Zeyde's voice.

"Come on, we are going to get stuck in traffic," he said to Bubbe.

It seemed like hours later. I thought his beat up Chevy had been towed to the emergency ward.

"*Got in himmel!*" Bubbe exclaimed. "*Vos iz mit dir?* We still need to pick up Alexia's belongings at her house. Driving all day to get home is going to take us another eight hours. Thank *Hashem* Rabbi Goodblatt has offered to take on the preparations for *shiva.* And, *okh un vay,* Alexia can hardly hold herself up," Bubbe scolded.

"I searched for an hour before going to security to report it stolen. You can thank *Hashem* the guard offered to drive me around the lot."

"You had to drive around the lot?"

"What? *Er drait zich vi a fortz in rossel*, in circles, in circles in circles!" Zeyde yelled. "I couldn't find the *meshugener* car. You're the one who insisted our car was in the orange area before I went to get it."

"It wasn't?" Bubbe questioned.

"Green zone," Zeyde said.

"Oh, I'm sorry," Bubbe said, her eyes drifting away from Zeyde. "Shall we get going?"

We headed for the highway leading to Spring Falls. I began to relax, cherishing the idea that I would sleep in my own comfy bed that night. As my grandparents hurried me to pack my things, it sank in that my stay at home would be rushed because of my parents' funeral.

CHAPTER III

Driving on Shabbat

The first thing I did when we got to my house was run to our pasture. I plunged into a front handspring that spiraled into a summersault.

"*Oy gevalt*, Alexia. Alexia, come back here!" Bubbe yelled. "The doctor told you to keep calm for the next couple of days. No tumbling."

"But this is the last time I'll be here," I yelled back.

"We'll talk about that later," Bubbe said when I met her and Zeyde at the front door. "We've got a lot of things to gather before we leave, and it will be early in the morning. I don't mean to be a *nudnik*, but—" she paused and shrugged her shoulders, "—we don't have much time. Oh, yes, be careful of what you choose— just bring what's important."

"What's a *nudnik*?" I asked.

"It's someone who's a nag...a pain in the neck. This is a difficult thing to do, and I don't want to make it harder on you than is necessary, but just get what you plan to put in your bedroom. Our house is not as large as yours, and we don't have the time to figure everything out right now. Oh my."

When we entered, Bubbe's eyes were fixated on a beeping answering machine. She pushed a button. Then she hurried to her purse and pulled out a pen and paper to write with.

"Hey, Jude, you stood me up. I heard what happened with Bob...José. I call him Bob because I hate the name José...long story. You got to calm down that hubby of yours. Bob's English isn't the greatest, and he's got his quirks, but he's a wealth of knowledge. You'll like him when you get to know him. It's my fault, I told him to smuggle the patent number off of Timmy because I wanted to surprise you. Meadon Instruments is extremely interested in manufacturing it - biggest manufacturer for astronomical instruments. So, don't make any deals with those small timers next week. I'll tell you about it when we talk. No hard feelings. Call me—we need to discuss the building plans. Sorry, I have to cancel our meeting on Monday. I'm on route to my hotel in Italy—some scandal with a concierge. I'll contact you as soon as I know more." The first message ended.

"Happy Birthday, Alexia. I hope your ankle is healing. It only looked like a bruise. You made your master proud. I won't be in the *dojo* on Monday. *Sensai* Wokjo needed me to meet him in Tokyo, but I'm very proud and will talk to you as soon as I get back." After listening to his voice, I wondered why everyone, all of a sudden, had to leave the country. Then I pondered the possibility of never seeing Master Luna again.

"Happy Birthday," echoed and echoed and echoed. The repeated calls from Bill kept coming. I stared at the machine. Bubbe glanced at me.

My body felt like a ten-ton weight. A river cascaded down my face, and I couldn't speak. Through blurred vision, I saw Zeyde take off his gloves and lift his matching polka dot earmuffs and his multi-colored jester hat. As he moved toward me, he rubbed his hand against his bald head. While his eyebrows furrowed and chubby lips pouted, his flabby cheeks wobbled. His cool palm caressed my drenched curls. I burrowed my head in his chest, and he held me until I calmed down. Then he led me up the stairs.

"Why don't you rest in your room for a bit, and as soon as you are able why don't you choose the things you want to take with you? We've got a big day ahead of us tomorrow."

Stumbling to my room, I quickly became tortured having to decide among all of my pictures, karate gear, and clothing. Plus, I had all my art tools and sewing accessories. My karate gear was important, but I doubted if my grandparents had the money it would take for me to continue my training. Plus, nobody could replace Master Luna. But, I couldn't leave the karate helmet Tutti gave me. There was no way I could give up karate completely. I'd just have to practice on my own. As I stared at the spiffy outfits Mom and I had made, I realized that most of them would have to go into storage. My grandparents' attic was half the size of my bedroom, if that.

I was up all night trying to figure out what was essential. I snuck into my parents' room so that I could find Dad's art deco box—that was definitely crucial. It was underneath his shirts, just like he'd said. Removing it with the utmost care, a chill ran through my spine. I scanned the place where I'd snuggled with Mom and Dad on many nights. The scent of Mom's Oscar de la Renta still filled the room. There it was—standing like a statue in the center of Mom's vanity inside her antique crystal container. I wondered why she hadn't placed her perfume back on the ledge with her other fragrances. After all, she was neurotic about everything— especially order. If anything were missing from its proper place, her hands would flail and a shriek, sounding like a wounded monkey, would erupt from her throat. I hurried to set it back in its designated space. Then I thought that if she had left it out the night of my tournament, or even the day after, my competition must have really distracted her. I hoped it was because she was proud of me. I raised the elegant container and inhaled the delicate smell, holding it close.

I crept back to my room. I threw my shirts into one of my suitcases. I picked up the heap, dropping it on the lioness rug that covered my bamboo floor. With care, I placed the deco container inside the suitcase and stared at it. Then I wrapped the perfume bottle in a thick wool shirt so it wouldn't break and placed it next to the box. Next, I replaced each shirt after it, flattened and folded with care. I smelled my hand, touched the blouse that lay on top, and took a moment of silence.

Time was of the essence. Searching the room and eyeing each picture was overwhelming. The Bruce Lee print was a definite, but having to leave any of the other pictures behind was heart wrenching. That night was the last time I would get to sleep on my snuggly queen-sized bed with my down comforter and six puffy pillows. Can you believe I passed out on top of a bunch of clothes on the hard wood floor? When Bubbe banged on my door to wake me up in the morning and told me to meet her downstairs as soon as possible, all I wanted to do was bury myself in my bed. It was too late.

"Can I come in?" Zeyde asked s few moments later.

"One second." I changed into a sweatshirt and jeans. "Come in."

"Did you sleep okay?" Zeyde gave me a kiss. "Why don't you go help Bubbe with packing the food, and I'll take your things to the car." Then he paused in shock as his eyes scanned my belongings. "You want to take all of this?"

"I limited a lot."

"Your pictures are fine, and you need your clothes, but these toys and costumes and extraneous things are a bit much."

"I can take my sewing machine and some material though, can't I? There's no way I could survive without it. Mom gave it to me, and we created amazing things on it."

Zeyde covered his chin with his hand.

"Please, please, please," I pleaded.

"Most of this stuff will go into storage, so don't worry about losing it, we are just a little hurried right now to sort everything out."

He crumpled his eyebrow as I continued clasping my hands, hoping that he would have pity.

"Who am I to deprive you of your *chatchka*, but you've got to make some gloves to match this hat."

I agreed as he knuckled my hair.

***

After the last bag of clothes was stuffed into the station wagon, we wriggled into whatever space was left, and began our eight-hour trek into the city.

"Tutti's grandpop died, and they didn't have the funeral right away," I said.

"Tutti's not a Jew," Bubbe said. "Jewish people are buried as soon as possible out of respect for the connection of body and soul. Though a person passes, it takes time for the soul to leave, and we want to say good-bye to your mom and dad as a whole."

"Why can't we have it in Spring Falls? Our friends are here, and it would make things easier. Plus, my parents would have wanted it that way."

"We thought about that. It would be easier and some of your parents' friends offered. But, your parents stated in their will that they wanted to have the services where your mom grew up. We wouldn't do anything against your parents' wishes."

"But this is our home." I believed what Bubbe had said, but it made no sense.

"I'm sorry," Bubbe and Zeyde said at the same time, and then there was silence. As we left, I looked back at the house where I had grown up. A **For Sale** sign had been stabbed into the lawn.

"The realtor was supposed to wait until after we left before she put up the sign," Zeyde whispered to Bubbe. Zeyde was so hard of hearing that he didn't realize that when he meant to use an inconspicuous voice, everyone heard every word. I always knew he was trying to whisper, because his voice became airy and deep. Bubbe was kind of like that, too. I wondered if that was what happened to people when they got old.

"That's what I told her. She obviously didn't listen," Bubbe said.

"It's okay," I said, hoping that my grandparents couldn't see my tears.

"Oh, did you say something?" Bubbe asked.

She began to turn her head and body toward the back seat and sputter some words, but Zeyde rubbed her arm gently and shook his head. Time passed. I heard Bubbe complain about traveling on *Shabbat*.

"You know we are not supposed to work or travel or exert ourselves in any kind of way," Bubbe said.

"What are you, *meshugener*? Jews do have sympathy. *Shabbat* may represent the seventh day of creation where *Hashem* rested, but *Hashem* also does realize that there are exceptions. Don't you think your daughter's dying might be one of them?" Zeyde's voice became raspy and strained.

I saw Zeyde lift his head and position his rear-view mirror in my direction. Curling up in a ball and pretending I was asleep was an easy way to avoid conversation.

"Rabbi Goodblatt is such a *mensch*," Bubbe said. "Taking responsibility for Jude and Jesse's *levayah* is a blessing.

"Don't forget your precious cat, Scruffy," Zeyde added.

"*Oy vey*, I hope that little fuzz ball doesn't get into too much trouble."

"What do you mean by my parents' *levayah?*" I asked, letting curiosity get the best of me.

"Oh, so you're awake?" Zeyde asked.

"*Levayah* means funeral in Hebrew," Bubbe explained. "Now that you'll be living with us, you'll be learning more about your heritage."

"But don't you speak Yiddish?"

"We basically do, but sometimes we mix it with Hebrew," Zeyde said.

We drove many miles in silence.

"And strolling through Steinbeck Park is exhilarating. You remember the square a couple of blocks from our bakery? It's got that cute little pond," Zeyde continued.

"You mentioned it when we were in the hospital. *Hashem must've known I was coming.*" I didn't mean to be rude. It just came out. Again, the car filled with silence.

"Do you remember Rabbi Goodblatt?" Bubbe asked.

"Sort of, he used to stop by your house a lot when we'd visit."

"Did we ever tell you that Rabbi Goodblatt was a karate champion in Israel?" Zeyde asked.

"No," I said, but when I thought about it, something might have been mentioned.

It's just that my grandparents were beginning to irritate me. It was obvious I didn't feel like talking, and all they did was ask questions—as if I were interested in anything that had to do with Judaism. To top that off, I didn't want to think about having to stop my karate, and never seeing Master Luna again. Indicating that their rabbi could be my *sensai* was stooping lower than a sewage pipe as far as I was concerned. No matter how interested I was in martial arts, there was no way I was going to let them play me like that. Why couldn't they just leave me alone?

Thank God everyone remained silent except when there were some bathroom stops and Bubbe offered a prayer and some *challah* sandwiches, but other than that the ride was calm. And, the food was the best part of the trip. Bubbe made the sweetest, most scrumptious *challah* bread. I could probably eat a whole loaf if I didn't stop myself.

When the sky turned orange and the sun began to fade, the tranquility was broken. Bubbe lit a candle and said a prayer in Hebrew. She put the candle on top of the dashboard, holding it firmly to protect it from Zeyde's swerves.

"Don't you think that's a little bit dangerous?" Zeyde blurted out.

"But it's *Shabbat*," Bubbe replied.

"Not when someone's life is in jeopardy." Zeyde's voice was stern.

"You don't have to speak to me like that, especially not on *Shabbat*."

"How was I speaking? I was just saying that lighting a fire in a moving car is not a brilliant endeavor."

Bubbe crunched her lips and then blew out the candle, threw it back in her bag, said a prayer in Hebrew, and slapped her hands on the dashboard.

"Come on, Lilly, I didn't mean anything. *Shabbat* is a day of peace and tranquility. We're in a difficult situation. Let's make the best of it."

"I know, you're right."

Still keeping his left hand on the wheel, Zeyde pulled Bubbe's hand to his mouth, and touched his lips to her palm. A small swerve caused Bubbe to smack her hands right back on the panel. A quick glance at each other ended the spat.

Flurries dropped from the sky late Friday night as we arrived. Though we could get to my grandparents' apartment through their bakery because it was connected, we entered by the side doorway. Zeyde carried my bags up the never-ending stairs, through their living area, and up to the attic. When they opened the door, they raised their arms as if they were presenting a palace.

I thanked them. I knew that I would have to change some things later on. The bed was right under a slope in the wall, and there was no way I wanted to wake up banging my head every morning, but at this point I just needed to lie down.

"I know people usually wear black to funerals, but I think my parents would've liked me to wear something colorful. You know how Mom liked to be different. Can I wear something bright that I designed with my mom?" I asked.

"Oh *bubeleh,* they'll be a lot of people from the neighborhood, and though the people from Spring Falls understand your parents, some of the people here might not. It might be better if you wear black for the funeral," Bubbe answered.

"You look like you're about to drop into oblivion," Zeyde said as he lifted my face in his hands and kissed my forehead. "*Oy vey,* Lilly; let the child get some rest."

As soon as the door shut, I plopped into the bed, kicked off my jeans, and closed my eyes.

CHAPTER IV

The Baron Butt

Waking up disoriented, I sat straight up to gather my thoughts. *Wham!* My head slammed right into that sloping wall near my pillow—just like I had predicted.

My head throbbed, and there was a crick in my neck. My hands pushed against my long wavy hair as if it could make me feel better. Sleeping on cardboard would have been more comfortable. I missed sinking into my comfy mattress, surrounding myself with my feathery pillows and hugging my down comforter. At least I had packed our Mickey Mouse blanket. It wasn't quilted, but it reminded me of home.

I was stuck in a plain, boring, colorless attic. The puny single bed was supported by a cold metal frame and accessorized with one flat, lifeless pad. I could've pounded myself for not asking Zeyde to bring my bedding. There was no hope for my canopy forest bed. It wouldn't fit. My comforter and puffy pillows might have been bulky, but I could have made them work, at least some of them.

This place was a cramped closet. People taller than six feet would get their head chopped off by the ceiling fan. The only good thing was that the room was separated from the rest of the living space and I wouldn't be bothered, but it sucked that I couldn't do full-blown *hyungs* like in my old room.

But not today, my body ached. Not to mention, the room was small. Some movement was possible, but I was going to have to face the funeral tomorrow and lacking the energy to confront my minimal surroundings overpowered me. Unpacking crossed my mind, but my body felt like metal chains were weighing it down.

Spread across the bed, I slept. Bubbe called me down to eat, but I wasn't hungry.

"*Shabbat Shalom,*" she said when she bought some food to my door. I took it into my room, but just looking at the plate gave me heartburn. "Today is a day to rest. Don't worry about unpacking until after the first day of *shiva.* I'll get someone to help you after."

And, that's what I did. I stared at the slope and the window that opened to the sky. My birthday, the Ming Championship, and that Sunday repeated in my mind. In between, I slept. Like a bad commercial the day passed by.

***

"We must hurry, Alexia!" Bubbe yelled as I began to roll my neck, forcing myself out of the bed.

"Ugh," erupted from my throat.

I knew that I should've unpacked yesterday. Running to my suitcase, throwing my clothes everywhere, I searched for my black, formal outfit. It had to be somewhere. I remembered taking it off the hanger and neatly folding it in my bag. My mind was boggled. Everything was interfering with everything. Where was that stupid dress? Tears started filling my eyes. In frustration, I grabbed a group of clothes to throw them at the open closet. As they scattered on the floor, I noticed something hanging—my black dress.

They could've told me! They must've unpacked them while I was sleeping.

I scanned the room. The plate and cup that were beside my bed were gone. A quiver passed down my spine. They were in my room without me knowing.

After a quick wash and searching to find my undergarments, I inspected the long, soft black top, making sure there were no stains. Then I unhooked the mother of pearl buttons so I could slip into it. After making sure my velvet skirt was not crinkled; I slid it over my hips and attached it to the blouse's shiny shell snaps, transforming it into an elegant ensemble. Turning the waist a smidge, each zigzag diagonally flowed downward. The gray cashmere sweater that accompanied it assured warmth with a touch of elegance.

Luckily, I had gone to a black-and-white ball at school. Tutti made me go. Not that I wouldn't have gone anyway. But, there was this girl Wanda's older brother who had big blue eyes and massive muscles. All Tutti talked about was how to get him to ask her to dance.

Mom and I spent hours attaching an exotic translucent silk fabric that we found at a flea market, to plush delicate velvet. Mom said that she was saving it for a special occasion. My other clothes were variations of blue, purples, and startling greens. If it wasn't a radiant color from the rainbow, it didn't exist in my wardrobe, except for some leotards and stockings I had from gymnastics.

"Don't worry, everything will be taken care of," a woman was patting Bubbe on her back when I entered the living room.

"Why don't you meet Zeyde downstairs, and I'll be right there and we'll go to the synagogue," Bubbe said to me pinning a black ribbon to my sweater. "This shows that you are mourning."

A lump filled my throat and a spinning wheel turned in my stomach. I wanted to run upstairs and hide under my sheets, but instead I forced my way towards Zeyde.

"Lilly, come on. We don't want to be late," Zeyde yelled. He sighed and wrapped his arm around me and gave me a squeeze. "She always does this." Shaking his head, he yelled up the stairs again, "Lilly!"

Bubbe, finally, tottered down the stairs out of breath.

***

Zeyde rolled his eyes, and we made our way in silence to the synagogue. Rabbi Goodblatt was there to meet us and led us to the sanctuary where the services would be held.

Blah, blah, blah is all I heard Goodblatt say. I just didn't feel like listening to other people talking about my parents as if they knew them really well. People started to take their seats. I searched for Tutti.

"Bubbe, is Tutti coming?" I asked.

"Her parents said she was."

Zeyde smoothed his hands through my hair and patted my shoulder. My eyes weaved in and out of the crowd. Other people from Spring Falls were there. Where was Tutti? The rabbi began speaking about Mom growing up and meeting Dad in college, and how she stood out in a crowd. My ears opened a little when I heard my name mentioned. Then it registered that the rabbi was talking about my parents in past tense. But it didn't feel like they were dead. They were still in my heart and I sensed that they were near.

What if the hospital made a mistake? Maybe they switched bodies, and my parents were in intensive care? That happened in a Shirley Temple movie. Shirley Temple had to go to an orphanage and was treated like scum, but then she found her dad and it was a happy ending. I knew I wasn't living in a Hollywood movie, but never seeing my parents again didn't seem real either.

I felt a nudge.

"Come on, *bubeleh*, we need to lead everyone to the cemetery," Bubbe said as she led me down the center of the sanctuary. My hunt for Tutti was useless because the place was packed. Most of the people I didn't even know, nor did I want to see. I stared at the rug and followed my grandparents outside to a limousine.

I'd been in limos before. The last time, Dad rented one as a surprise get-a-way and took us to The Plaza Hotel in New York City where we saw *Cats* and ate at this fancy restaurant. The stretch Mercedes was really neat, with a TV and food and the coolest sound system.

This Lincoln was just long and black and blech. Annoying honking flooded the streets, and it took forever to get to the cemetery. When we got there, my grandparents led me as we walked behind the pallbearers. Daddy's best friend, Scott, was there. There were only a few faces that looked sort of familiar. I didn't see Bill or Bob—José. Master Luna didn't even come. It took forever to get to the burial site because the pallbearers kept on stopping for some reason. Everyone was wiping their eyes and holding hands. I couldn't take it anymore and just kept my head to the ground.

My last martial arts performance in our yard—when Mom had to get the perfect photo and Dad had to make sure he locked up his new invention before we left for ice cream—went through my mind. *Please don't go. Don't go. I want to share some chocolate one more time. Mommy, you can nag me as much as you want, just don't go*. My throat swelled, as if tiger-nails were clawing it, and I imagined the shower of water falling from my eyes coagulating into icicles. I just wanted to go home to Spring Falls and cuddle with my mom and dad and watch Bruce Lee's *Enter The Dragon*.

Everyone was supposed to shovel some dirt into the grave for last farewells. I couldn't.

"My *bubeleh*, it's like throwing a kiss and letting them go," Bubbe said.

"It's like hurling mud in a hole," I responded..

"Bubbe is just trying to explain the Jewish tradition," Zeyde said, placing his arm around me.

"There's no way I'm throwing mud on them."

"It's a way to let them go," Zeyde said, rubbing my shoulder.

"I don't care, and I don't want to let them go." I pushed his arm away.

"Okay," Zeyde said. "It's okay."

But it wasn't. Saying good-bye was like saying I had to forget them, and there was no way I was going to do that.

***

The limo driver drove us back to the house. As I followed Bubbe to the doorway, she washed her hands with water from one of her antique bowls that had been placed outside on a stool. She turned and stared at my hands then raised her eyebrows and nodded towards the bowl.

"Three times, switching hands," she said directing me. "Water represents life," she continued with a soft tone.

Icicles hung from the Baron Bakery sign, and I was freezing even though I wore my thickest sweater under my down jacket. Never ever in a million years had I been cold in my purple down coat, not even way up in the mountains. To take my gloves off before I got warm seemed ludicrous. Then to dunk them in water was even more absurd. I felt like my head was spinning like the teacup ride at Downey Park, except this roller coaster wasn't fun. I wanted to tell Bubbe a thing or two, but my flair had faded and my frame of mind couldn't cope with confrontation. So I dipped my hands in the water, wiped them with a towel, and thumped upstairs to the apartment. I threw my coat in the closet and was ready to run to my room when I was struck by what I saw.

"We have Rabbi Goodblatt to thank for this, although I didn't get much sleep," Bubbe said as she led me to the living room and then the dining area. "*shiva* is kind of a food fest, where people fill their stomachs, drink and remember."

How all this had been prepared was a mystery. The living room was filled with rich luscious cheeses, ripe sweet fruits, brisket and tender sirloin, *kugle, challah*, and there was even Bubbe's Baron Booming Caramel Confection Apple Cake in the center of a huge assortment of pastries.

Something caught in my eye, and I couldn't get it out so I went to the large intricately framed mirror. Why was it covered by material? I raced to the guest bathroom, but that mirror was also covered.

"Bubbe, why did you cover the mirrors?"

"During *shiva* Jewish people cover mirrors because they should be mourning and not concerned with their own appearance."

"That makes no sense. What if you're trying to see what's caught in your eye or something itches you and you need the mirror to see what it is?"

"Then you ask your grandmother for help."

I pointed to where my eye was irritated, and Bubbe pulled down the skin underneath my lid and found a lash floating.

"See, no problem and no need for the mirror."

"Thank you, Bubbe. Is it okay if I go to my room?"

"Oh, *bubeleh*." Bubbe took my cheeks in her hands and pressed her lips all over my face. Her breath smelled like some kind of sweet liquor. "Everyone will understand. Go right ahead. You can join everyone when you're ready."

***

I nodded—anything to get away. Maybe some physical therapy would help. As soon as I got to my room, I rushed to the heating vent to warm up. The sight of another cloth covering my mirror in my room jolted me.

"Bubbe, Dad wasn't Jewish, and Mom didn't practice. This is supposed to be for them, not you." Bubbe wasn't near, but I had to let out my frustrations. I gritted my teeth and then burst into tears. "Mom, Dad, I need you!"

Nobody was around to comfort me, so I calmed myself, taking deep breaths. I shut my eyes and leaned back to stretch out on my puny bed and drifted off. Waking up disorientated, I sat straight up. My head pounded into the sloped wall.

My poor noodle was going to turn into mush.

I heard a knock at my door. At least an hour had passed, but I still was not ready to face anybody, especially not Bubbe needling me to join the guests.

"Could you leave me be?" I weakly shouted through the door. "I really don't want to see anybody."

"Oh, *bubeleh*, I'm sorry you have to go through this," Bubbe said. "Seeing your friends and family might make you feel better."

I went to the door and cracked it open. "Half those people I don't even know. And covering all the mirrors—Bubbe, you're taking this too far. Dad hated this religious stuff."

"Well, your dad married your mom. She is Jewish because Zeyde and I are Jewish. And Zeyde and I have a Jewish household." Bubbe paused and took a breath. Then her eyes met mine. "Come on, *bubeleh*, stop being an *ongehblozzen*." Her voice was soft, but *ongeh*-whatever didn't sound so good. "I know it's hard, but you've got lots of friends and neighbors that drove a long way to sit *shiva* with you."

"I don't even know what *ungerotzen* is."

"*Ongehblozzen* is someone who is full of herself—I don't mean to be harsh, but that is how you are behaving. This is a time to mourn, pray, and honor your parents' lives. Sulking about how we do *shiva* doesn't help. You would never behave like this if your mother were here."

"If Mom were here, there would be no need for all of this."

Bubbe was silent. Her lips hardened as she nodded her head.

Bubbe's words pierced my heart. Why did she have to be so blunt? You would think that she'd give me a little break. Like a reminder of my parents' death is going to help matters. I groaned.

Why did she have to be right? She was always right. Just like my mom. I couldn't help but kick the suitcase.

"*Oy vey gevalt,* your mother would roll over in her grave if she saw how you were acting."

Then there was silence. A sword twisted between my ribs as I contemplated my mother's activities down beneath the earth.

When Mom was alive, she only ate kosher food and celebrated *Shabbat* when we visited Bubbe and Zeyde. But, we never observed Judaism in our own home. I remembered the last time I visited my grandparents. It was Passover. Actually, the dinner was kind of fun. We read this book called the *Haggadah* about how God told Moses to guide the Jews to freedom. And, we got to eat these flat breads called *matzah* and this nutty, fruity spread called *charoset*. At the end of this totally cool story, Zeyde hid the *matzah* and when I found it, he gave me five bucks. But, as soon as all the religious stuff was over and we got in our car to leave, Dad headed for the next town to buy a ham hoagie and any other non-kosher edibles he could get. Mom went along with Dad's rebellious antics because he was totally cool and kind of charming when we were with Bubbe and Zeyde.

On the other hand, Mom did light candles and say a little prayer on Friday nights. But it wasn't like any kind of Jewish tradition. Mom belted out tunes in English—it could have been a Beatle's song, a Jamaican jingle, or something she made up.

"Judaism wasn't a part of Mom's life except when we visited you."

"Well," Bubbe said and then paused. I heard her take a breath before continuing. "You are here now. And just because your mom didn't practice, doesn't mean she didn't believe in and value Judaic principles. It's just that she followed the theories in a different way. Sweetie, it's just the way it is. Your mom was a Jew, and so are you."

Neither of us said anything more for a moment. If a pin dropped, it would have sounded like thunder.

"I won't bother you anymore," she said. "I just knocked on your door to tell you that Tutti was looking for you. Should I tell her you won't come down to see her?"

I looked toward the door and quickly hurried to stop Bubbe. Wiping my slippery face, I turned the knob.

"Oh, my *kinderlekh*," Bubbe said embracing me. Though my ears were being crushed, I allowed my grandmother to smother me between her big, billowy boobs.

"You come down when you're ready," Bubbe said as she gave me a final squoosh.

"Tell Tutti that I won't be long," I said, sniffling as I tried to regain my breath.

Bubbe nodded. After trying to scoop my thick curls around my ears, Bubbe reached over and dried my tears, pressed her lips against my forehead, and turned to leave.

Was this for real? Why wasn't she freaking out? If anyone ever talked back to Bubbe, she'd go wild. I mean, whenever she thought I was the slightest bit disobedient to my mom, she'd call me a spoiled brat and spew out tons of Jewish words and go haywire. My eyes followed her. Mom must've inherited her kooky mannerisms from Bubbe. They were like identical twins. Even their figures were the same. Except, Mom was a lot skinnier. Bubbe's bottom looked like two oversized beach balls ricocheting against each other. If Bubbe had any idea about the field day my parents launched when her bouncing backside came into play...I quivered just thinking about it.

"Where did Bubbe get a butt like that?" Dad would say to Mom as he patted her rear end.

"My dad married her for that butt—" Mom would retort, "—thank you very much."

"I didn't say there was anything wrong with it. I like it."

At that, Mom would shake her hips.

My tears were like a runaway train, but as I moved my thighs from side to side, a giggle jumped from my mouth. People used to say that Dad got a double whammy when he had me; they said he had made a clone of Mom. Thank God my likeness had nothing to do with the Baron Butt. At least, I hoped not. I knocked into a table, which caused Scruffy to meow.

"Where did you come from?" I said with a shrug and shooed the pest away. I uncovered the mirror. Bubbe would never know.

Then I turned my back to the reflection and looked to see if my little tush was as big as Bubbe's, or Mom's for that matter. Reassured, I recovered the mirror.

I heard a screech from Scruffy as she darted out the window and down the fire escape.

Scruffy had it so easy. She could just flatten herself and jiggle through a partially opened window to escape. It would be utterly cool if I could sneak down those metal rafters so that I could be freed from the tortures that I was about to face. Too bad I didn't have a car. Then again, I was only twelve, and driving was against the law. Plus, not having enough money was a barrier, and plunging into that pile of trash at the bottom of the ladder was totally gross. Also, who knows when I'd get to see Tutti again?

Watching the mass of fur fly down the stairs was my only alternative. Plunking down on the bed was a relief. I pulled off the cat hairs and I looked at my open luggage. A corner of the art deco box peeped out from the shirts.

With extra care, I opened the legacy and stared at the contents. We never got to refill it with Milky Ways.

I closed my eyes and pictured Dad hugging me. It would always be our secret.

Bubbe could never find out about the candy bars because they were store-bought, and Bubbe had a hissy fit if everything wasn't either fresh from the grocer or made from scratch. I didn't know if Hershey treats were included, but I wasn't about to take any chances, and Bubbe didn't have to know.

I gently rested the box in the drawer where my neatly folded shirts were going to be organized. Then I unrolled the wool shirt and placed the perfume bottle on top of the portion of the table I would call my vanity. The sewing machine would be positioned on the work area section. As I lifted it, there was a relapse of pain, but the excitement of making this room my own softened my soreness. Mom and I had created lots of clothes together, including the gray sweater I was wearing. I nuzzled my nose in the floppy turtleneck and snuggled my arms against my body. Then I sneezed.

"That damned cat."

I lifted the stage make-up my mom had given me from a pocket inside one of the bags, and I organized each item in a drawer that was located underneath the covered mirror.

"Okay, this actually might be kinda cool," I said, not believing, but trying to make myself feel better. "It's not as large as my old work area, but it's still good, and maybe I can gather some strength to organize some of this stuff." But, I was kidding myself. I felt as weak as a fly that had just been swatted.

When I spotted my Bruce Lee picture, the one my parents had surprised me with the day after the Ming Tournament, I tried separating it from the rest, but a small sting in my back caused me to freeze. I had to concentrate in order to drive any pain I was carrying away. My focus had to center on my karate. Nobody could take that from me.

I spun around. Avoiding the side bureau, I leapt into a spinning crescent kick. As I landed, my leg lifted above my head and cut straight down in front as if I were breaking an imaginary board. Then I dodged a standing lamp, moved forward, and as I pictured attackers coming at me with huge poles, I blocked them with several upper arm blocks. As I hopped to the side, I completed a jumping roundhouse, laterally lifting my leg and thrusting the top of my foot forward. Then I stepped into a front kick, causing my foot to smash into my second invented target. After taking a couple of breaths and readjusting my position in order to avoid knocking into the work table, I finished my final move by ducking the sloped wall, turning my head behind me, and bending to sweep my leg around in order to trip my opponent. As I finalized my routine by flattening my right hand above my head, my pinky led my fingers downward and I visualized a clean break for my third wood slab.

Envisioning my parents standing inside the covered mirror, beaming with delight, my energy surged. Practicing those moves nonstop for months, across the living room, when we shopped, in the park—you name it—had paid off.

I took my black belt from the suitcase and with care tied it around my karate uniform. There was no way I was going to leave my *dobohk* behind, even if Master Luna wasn't my instructor anymore.

There was a knock at the door. I hid my karate uniform in the back of the closet.

"Who is it?" I asked, dreading another interaction with my grandmother.

"It's me, Tutti. Your grandma told me to wait patiently, but I really missed you and wanted to see you. I tried getting your attention at the funeral, but I guess there were too many people."

"Oh, I'm sorry." I rushed to the door and opened it.

We hugged, and when we parted, Tutti twisted her skinny knobby knees that were covered with the multi-colored stockings that I had made her for her last birthday, and around her neck was the scarf that matched. Her bright cherry hair outlined her freckled face and infectious smile.

"Those stockings and that scarf have got to be the new Bonet Sensation," I said snapping my fingers.

"I think they are one of your top fashion statements. They are totally warm. They're not black, but everything else I'm wearing is."

We hugged again. "Sorry I never got to say good-bye. They imprisoned me in that dreary hospital 'til right before we left."

"Yeah, my parents told me. I wanted to visit, but my parents said that it wasn't a good idea. I'm sorry about all the stuff you're going through, but at least I get to see you now. Hey, you took that Bruce Lee print with you."

"There was no way I was leaving that behind."

"You know, your mom had your surprise planned as soon as she found out you were going to be asked to the Ming Tournament. You kept on asking me if it was too outrageously expensive to ask your parents for it. Personally, I thought it was. But, when your mom asked if I knew what she should get you for your birthday, I figured I'd mention it, just in case. She didn't even bat an eye. You tortured me."

"I did not."

"Yes you did, and you drooled every time you passed by the antique shop. I've never seen a picture excite someone so much." Tutti giggled and jumped around, singing, "I'm so excited...I'm so excited."

"I didn't drool," I said while I gave her a playful nudge.

After she was finished teasing me, we sat down and both gazed at Bruce Lee.

"Your mom was totally revved when I told her about that print and asked me to go with her to get it. The guy at the store said it was really rare and a collector's item. I know your mom annoyed you, but she really loved you."

"I know...I really loved her." My eyes didn't want to leave the floor. Holding my breath didn't stop the tears from drenching my skin. "I shouldn't have given her so much flack."

Tutti wrapped her arms around me, and my body collapsed into her. As I regained strength, her grip loosened, she looked toward me. I couldn't speak. Then, all of a sudden, she waltzed over to Bruce Lee.

"Your mom was going to give it to you on your birthday, but then decided to give it to you after the tournament. She wanted to make sure; you got a trophy, even if you didn't win anything at the competition. It was a last minute decision, and she was afraid you'd suspect something. She specifically told me to distract you at your little party."

"So you were in cahoots with Mom?" I said.

"Didn't do a bad job either. Not once did you ask about your parents' birthday present." Tutti beamed so brightly that I thought she was going to burn a whole in the floor. "She wanted you to know that you were a winner no matter what. And, totally cool, you won. You beat all those people." We both glared at Bruce Lee. "Where are you going to put it?"

"I thought it would look kind of neat hanging on the wall where that slope is, above my bed."

"I never would have thought of that. That'll look awesome. Oh, and Bubbe told me that the rabbi downstairs does martial arts too. Totally, cool; you two will have something in common. He said that you're going to have a *bat mitzvah*. That's incredible."

"What, a *bat mitzvah*? You've got to be kidding me. This is all getting way out of hand." I plopped myself on the chair by my worktable. "My grandparents are destroying my life. If I was going to have a *bat mitzvah*, my mom would've planned for it."

"So you're not going to have one?" Tutti sounded disappointed.

"I don't know what I'm going to do," I said. "It's just that this is a really Jewish neighborhood, and I don't know the first thing about Judaism. What am I going to do?"

"You know a lot more than most." My forehead furrowed. "It'll be okay, and the people seem really nice, and you get to learn about your history. That's amazing. Plus, there is this one really cute boy I saw. You gotta come down and check him out." Tutti pushed me toward the door. "And that rabbi, totally in another dimension. He looks like some character from the sixties. He's got a ponytail and those long curls hanging by his cheeks, and what are those things called that Jewish men wear on top of their heads? He wore a plain black one during the funeral and in the synagogue."

"*Yarmulkes,*" I answered.

"Yeah, *yam-locos.* But he has beautiful flowers embroidered on the one he's wearing now. Usually it would be too girly for a man, but it's not. It's kinda high style vogue." She looked like she was checking for a response, but before I was able to say something she continued. "When he talks, he has an old-fashioned Yiddish or Israeli accent or something. And when he came in, he put his keys down so that he could try and find something he had for your grandma. When he finally found a card for her, he forgot where he placed his keys and while frantically searching for them he tripped over your Bubbe's cat."

"Scruffy," I said quickly so I'd get at least one word in.

"That's right, Scruffy, and the keys magically appeared by his nose. Then he looked up and said some funny Jewish words, crossed his eyes, and ended with, 'See, *Hashem* works in mysterious ways.' I don't know who *Hashem* is, but everyone was laughing."

I wanted to explain to Tutti who *Hashem* was, but her ADHD was getting the best of her and she ignored anything I was trying to say.

"You kinda had to be there. Then he said something so sweet. He said that your mom had made the *yam-loco.* It was a present before she left for college. You've got to see it. It's totally fab—you know it's got your mom's distinctive touch." Tutti grabbed my hand and began tugging at me again to go down the stairs. "You've got to meet him."

CHAPTER V

Shiva

At the synagogue, everyone was dressed in dark clothes and one man had fringes hanging from a white shawl. Actually, many of the men had white strings that were suspended underneath their jackets, even some women. They reminded me of that movie *Fiddler on the Roof* where every one wore those Jewish fedoras and *yarmulkes* and had strings hanging from their shirts. Dispersed were some people from my neighborhood. How they all fit into my grandparents' apartment was beyond my comprehension.

"Your grandparents know a lot of rabbis," Tutti said.

"I don't know if they are all rabbis, but they might be just super religious. Dealing with all this stuff isn't going to be easy." I said. "Bubbe wouldn't even let me wear one of the cool outfits I made with Mom. I mean, I went to a synagogue once or twice before, and I've learned a little about being Jewish, but not like these people. It seems like everyone wears the same type of clothes. See those shawls they're wearing? They are called *tallits*. There is no way I'm ever going to dress like that."

"I kind of think they're cool, like something you would find at a high-end boutique. Oh look, that guy has something underneath." Tutti pointed me toward a man dressed with the entire Jewish garb. "See it swinging?"

"Those knotted things attached to the *tallit* are called *tzittzit*. I didn't realize my grandparents were so devout, and that there were women rabbis too."

"Women rabbis?" Tutti's eyes widened.

Well some of them were wearing *tallits* at the synagogue. I thought only rabbis wore *tallits*. Either which way, I've never seen so many religious get ups in my whole life."

One of the men dressed in black with round, thick glasses and sandy-colored curls hanging from his cheeks was laughing and waving his arms while he told a story to the crowd. A lump of dip or something was hanging from his chin. The people around him were clapping their hands with amusement and didn't seem to notice the goop on his face. Some children raced through the mob and continued chasing each other around and under tables playing tag. Nobody flinched at the madhouse.

"I kind of remember that guy over there," I said. That's Rabbi Goodblatt. He always showed up when I used to visit my grandparents. Hey, isn't that the *yarmulke* you were talking about? I think I've seen it before."

A crowd of people flooded around me. Watching Tutti stand there patiently waiting for me to do my duty magnified my anxiety. My lips bobbed from one cheek to the next, foreign arms draped around my body, and wishes of sorrow soared in and out of my ears. When I was just about to grab Tutti to make our getaway, Bubbe offered us some raspberry *rugellah*. Tutti wasn't about to resist the bite-sized, sweet, doughy treats, so I submitted and took some also.

"Rabbi Goodblatt! Rabbi Goodblatt!" Bubbe called. "Thank you for such a beautiful ceremony."

Tripping over his feet, Goodblatt rushed over to greet us. "Oh my, *shana punim,* you remind me so much of your mother. I have a feeling she would have done the same as you at the cemetery. You have grown up." Goodblatt pinched my cheeks. "You are coming to the next *Shabbat*, aren't you? Your mom got a kick out of this story. It's a *Parsha* explaining how obstacles can become blessings. Do you know who Jacob is?"

I shrugged my shoulders assuming that Jacob most likely was somebody in the Bible.

"Well, he is one of the patriarchs in the Torah. When he was born, his twin brother blocked him from leaving the womb with his foot. Jacob had no choice but to push against his brother's heel, which aided his ability to be born. It shows us how barriers can cause us to move forward."

Thinking about babies kicking each other in amniotic fluid was totally disgusting. I had enough to deal with, like that fur ball that was rubbing her body against the rabbi's leg. Goodblatt picked her up.

"Little Scruffy helped me find my keys," he said as he rubbed her belly and nuzzled his nose against hers. After taking a moment to cover his face and sneeze he turned toward me. "I hope I am blessed with your presence at *shul*."

"Of course we'll be there," Bubbe said.

"*Halal*," he said as he bowed to Bubbe and then he focused on me. "Oh, by the way, Alexia, I heard you're going to be studying for your *bat mitzvah—mazel tov*."

I glanced at Bubbe. My tongue tangled. So, I grinned graciously.

"When your mother had her *bat mitzvah*, how your grandparents *kvelled*," the rabbi said. "It was a beautiful sight. You've got that glow, just like your mother. Did I ever tell you that she made me this?" The rabbi pointed to his cap. "She was a talented and amazing lady.

As they finished their conversation, Scruffy moved next to the rabbi, sneaking licks of cake crumbs from the floor, and Goodblatt accidentally stumbled over her again.

"That cat, she must be trying to warn me about something," Goodblatt said as everyone laughed.

The distraction gave me enough time to grab Tutti's hand and pull her behind a pillar without anyone noticing.

"Let's go hide somewhere in the bakery. It's like a maze in the kitchen with all the aisles of pots and pans." I crept toward the stairway leading to the bakery, making sure Tutti stayed close behind me. "And wait 'til you see the front part where the people order the pastries. It's small, but adorable. It used to be just take-out and deliveries, but remember those chairs that Mom designed for Bubbe?"

"You mean those cool-looking stools with leopard material for seat covers?"

"They totally increased The Baron Bakery business twofold. Zeyde said that People started hanging out at the bakery. And, he wouldn't stop saying how," I placed my two fingers by my face making a quotation sign, "*Bubbe kvelled*."

"You're a lot like your mom," Tutti said and bumped her elbow in my side. "You are really going to liven up your grandparents' lives."

"I need a breather from all of these people. Come on, you've got to see that photo of Bubbe and Zeyde I told you about. It's hanging on the center wall in the bakery so everyone can see it when they enter. You've got to check it out."

"Okay," Tutti said. "Oh wait—look—there's that hot-looking redhead I was talking about. Oops, he just spilled grape juice all over himself."

I heard her, but I got distracted when I saw this black-haired boy helping a little toddler who was crying because he couldn't reach the sweet, nutty pastry called *schnecken*. Holding on to his *yarmulke*, the boy began making faces, gave the cutie pie one of those sweet buns, and then did a little tap dance. The toddler's tears disappeared, and the mother ran over to thank him.

"You are such a little *mensch*, David. Your parents must be proud," the mother said as she lifted her baby.

The boy named David shrugged, and then blushed as he chanced a gaze toward me. My stomach flip-flopped and I didn't know what to do, so I snatched Tutti. I didn't want him to think I was spying on him or anything.

"Come on, let's go to the bakery," I said.

***

We ran down the stairs and halted underneath an archway. The door was already open. Pride surged through my body as I watched Tutti absorb her surroundings. She wandered through the kitchen to the parlor. On the left was the countertop I had told Tutti about lots of times. The two stools that my mom had designed were on the right and each seat had black-wired, wide backs to lean on.

"Dad worked hours upon hours to construct these chairs—he had to meet Mom's specifications. She spent hours trying to find that plush fabric. And, see how the black and brown iron swirls down the center?"

"I remember when your dad was molding all that stuff together. He said that the black-wired, wide backs were perfect, but he was afraid your grandma wasn't going to be happy with the polka-dotted kitty look."

"Yeah, he thought Bubbe was too traditional to understand Mom's style."

Tutti's dimples perked.

"Okay, you've heard this a million times," I said and Tutti cleared her throat. "A zillion times, but this is the real thing. You finally get to see everything in real life."

"I know. It's totally cool. I'll never forget when your mom convinced your dad that you grandparents weren't as old-fashioned as he thought. When he said that he'd construct the chairs, she couldn't contain herself. She jumped on him, wrapped her legs around him, and he tumbled to the floor. Then she smooched him all over." Tutti's braces sparkled.

"Here are the stools." I pulled one over for her to sit on and plunked myself in the other. "We gave them to my grandparents on their 50th anniversary. You should've seen Bubbe and Zeyde jump out of their socks. They were so thrilled." I patted the furry seats.

"They've been in the bakery ever since." Tutti said, finishing my thoughts.

We took turns spinning each other.

Then she stopped me and cleared her throat. "You're forgetting about the story?"

"*A bisseleh chain iz shoin nit gemain.* Do you remember what that means?"

"Does an Italian eat meatballs? I've only heard this rendition more than you've karate chopped the air." Tutti placed her hands on her hips while she leaned her head to the side. "A little charm and you want to be ordinary."

"A little charm and you are not ordinary, smarty pants," I said imitating her motions.

"That's what I meant, double extra large smarty pants—except I didn't know *smarty pants* was a part of the translation," she said wiping off pretend spit.

"Okay, okay. Shall I continue?"

"Is my hair red?"

"Okay, when Zeyde sat on the stool for the first time, he pointed to my mom and said those words. He was really proud of her."

"She was pretty amazing."

"Yeah."

"She could make a doghouse look like a palace."

"Yeah, and all she needed was some cardboard." We both smiled.

Tutti spun her chair.

"Your turn," she said.

"To talk or turn," I said.

Tutti swiveled and I followed. She quickened her speed and there was no way I was about to trail behind. When we stopped our bodies swayed.

"Enticing people with funky chairs so they would hang around and drink coffee—maybe buy some more pastries—nobody would ever think of that, but my mom."

"She was brilliant."

"I never gave her enough credit. Bubbe sure did. *Where did you get all that talent?* Bubbe always asked her. Then she'd sing *Halleluiah.*" I started to stare off into space, picturing the memory.

Tutti jerked me back to reality. "And you got your finesse from your mom," she said.

"You're a goofball," I said.

"And I thought you didn't know anything about Judaism. If that's the case, how do you know all those Jewish words?"

"First, I saw *Fiddler on the Roof,* and second *goofball* isn't a Jewish word."

Tutti stood there and cracked her knuckles.

"And, *halleluiah* doesn't have to be Jewish."

She crunched the knuckles in her other hand and I winced.

"Well, if you're referring to those other jazzy words, they're Yiddish...I think. I told you that Bubbe and Zeyde have taught me a little. Mom used to zing some at me. I just know a few like *mazel tov* and *mensch—oy vey—*okay and some others, but the people here are super Jewish."

"Don't you think that's better than butterscotch? I wish I knew something about my heritage. You've taught me more about your background, than I even know about mine. You explained to me what *motzeel tuff* meant that time when we watched that movie on Judaism. It means congratulations or something, right?"

"Yeah, and I think *mazel tov* also means good luck."

"See, you're going to learn so much, and then you can teach me." Tutti stumbled staring at the glass plates on top of the pastry bar. "Hey, to the right of that Formica counter, right next to that cash register, is that where your grandmother displays her cakes?"

"How could you tell?" I asked. The empty cake plates were in plain view.

"Does she put Bubbe's Baron Booming Caramel Confection Apple Cake here?" Tutti pointed to the center dish.

"That's the primo place for the cherry cheese danishes. Did you have one? She always forms them like a pyramid right next to the register."

"I had two. They were the best. As a matter of fact, I think I had too much of everything."

"And that's my favorite of all my mom's photos." I pointed at the portrait of my grandparents hanging high above on the wall. "My mom captured the crux of Bubbe's craziness." We laughed. "Look at the way she is threatening Zeyde with a rolling pin above his head."

"I'll never forget that weekend. I was fuming with rage because I was supposed to be in this neat karate exhibition, but Mom said it was more important to visit my grandparents. *They may not always be around and you should always appreciate every moment you have with them.* Pretty ironic, huh?"

We were quiet.

"You know, your grandpa's got that wink and, oh my God, how he holds your Bubbe—like Conrad Birdie, you know that suave rock star in that musical. Your grandpa is not so young, but he's got that pizazz. And your grandma—that surprised, cross-eyed gaze is hilarious."

"Yeah, my grandparents are like a comedy routine. Do you think married couples just get that way after being together so long?"

"I don't think so. My parents aren't like that. When they fight, they don't speak for days and everyone hides behind doors. It takes a while before they come out and enjoy each other again. I like the way your family handles the garbage. They lay it out so it can be thrown away and they open a new bag to fill without hesitation."

"Yeah, Mom always said that holding on to trash stinks up a room. Even though they had loads of little arguments, the rubbish was easy to ignore, because once it was out of the bag, there was no use for it."

"This picture is a perfect example," Tutti interjected.

"My parents were having one of their little spats. Then, Bubbe and Zeyde began squabbling about Mom and Dad's dispute. This distracted my parents who then concentrated on calming my grandparents down, which caused them to forget about their own argument."

"So one moment your parents were throwing garbage at each other and then, all of a sudden, your grandparents decided to take over the haul, and your parents gladly gave it away."

"You could say that. I thought my mom was going to clean up the spill between Bubbe and Zeyde, but she just raised her hands. 'I had enough. I'm going upstairs to figure out this new camera attachment. Make sure they don't kill each other,' as if her hands were washed of any damage, and she was allowing her parents to have their turn. Then, she started climbing the steps."

"I wish I could've been there to see your grandma chase your grandpa."

"You would've been dumbfounded. As soon as Mom left, Bubbe started chasing Zeyde, threatening him with that big dough masher. It was if they didn't even know Dad and I were in the same room."

"It sounds like your mom was a lot like your grandma.

"She was. You know how Dad was impulsive? I'll never forget how he raced toward the stairs grasping the handle for balance, yelling up to Mom, *Jude, Jude, it's the picture of a lifetime, don't miss it—hurry.*"

"She was immersed with her camera trying to figure out how it worked, right?" Tutti said.

"Did I ever tell you that she was absorbed in her new gadget, trying to figure out something about some contrast button somehow."

"Hello," Tutti said sarcastically.

"How about her racing down the steps when she heard Dad and getting to the kitchen just in time to catch Bubbe trying to whack Zeyde over the head."

"I'll never forget you telling me when she said, '*Jelly Belly, this is perfection.* I could picture her snapping the button on the camera." Tutti pretended to push a lever. "And, then waving it in the air." She waved her arms above her head.

I straightened the masterpiece. "You should've seen Bubbe, when she saw Zeyde hanging the picture. There was no way she wanted anyone to see it. The fit she threw was worse than when I tricked you into eating those chili peepers. When she demanded that Zeyde burn the film, he just laughed and pulled out his empty pockets."

"Just like you giving me that empty glass of water when my mouth was on fire. I thought you got that rascally behavior from your dad but now I'm not so sure. Look at that wink. Your grandpa has that mischievous glow."

"You should have seen Bubbe. *Where is the koved?*" she shouted. "That means respect."

Tutti crossed her arms and glared at me.

"Okay, so I know a few words, but that doesn't mean I'm a Jew." I mimicked her motion.

"Well, aren't you supposed to be Jewish if your mom's Jewish?" she asked.

"I guess, but..," she interrupted me.

"It doesn't matter, go ahead."

"Gee, thanks." I said as I tried to remember where we were in the story. "Oh yeah, Zeyde's response, it's the coolest. *You're always kvetching how I don't respect you. You are a mensch.* Then he continued on in Yiddish, saying that he'd never want to disrespect her, *Zol* something or other—Yiddish phrases that I think were supposed to mean something extra nice. I wasn't sure because *I'm* not Jewish." I paused to make sure Tutti got my drift. She crossed her arms waiting for me to continue. "Well, he insisted that she was the boss. Then he turned her around and gave her a big fat kiss."

"Your *Zeyde* knows how to handle your *Bubbe*. That must be because they've lived together so long?"

"I guess so. Bubbe acts like a deranged sociopath sometimes, and I don't know how Zeyde does it, but he humbles himself and announces how incredible she is and she falls for it every single time. My parents were kind of like that too."

"Not mine. My parents become raving lunatics and don't speak to each other for a few days. They're both too stubborn to give in to the other. They end up pretending nothing ever happened. At least your family knows how to release their pent-up rage."

"Yeah, but their outbursts are never-ending."

"They're a perpetual whoopee cushion. You've got to admit the hot air they blow is pretty funny. You're going to have a blast living here," Tutti insisted. "Saturday cartoons aren't half as entertaining as your Bubbe and Zeyde, and you'll learn Hebrew or Yiddish, or both. It'll be better than chewing on those gooey chocolate bars."

"Excuse me, are you insulting my treasure trove?"

"This place is not home like you know it, but it's going to be better than you realize."

"Come on, every one here is way too Jewish. Creepy smelly rats have replaced the cute little raccoons that used to ravage our trash, and instead of finding pink adorable rabbits nibbling in your garden of carrots and parsnips, a grimy stinky vagrant pukes and defecates in the alleyways and on the grates. See that." I pointed out of the window. "Beer cans and cigarettes pollute the streets. Plus, no one has personality. They're like those old TV sets that have no color; a vast hole of nothingness."

"Lighten up, Miss Drama Princess. It's a funeral. The color scheme is supposed to be dark. Come on, the rabbi was kinda different with that ponytail and crazy hat. Plus, you can come visit me anytime on the weekends or on holidays. We'll pick you up at the train station. Just give it a chance." Tutti's eyes were fixated on me and she wouldn't let up with her stupid arguments.

"Okay, okay. But, promise me that we won't lose touch."

"Just because we live far away, doesn't mean our friendship disappears. Best friends forever, remember?"

"Yeah."

"You can do better than that." Tutti put her hands on her hips.

"Well, I guess exploring the ins and outs of this place won't be so bad, and I could stay up late at night creating stories about these people and send them to you."

Tutti did a little jig and hugged me. With all my might, my arms pressed against her. I didn't want to let her go. Bubbe yelled for us, so we went upstairs.

***

The door opened and we searched the room.

"Everybody's gone," Tutti said.

"And we have to get going too," her mother said.

Holding back my tears, I watched my best friend leave, not knowing when I would see her again.

After helping my grandparents tidy up, I went to my room. As I dropped into bed, darting spasms ran through my body. My eyes were heavy, but I needed to taste something from my special box before I'd allow myself to sleep. While cherishing the melted chocolate around my tongue, the paper crackled next to my heart. Freeing a hand, I grabbed the picture of me with my parents under our fig tree. Wandering above, my eyes searched in and out of the rooftops. The stars were somewhere up there.

CHAPTER VI

Coping

An avalanche of mixed up circumstances had fallen and I was lucky my grandparents offered shelter. They had spoken to me about taking off a semester of school to mourn and recuperate from what had happened, but we all agreed that my parents wouldn't have wanted me to stop my education and school would help me adjust. So, though I only had a few days until winter break was over, Bubbe worked vigorously so that I could enter classes on the first day of the semester.

"You might want to change your outfit. Its your first day: the kids are more conservative than you are used to," Bubbe said.

"My mom and I made this outfit on my sewing machine. When I wore it at the school in Spring Falls, it was the rave. The bright-colored birds of paradise might charm the kids at this new place. See—look how they dangle across the various shades of green. Don't they make you smile?" I pirouetted.

Bubbe's eyes widened.

"It flows, don't you think?"

Bubbe flinched and then smiled with her crooked teeth clenched together. There was a pause.

"Can you see how we sewed these pastel flowers on the stockings? Don't you think it will make the other kids curious?" I thought I could make Bubbe agree that my originality might engage my classmates. "The lilies and petunias on the leggings could be conversation starters."

The strength in my voice dwindled as I watched Bubbe's face blank. However, she did touch the velvety flowers on my legs. I thought I saw her crack a smile. But, whatever I thought I saw meant nothing.

"*Bubeleh*, your innovations are wonderful. But the children around here are more traditional than you are accustomed to. Maybe you should introduce your creativity a little bit at a time so they can get used to you."

"*Oy gevalt*, let the child be," Zeyde said as he pinched my cheeks and gave me a kiss. "Never lose your *chutzpah*. It reminds me of your mother, and if people don't like it, they're *bobkes*."

"*Bobkes*?"

"Worthless."

I was relieved that Zeyde understood me.

Scruffy zoomed in from outside, shaking mud on my leggings. The damage this one cat could accomplish was beginning to grate on my nerves. I wiped the mud off my flowers as best I could and threw on my comfy purple down jacket. I didn't care. Tutti was right. I needed to take on this new world with zest and zeal. Flipping out the map Bubbe had made, I marched down the street.

"Your line-up number is 6B and don't forget your scarf and mittens!" Bubbe called.

Though Bubbe's voice was clear as a sunny spring day, it was too late for reminders. Flying out of the door and forging ahead consumed my mind. My pockets would keep my hands warm.

***

As I passed litter in the streets and saw graffiti-covered buildings, my brain filled with ways to revive the neighborhood. Some of the windows were covered by rotted cardboard, but that was an easy fix. Captivated by the brick and stone buildings, I studied the intricate details that appeared as my eyes followed the details upward. Gargoyle heads stuck out of walls, and various carvings decorated the sandstone. When I inspected several thick railings, I noticed a twirling design when they reached the sidewalk; they were more like sculptures than simple hand rests. The possibilities in this neighborhood were endless, but why did it get so junked up in the first place?

The store ahead of me was a bland, brick, square with a shabby black and white sign that said *Beakman Boutique*. It had horrible knock-off clothes on one side and religious garments on the other—totally weird. But my priority at this point was not to be judgmental. On the other hand, that Beakman's was a disaster.

Some girls about my age were walking in front of me, going in the same direction. They were all wearing tacky, fake-leather, bloated coats, like they were bought at some no-name outlet. Even their mittens and hats were made out of cheap phony fur. On the other hand, the girls seemed cheery enough, laughing and immersed in animated conversation. But then again, people are a lot like they dress, and those girls were really goofy-looking. Stopping myself from being too critical, I decided to try and make new friends.

However, no matter how much I increased my pace, catching up to the girls was impossible. I didn't realize that the accident had weakened me so much. A girl with a French braid turned her head and I waved, but she didn't gesture back. My body still had remnants of pain, so I slowed my pace and let the girls go on their way. If they were rushing to the same school, we would meet anyway.

When I arrived at Shalom Middle School I was stunned when I saw a huge, plain, brick building surrounded by a massive gated cement area with a metal playground. There was a jungle gym and a slide in one corner and groups of kids gathered in separate clusters in another.

In Spring Falls I went to a private school located on plush green grounds that used to be owned by Prince Shasta. Though the construction was large and spread out, it had the charm of a quaint castle. Blueberry bushes, sunflowers, along with other amazing flora and fauna surrounded the location. There was a sparkling outside pool, tennis courts, and a football and baseball field in view.

Shalom Middle School was a barren, concrete-encrusted block and it seemed like kids were swarming everywhere. I wondered if I'd ever meet up with those girls again. I found my own space and waited for the buzzer to sound while I observed. Among all the commotion, I noticed that the girls who were racing ahead of me were a few feet from where I stood. They glanced in my direction and pointed.

When the buzzer sounded, everyone scuttled to an area in front of the entrance to the school and lined up behind the adults, who were holding up numbers. The girl I had waved to and her friends scurried behind a skinny woman with thin, stringy hair. She was holding a banner that said 6B. When I moseyed toward my assigned line, I overheard the girls talking.

"That girl looks like she grew up with the Beatles or something," the girl with the French braid whispered loudly.

"Well, her dress is kind of unusual," another girl replied.

"Hey, Roni, do you think she's from some other country?"

"No, she's just strange. My mother knew her mother when she was younger."

I heard someone behind me.

"Don't worry about Roni and her crew. Their bark is worse than their bite."

I turned and it was David, from *shiva*. He smiled. My legs felt weak, and I sort of stumbled and then waved trying to cover up my awkwardness.

***

The teachers led everyone to their classrooms. Thank God my room had lots of windows, even though all I looked out to was an empty lot with a stark playground.

Names were pasted on the front of each desk. My desk was planted in the middle of the room. After introducing herself as Mrs. Schmultzer and explaining some rules, like tending to our own business between classes, and being respectful to our classmates, the teacher pointed me out as the new student.

She then asked the other children to introduce themselves and chat about their winter break. I tried to wait until the class was over, but my bladder was going to burst so I raised my hand. I was thankful when Mrs. Schmultzer called on me, but when I asked to go to the bathroom, the other children laughed.

"Hush, hush," she said to the class. Then she turned to me. "It is important you listen in class and go over the rules and regulations in this classroom. As I said before, you must relieve yourself on your own time. Your time with me is to learn, and your breaks between classes are your own."

This woman was out of her mind. At Spring Falls, the teachers never had a problem if we had to go to the bathroom. If you had to go, you had to go. I didn't realize that *tending to our own business* meant we had to let our bladders explode.

"Now, why don't you tell us about yourself?"

I have to pee, I wanted to say. Instead the robot in me came out. "Yes, Mrs. Schmultzer. My name is Alexia Bonet, and I just moved here to live with my grandparents. They own the Baron Bakery."

"Is there anything else you would like to add?" the teacher asked.

I shook my head, not knowing what else to say.

David raised his hand, diverting Mrs. Shmultzer's attention. When she called on him, stiffness released from my spine. While all the attention was diverted in his direction, my lips formed a thank you.

"This vacation was great. You know that kosher Chinese restaurant down the street? Well, my dad took me there when it opened. We were discussing whether there were Chinese Jews. I said there were, and my Dad said that there weren't. So I asked the waiter whether he knew if there were any Chinese Jews. The waiter said *Aw, one secon pees. Leh me check.*"

David was really funny the way he imitated the Chinese accent.

"He goes in the kitchen and comes back," David continued. "He says, *I hab the answer to you queston. We hab orange jews, tomato jews, and cranberry jews.*"

The classroom filled with laughter, and I was relieved the focus was off of me. I noticed a short glance from David and smiled. Mrs. Schmultzer joined the fun, but explained that it wasn't nice to make fun of other people's ethnicities. This woman was lamer than I had thought. David wasn't even making fun of the waiter's ethnicity; he was making fun of his accent. Meanwhile, I was afraid I was going to pee in my pants, so I crossed my legs and began to doodle on my notepad, hoping to distract my necessary function. When the bell rang, I zoomed out the door.

Art class had possibilities. Mrs. Zendeck had a fun, bubbly personality. Her long, straight, blond hair had a few braids tied with tiny, colorful animal clips, and her smock was painted in a surrealistic style with magenta and wild-colored blotches. One of the kids asked her if the blots were supposed to have meaning and she told him that he should decide for himself. Listening to her deep, soft voice was soothing. After she handed out aprons, paints, and patches of fabric, she told the class to craft whatever moved them. When we were finished, she told us to bring an object we wanted to decorate, whether it was a t-shirt or plate or cloth. With a parent or guardian's approval, we were allowed to choose our next project.

I mixed paints and cloth and constructed a three-dimensional teardrop sliding down the side of a face.

"You've got talent," Mrs. Zendek exclaimed. "You might think of entering something for the art festival."

This was more like a class I could've had at Spring Falls. I was starting to feel more comfortable until I heard an irritating voice.

"Mrs. Zendek is just trying to make Alexia feel good because she's *new*," Roni said loud enough so that I could hear.

David moved beside me. "That eye is really neat. I like the way the tear dangles."

"You're going to be crying yourself to sleep after Mr. Hames' science class. Am I right, David?" Roni said.

"She's just trying to scare you. I mean, science isn't as fun as art, and Mr. Hames is boring, but it won't be that bad," David said.

The bell rang, and we switched to the science room.

"This is a stalagmite. This is a stalactite, and this is a speleo-them," Mr. Hames said as he coughed into his yellow, creased hands. Then he hoarsely repeated the names of other stones as he used his pointer guiding us to the pictures posted in a never-ending slide show.

The pictures showed rocks clinging to the ceiling of a cave, but I mean, how could you tell one rock from the other? Between the phlegm in Mr. Hames' throat, his monotone voice, and the mind-numbing subject matter, my brain became fuzzy, and I started looking forward to my cold, hard mattress in the attic. My yawns were unstoppable. When the bell rang for lunch, I darted out to my locker.

Everyone else did the same. They, however, drifted toward people they seemed to be familiar with. I figured that all I needed to do was start up a conversation with someone. There was a girl with short brown hair and thick tortoise-shell glasses standing by my side.

"Hi, my name is Alexia. I'm new to this school. I just moved -"

"Sorry, I've got to go," the girl said as she darted to the girls' room.

I gave up trying to make friends, and nobody made any effort to talk to me, so after school I zoomed home, scurried through the bakery, and zipped to my room. During dinner I had little to say. There was no way I wanted to listen to Bubbe saying, *I told you so.* Excusing myself and escaping to my room was my first priority. My pen went straight to the paper, writing Tutti about the horrid kids living in my neighborhood. Sleep was the only way to escape my dreadful predicament.

CHAPTER VII

Cherry Cheese Heaven

While I slept my feet dangled outside of the blanket, so I had to readjust my body repeatedly. Still they drooped, catching the cold air. Searching for extra pillows was futile, and instead of finding a comfortable position, I flipped and flopped. Mid-sleep, my brain waves crossed paths with the weirdest images. Usually my dreams were swallowed into oblivion, but this one had such an impact, that it stuck in my mind—not that it made any sense. Most dreams didn't, except to Mom. She always called them "night bubbles" and said that they meant something.

It began as I sat next to David in the bakery. I hardly even knew the guy, and he popped into my dream. He scooted close to me and wriggled his butt on one of the jungle seats down in the bakery. An elbow tickled my side. My spine quivered from a chill. Then, engrossed in Bubbe's famous Baron Cherry Cheese Danish, he licked his fingers as he leaned back in his stool. He winked at me. My body froze. The echo of a police siren whizzed by, but I heard no other noise.

Where were Bubbe and Zeyde, and why was David in our shop with icing all over his face?

The dream seemed so real.

I spun my seat and peeked out of the storefront window. All of the other businesses had their security gates down.

Why weren't any of the streetlamps turned on?

While exploring the outside through the large glass window, I squinted, adjusting my vision to the pitch-black night. My eyes focused, and I caught a glimpse of one of the beacons flickering in the pouring rain. It flashed as it sprouted arms and legs. Traveling down the street, it moved as if it were forming a *hyung*—and every time it kicked or punched, its light blinked. Part of its routine was sticking one of its flat feet under each gate and lifting it then pounding its foot in a puddle. When the karate form was finished, the figure went back to its original location, bowed, and froze back into a streetlight. The storm stopped. Then, the light died out. I waited for it to come alive, but the last little spark dwindled.

"Did you see that?" I asked David.

There was no answer. I was about to turn my stool back around, but the light turned back on and beamed brighter than it had before. I waited for the others to do the same.

Everything was still. I looked across the street at the Sherman Shoe Shop and then glanced upward, above the building. The man on the moon winked at me, and I saw a portion of the Little Dipper twinkling through the cotton-ball haze that coasted above. After wiping my eyes, my tongue caught a tear.

"Why are you crying?"

"I don't know." I missed my dad, but I didn't want to tell him.

"It's all right. I get scared too."

"I'm not scared."

"Come on, everyone gets a little nervous before they, you know, have the *b-day*."

"What are you talking about?"

"You know, your *bat mitzvah*."

"Who told you I was having a *bat mitzvah*?"

"Everyone knows," he said. "What's the matter? You're going to be an adult, and everyone is going to party and have fun. It's a *mitzveh*, and your *Bubbe* and *Zeyde* will be so proud."

"What about my parents?"

Oh, no. Making him feel uncomfortable was the last thing I wanted to do. To avoid the awkwardness, I turned my head. Dashing toward the stairs was on my agenda.

"They would've been super happy," he said.

He caught my attention, and I turned my head enough to catch his smile. I smiled back.

The dawn appeared, causing the streets to glow and golden rays to shine.

"You and I are the only ones here. Isn't that cool?" David said.

As I examined the bakery, I observed that no delectable delights were in sight. Nothing was displayed behind the counter, above the tables, or even in the exhibiting cases. No *knishes*, newly baked plump bagels, scrumptious breads, or any indulgences filled the shelves. David was holding the only thing that was edible.

"Where are all the pastries?" I asked.

"I thought you left this danish out just for me. There's nothing else."

The coffeemakers weren't brewing, but the warm, cozy aroma that usually filled the shop every morning sifted through the air. While enjoying the scent of coffee, I realized that the pots were empty, yet vapors flared from them. The mist flowed towards David and surrounded a canister of whipped cream. He pointed the cylinder towards the pastry.

How could he? To defile the most incredible baked good in the Country, if not the world, was like eating pork if you were kosher. It was sacrilege. People traveled for miles to relish the sweet, savory taste of the Baron Cherry Cheese Danish. Not even Dad would dare disturb the flavor—not even if he wanted to spite Bubbe.

Just a note—outside of my dream, when we used to visit my grandparents, I ate Bubbe's homemade whipped cream every chance I could get. My hands clenched and shook until I could sample every ladle and jar that it had touched. One day, as I spooned a huge helping of Bubbe's creamy delight on my danish, Zeyde grabbed my arm. It was the first time he lost his temper with me. At least he seemed angry. He was really big, because I was so tiny.

"*A mekheieh,* when you have got a good thing, do not tamper with it," he cautioned.

"But don't you put whipped cream on everything Bubbe makes," I asked with a quivering voice.

"Ah, but interfering with the Cherry Cheese is taboo."

He might have been teasing me, but I wasn't going to take any chances.

Back to David—I checked to make sure Bubbe and Zeyde weren't in sight before attempting to steal the container from

David. He dodged my move and gazed at me. Then he pushed the cylinder of Bubbe's mouthwatering, supreme creation away. I was relieved.

Nobody else in the entire universe made whipped cream as tasty and light as Bubbe did. There was a hint of orange flavor that was indescribable. Zeyde had suggested that Bubbe dabbed some Grand Marnier liquor in the recipe, but he must have been joking because kids weren't allowed any type of alcohol, and children from all over ate Bubbe's whipped cream. It even won Bubbe the "New York's Finest Sweet Treat Award." And when that happens, *Sweet Treat* gives out the prize-winning dessert topping to a whole bunch of kids all over New York.

David pushed the container of Bubbe's prize-winning topping away.

What a relief. Wait. Oh no! Where did that canister of Reddi-Whip come from?

David replaced Bubbe's finest with a store-bought whipped cream. Bubbe would have a nervous breakdown if she saw that can of chemicals in her store.

I stared in disbelief. David lifted the Reddi-Whip and aimed it at my nose. Then with a mischievous smirk, he eased the canister toward the Baron Cherry Cheese Danish.

"You can't—that's even worse. Bubbe hates Ready Whip. This is Bubbe's castle, and everything's got to be from all-natural ingredients." A few years before, my family visited Bubbe and Zeyde's and I'd secretly brought Jiffy peanut butter, some Aunt Jemima mix, and Nabisco's Double Fudge Oreo cookies into her house. I figured Bubbe could take a break from baking. Being wrong was an understatement. Bubbe ranted and raved, screaming and yelling, *"Oy vey Gevalt! Got zol ophiten!* What do you think this is? Only the freshest food is allowed in this household. Pre-packaged *drek*—who do you think I am? I make the jams and cereals and pancakes from scratch."

So when a downpour of Wal-Mart's Reddi-Whip plopped on my grandmother's renowned Cherry Cheese Danish, my heart skipped a beat.

David grinned.

All of a sudden, I started choking.

My brain blanked.

Was David strangling me?

I tried to loosen his grip by bringing my arms together and pounding against his thumbs. However, my hands got tangled up in a curtain, and I miscalculated the position of his body. Where all the material was coming from, I didn't know. Sweaty and hot, I struggled; trying to think what Master Luna would do in a situation like this. But then I realized that things were not as they seemed.

Sheets from my bed were tangled around my neck. My pillow was lost underneath my crumpled covers, and a crashing sound thundered from downstairs in the bakery. I sat up and collided with the wall. Gaining focus, I searched my room.

Scruffy flew by, leaping out the door. The picture of my parents hugging me at my last karate test had been knocked over. I unraveled myself and picked up the photograph, making sure it wasn't broken, and I sprinted downstairs to see what had happened.

CHAPTER VIII

The Neighborhood Punks

The shrill sound of the alarm filled the apartment and bakery. I stopped short when I noticed Bubbe and Zeyde at the bottom of the stairs. Zeyde embraced Bubbe as she wept.

"Oh honey, *neshomelah*, it will be all right," Zeyde repeated.

I crept down the stairs and peeked into the bakery. The windows to the shop were smashed.

That made no sense. There was nothing to steal. All the baked goods were gone. Bubba made her products fresh every day. After they closed the shop, I took the remains to the homeless shelter. It was part of my *mitzvah* project.

When Bubbe told me that I had a duty to do some kind of charitable service for the less fortunate as part of the process for my *bat mitzvah*, I got really annoyed. I mean, helping people out – I'd do that anyway? Why does it have to be part of a religious ritual?

"A shod, a shod," Bubbe said when there were pastries left. "Thank *Hashem*, that you are here to deliver them to the less fortunate."

Why she made a big deal out of me carrying over some packages made no sense because she had already been helping the needy for years. The only difference was that I was lugging the bundle instead of some hired hand.

As for cash, Zeyde deposited it in his bank each night. Plus, Bubbe and Zeyde didn't have much money to steal anyway.

Lying in the middle of the shattered glass were some rocks. One rock had a note tied to it. *This is just a warning. We will see you soon.* Graffiti-like handwriting covered the wrinkled paper. For a few moments we stood frozen, all three of us. I could feel the fear in my grandparents escalate.

"Crazy, crazy *meshugener* punks!" Bubbe yelled. "*Meshugeners!*" She pounded her arms on the table.

Zeyde tried to calm her down. Bubbe cried and cursed through hiccups. "*Oy gevalt, a klug! A klug tzu mir!* Woe, woe is me!" The pain in Bubbe's voice was unbearable. "Where is the *yosher,* the fairness, in the world?"

I searched for something to say, but no words were good enough.

"Those punks are *kopvaitik* kids—pains in the neck, I tell you!" Bubbe's movements were becoming so overdramatic that she reminded me of an episode where Daffy Duck drank too much caffeine and was ricocheting off the walls, ceilings and everything that got in his way. I don't mean she was funny or anything. She just didn't seem real. For a second, I thought that this could be a dream. But it wasn't.

"I can't stand it anymore; just last week the Cohen Deli, and before that Mel's Market. Now, they're harassing us. They've bombarded and ram shackled our homes and stores. Next they'll burn down our bakery if we're not careful. What do we do?"

I'd met Mr. Cohen the day before. He acted like he was real suave because he did magic tricks and said that once his store was fixed over, he'd give me butterscotch Tastycakes whenever I visited.

"Don't worry, your grandma doesn't have to know," he whispered to me. "I used to sneak a pack to your mom every time she came to our deli. You remind me of her. It's got to be your indomitable spirit," he said as he pinched my cheeks.

I don't know what it was about my cheeks, but old Jewish people liked to squeeze them.

"Would it be rude to ask for a Milky Way bar instead?" I asked.

"Oh, a Milky Way enthusiast—there's no reason to be bashful. Just stop by, and it will be on the house."

Anyway, it was pretty obvious how he'd made the quarter appear from behind my ear, but I got a kick out of acting surprised because it reminded me of Dad; although, Dad really *did* make things appear from nowhere. His tricks were impossible to figure out.

The fact that Mr. Cohen was David's grandfather made the attack worse—I mean, when people were really nice and you liked them ... it's just wrong to harm them. How anyone could be so despicable was beyond me.

"Calm yourself. It's over. They're gone."

Bubbe crossed her hands over her heaving chest.

"You're a fine person, a *mensch*, worthy of the utmost respect. They might want to scare you, but no one would want to hurt you," Zeyde said.

Bubbe and Zeyde continued on and on in Yiddish, I think. I wasn't sure what was Yiddish or Hebrew or mixed. However, I understood when someone was mad, upset, or cursing.

Sirens blared as police cars pulled up to the bakery. This was my chance to show my grandparents that I was a benefit instead of a burden. While Zeyde was soothing Bubbe, I strutted toward the police. Someone had to explain what happened. Zeyde stopped me.

"No, no, no—you're not to get involved with this. You've already been through enough," Bubbe said.

"Come on my little *bubeleh*, you go to bed, and let us handle it." Zeyde put his arm around me guiding me to the stairs.

"B-b-but—"

"Go get to sleep. You've got a big day tomorrow, my *punim*," Zeyde said as he pinched my cheeks together.

Before I made my way to my room, I overheard my grandparents whispering to each other. Though I couldn't figure out specifically what was spoken in whatever language, I understood enough to know that my grandparents were afraid that the punks would hurt me if I hung around the bakery too much.

What had happened to, *"We're going to have so much fun in the bakery?"*

Until this hoodlum thing was solved, that was out of the question.

CHAPTER IX

Return of The Punks

Sunday school sucked. Getting ready for my *bat mitzvah* was a huge task, considering the other people in my study group had been learning Hebrew their whole life. Plus, Roni was in my class, and that sucked double. She was a show-off, always raising her hand and correcting me when I pronounced a Hebrew word wrong. Also, whenever I raised my hand because I knew an answer, Roni would slyly haul her hand up as soon as I was done. With a haughty breath, she was sure to add whatever minor detail she thought I had left out.

Becoming an adult wasn't worth the pain and aggravation.

I wanted to quit. On the other hand, Rabbi Goodblatt was really funny, and I enjoyed his tutorials after class. When he shared stories—whether they were about the Torah, my mom, or karate—he acted out key moments with enthusiasm, and he would always stumble over or drop something.

I wasn't sure if he was what Bubbe called a *klutz,* or if he was being a comedian, because after my lesson we'd compare *hyungs*, and his movements were as slick as a leopard. Was he a bewildered bundler or a Master Luna in disguise? That was a question that I enjoyed contemplating.

Plus, Bubbe would go haywire if I quit. When she got mad, she hopped around like a rabid dog chasing after a squirrel and spurted out guttural lingo that sounded like a choking chimpanzee.

Hoping Bubbe had forgotten her plan about banning me from the bakery, I tied an apron around my waist and plunged into baker mode.

"No, no, no, no. You need to go and do your homework. We'll discuss your helping in the bakery later." She untied my smock and placed it across her arm. Then she patted me on the back, as if that would make me feel better. "Oh, by the way, have you met Roni yet? Her mother and Jude used to be inseparable."

"You've got to be kidding me?" I spurted out.

"What's that supposed to mean?"

"Roni is mean and snotty."

"Well, she must get that from her father," Bubbe said with a little snicker.

"What do *you* mean by *that?*"

"You see, it's probably not what it seems. When Rose, Roni's mother, got married to an Hassidik Jew, she began following her religion very differently."

"So?" I asked.

"Well, the Hassidik people have a strict way of following their faith. They are more conservative and sometimes don't understand more liberal practices. For instance, your mother married someone who was not Jewish."

"Why does it matter if you aren't Jewish?"

"It shouldn't make a difference, but people have other ways of viewing things. I think Roni's father thought he was being pious."

"Pious?" I questioned. "That's as stupid as calling yourself Italian just because you eat pasta."

"It does seem strange." Bubbe rested her hands on my shoulders.

"Maybe if you just keep on being yourself and show Roni how great you really are, she'll begin to understand you." Then she placed her forefinger under my chin. "Like Judaism, it's growing on you, am I right?"

Bombarding me was more like it. But Bubbe's welcoming warmth was comforting and avoiding awkwardness was preferable, so I agreed.

We promised Rabbi Goodblatt we'd go to Shabbat services and we haven't gone yet. You are going to love it. Everyone dances, and it's like a big party."

"Are you...pious?" I asked.

"Well, we like to follow the Torah and many of the rules, but we believe in changing with the times. We try to eat kosher, and follow the rules. But as you see, we don't go to synagogue every week. We just do our best and know that *Hashem* will understand. Back to you, my *bubeleh*. How is school? Have you met some friends?"

"I'm just getting to know people, and Mr. Hames, our science teacher, is a trip. He likes studying the innards of little creatures along with rock formations."

A pock-faced teenager entered the store. His hair was slicked back, and there was an eagle tattooed on the side of his face. He stared at Bubbe. Then another older punk with a huge hooked nose pierced by a colossal ring sauntered through the door. He went to a different corner of the bakery, and ripped a bag in order to grab a bagel. He stuffed it in his mouth.

"Can I help you?" Zeyde asked.

One by one, more hoodlums entered the shop.

"Yeah. You got onion bagels?" one of the hoodlums said. "We'll take those and all your money."

The punk pushed Zeyde over to the register.

Those weasels weren't going to bully my grandparents.

"Open it."

I moved toward the ring-nosed brute. Bubbe tried to interfere, but I avoided her touch.

"I'm his family. Try and make me suffer," I blurted out.

Zeyde went to stop the scumbag, but it was too late. His hand was clenched, and his fist was aimed at my face. I blocked his blow and kneed his groin. He turned and bent forward as he doubled up in pain. The loop on his nose passed through his legs as he groaned. I was about to chop his back when Zeyde clutched my arm.

"I'm sorry this has happened." Zeyde opened the register. "There is not much, but take what you will and let's not have any more trouble. My granddaughter is new to this area and does not understand. Our bakery is open to you, but please do not hurt our family."

"Zeyde," I protested under my breath as the sleazebags destroyed the bakery.

Zeyde gave me a glare that caused me to freeze. He pulled me over, pointed towards the scum and gave me a secret thumbs-up, but whispered to me, "Do not mess with those *meshuganers*—they outnumber us. I'm not letting anything happen to my *bubeleh*." He pinched my cheek.

Old Jewish people must be oblivious to their annoying habits.

"Hey, there's that funky rabbi," said one of the thugs as he pointed out of the window. "He's coming this way." The gang members rushed as they collected the cash. Then they gathered the bagels and whatever pastries they could carry.

"Don't forget, Levy's bookstore was burnt down last week. It could happen to you," the punks warned.

The injured bully glowered at me as he limped out and took a big sloppy bite of a Danish. As the punks exited, Rabbi Goodblatt entered the bakery.

"*Shalom*," the vermin said to the rabbi as they left the store.

"*Shalom*," the rabbi said. With his thick Yiddish accent, he asked Bubbe for a delicious poppy seed bagel and a famous cherry cheese Danish.

"I'm sorry, we are out of stock right now," Bubbe answered with a quivering voice.

The Rabbi glanced around the room. "*Got in himmel!*" Goodblatt said. He sprinted outside. When he returned, he said, "You need to call the police."

"Please don't go to the police. Those *parekhs* are unreasonable," Bubbe pleaded.

"Oh, Lilly. They ransacked your home. You are a Jew. We've survived deprivation for centuries. Since the beginning of time, Jews were persecuted until they were able to stand up for their rights. In order for a problem to be solved, it needs to be revealed and confronted."

"Alexia is all we have, and we don't want them to hurt her. Even if the police pick up one *drek*, another is bound to strike. The Cohens, the Schmacklers, and the Steins all reported their troubles, and the police locked up some of those *meshuganers*, but they got released, and they continue bombarding the stores, and it goes on." Bubbe started to cry.

"I understand. I understand. You need not worry. I won't do anything to cause harm. Why don't you go upstairs, relax, and we'll talk more at another time," Goodblatt said.

"Just think about the good—*yetzer re*—how amazing your granddaughter is doing in Hebrew school. She is zooming through her lessons like lightning." Goodblatt took our hands, and we prayed. *"Shalom,"* Goodblatt said as he winked at me and strolled away.

CHAPTER X

Not Again

The following night as I tried puffing up my pillow, a brush against the slanted wall reminded me that moving my bed was a priority. Procrastination was not an option. However, my body felt too heavy to fully address the situation, and rubbing my prior bump and shutting my eyes were preferable alternatives, though, a little prayer was doable.

If You are out there, and I think You are, could You protect me from whacking my head on that wall and getting brain damage? And by the way, thank You so much for putting Rabbi Goodblatt in my life. Picturing Goodblatt tripping over himself, I comforted myself with a pillow cuddle.

But, I couldn't fall asleep, so I stared at Bruce Lee's perfect kick above my head. Then my eyes scanned my surrounding space, remembering my animal filled bedroom with its forest surroundings.

"Will you draw a honey badger scaring off a lion on that wall?" I remembered asking my mom.

The next day my mom was in my room painting. She handed me a brush to help. My living area became a totally cool jungle. It took us months. Maybe Bubbe would let me paint the walls. I could pretend my mom was by my side giving me pointers. On the other hand, decorating this room wouldn't be any fun without Mom. Plus, there wasn't enough space. This place was puny.

Rolling out of bed and standing, I felt like the Jolly Green Giant contemplating a garden of one pea. Meandering to my dresser, I wondered if I'd ever see my fuzzy buffalo chair or the giraffe coat rack again. I started to open a drawer from the old, beat-up cabinet, but the tiny knob began to squeak. After halting for a moment, I continued with care. My precious box of chocolates rested between my aqua and lavender sweaters - a treasure chest filled with sugary riches.

Eating a piece meant re-brushing my teeth. That took too much effort. However, brushing extra hard in the morning was an alternative. So I pranced back to bed, nestled my blanket, and savored one small bite. While holding the remainder close to my heart, I searched the stars. Pulling up my cover and snuggling my pillow, I curled into a ball. My eyes closed, and I entered my dream world. Birds tweeted, and the smell of spring entered the air. A blooming magenta magnolia tree tipped in the wind.

Oh no, it was going to fall. The roots started to rise from the earth, and it toppled to the ground.

Sitting up and whacking my head made me arch my neck backward to see the skylight and wonder if He ever listened. However, there was no time to contemplate any damage that my brain had encountered because a muffled noise rose from down in the bakery. Those idiots had returned.

***

I tiptoed down to the living room and past my grandparents' bedroom, making sure that they were asleep. Then I crept down the rest of the stairs to the bakery hoping the swiftness of my pace diminished the creaks. Placing my ear on the door, I didn't hear any sound. I slipped my hand behind the picture in order to retrieve the bakery key, then unlocked and opened the door trusting no noise would escape.

Meow!" Scruffy cried.

"Scruffy," I growled under my breath. "You're going to drive me crazy."

"We told you not to mess with us," someone said. I suddenly felt dizzy and fell to the ground.

Scruffy's fur brushed against me, but I couldn't move my arm to push her away. A siren rumbled in the background. The soft aroma of my grandfather was near, along with the sweet doughy scent of my grandmother. I tried to force my lids open, but everything was blurred.

"*A klug!* Woe is me! *A shreklekheh zakh!* What have they done to our *Kinderlekh?* What are we going to do?" Bubbe wailed. "*A magaifeh zol dich trefen.*" Those words were a foreign language, but I knew Bubbe was cursing the punks.

"*Neshomelah,* calm down—Alexia needs us now. We'll deal with them later." Zeyde bent down, coming closer to my side.

Though my mind was foggy and my eyes were half shut, I understood what was happening. I tried to reach out to my grandparents to tell them I was okay, but moving any of my limbs was like lifting a ten-ton weight with my pinky.

"Those *meshugeners* will stop at nothing. We should have listened to the rabbi and said something before," Bubbe shrieked.

"The paramedics said that she would be fine. If we rile up those cockamamie *schmucks,* they could do worse. We can't afford for them to destroy our home and business—and God forbid if they did anything else to Alexia," Zeyde replied."

"All right already, I won't say anything, but I just get *fardeiget*—well, you know how I get. My head spins in fear."

Bubbe and Zeyde told the police and the paramedics that I must have bumped into something in the dark.

"Maybe some pots and pans fell on her head," Zeyde said.

"Her mother warned us about her sleepwalking," Bubbe added. When the officers pointed out the broken glass, Zeyde said, "Some kids were playing ball. We didn't get a chance to fix it. What can you do?"

I tried to shout out what had really happened, but no sound came from my mouth.

***

I woke up in a hospital room to a doctor telling me that I had a slight concussion. My poor brain couldn't take any more.

Over the next few hours I went back and forth, in and out of consciousness. Bubbe or Zeyde stayed right by my side.

"I'm sorry," I told them once I could speak again.

"*Gooteh neshumeh,* oh you are a sweet soul. Please no *shpilkes* about any of this stuff," Zeyde said squeezing my hand.

I winced and Zeyde lightened his touch.

"Oh, I'm sorry. I was just so excited to hear your voice. We are the ones who should apologize." Zeyde kissed my hand.

I shook my head, not understanding.

"We want you to enjoy your life with us," Zeyde said. "These cursed kids—going around destroying good people's homes and businesses. It doesn't make sense." Zeyde's hand weaved through my hair.

"Why didn't you tell the police?" I asked as I tried to lift myself.

"We wish it were that easy. Those *Yungatshs* are *oisvurf,* and they squirm out of whatever trouble they get into."

The room began to turn, so I rested back on my pillow.

"What is a *yungat* and a *oisurf*?" I asked, as Zeyde continued to smooth my curls.

"I'm sorry. I keep forgetting you are not so familiar with our Yiddish. I was just describing how horrible these hoodlums are. We are going to have to be careful or they could cause a lot of damage."

All of a sudden my haziness started to clear. "How about telling Rabbi Goodblatt? He'd know what to do."

"Not a peep. You must promise. If you say something then it will come right back," Bubbe said.

"Bubbe's nerves are getting to her. The rabbi knows what is going on. I think he is trying to figure out what to do, too." Zeyde wrapped his arm around Bubbe.

I watched her take a big breath. Because of my weakness, attempting to lift myself up in order to calm her trembling body was unsuccessful.

"Bubbe, Mom always said that bozos like that are wimps and that their bark is worse than their bite. Mom knew what she was talking about. They have no right to be that way. If we band together we can get those—what do you say, *schmucks*?

Bubbe winced and gazed at me as if I had just eaten a rattlesnake.

"I mean the whole neighborhood, especially the rabbis, can't just let this stuff happen."

"Excuse me, little girl. That 's' word is not to be repeated."

"You mean sh..." Zeyde covered my mouth.

"Even if we've used it before, that doesn't mean you should." Zeyde widened his eyes. "That boy's thwack was harsh. His message was sharp and to the point." Then he patted my head. "We know it is hard for you."

"Hard for me? What kind of life is this? You say you want me to have a *bat mitzvah*, but what's so great about celebrating adulthood in a neighborhood that allows stupid punk bullies to control all of the grown-ups?"

"We understand." Zeyde placed his hands on my shoulders.

"Men and women are supposed to stand up for the ones they love. This place is filled with zombies who accept the dirt that's kicked on them," I said, feeling as though clouds of steam were gushing out of my ears. I helplessly slumped into the bed. Bubbe reached for the button to call the nurse, but I pushed her hand away. "I'm okay. Don't go. It's just that my mom wouldn't have let this happen."

"Your mother was not in this situation," Bubbe said.

"But she was in a similar one. Once while Dad was on a business trip, her boss decided to give Mom a visit with the guise of going over some important work from the office. He tried to kiss her. You know, like with his tongue and everything. Mom kicked the guy in his you-know-what, even though she knew he'd fire her for it—and he did. Afterwards, she told me to never give in to a tyrant, no matter how powerful they may seem."

"She never told us about that," Bubbe said.

"She probably didn't want to bother you with something she could handle herself. And anyway, she ended up getting an even better job, and when she threatened to file charges, her boss ended up apologizing and giving her a great severance pay."

"Oh, yes, now I remember. Your mom was tough, but that was a different circumstance. Her child wasn't being threatened," Zeyde said.

"But she stood up for her rights. She always said that there was good in the bad and bad in the good, and sometimes you have to defend the good in order to keep the bad at bay." I had their attention. "Maybe if you didn't let those hoodlums take advantage of you, they'd stop harassing you, and now that I know they're such deceitful *meshugeners,* they'll never get me again." Waiting for some type of approval, I straightened my spine.

"That's what Mr. Cohen told us," Zeyde said. "He was fed up like you and became an informant. He and his wife were about to testify when they bombed his deli. Thank *Hashem* the fire trucks were around the corner. Otherwise, you would have never met that boy David." My back curved back to its original position.

"Alexia, you are our only granddaughter," Bubbe said. "You mean *everything* to us. We are not going to let anything happen to you. The police just need enough evidence so those punks are gone for good. We just have to be patient."

The nurse came in to take my blood pressure and pulse.

"Oh my, your blood pressure is high," she said to me and then turned toward my grandparents. "Alexia needs to relax for a while. Why don't you come back later when she's had some rest?"

Bubbe and Zeyde agreed. As they left, I used all of my might to reach out to Bubbe.

"You just need to strive for the best, and somehow it all will balance out—that's what Mom always said. These people in our neighborhood are giving up, and there's no balance in that. If we let them, those punks will destroy everything in this town." I sounded preachy and corny, but I really meant it.

"I'm not disturbing anything, am I?" Goodblatt peeked his head in the door.

"You are always welcome," Zeyde said. "Word gets around fast, I might add."

"I've got connections." Goodblatt smiled.

"Don't say anything right now—not even to the rabbi. We'll discuss it later," Bubbe whispered.

When I gazed over Bubbe's shoulder, Goodblatt winked at me on account of Bubbe not realizing how loud she was whispering.

"I heard the story about your mother through the door. I didn't want to interrupt. She was a magnificent lady and had *chutzpah* like you wouldn't believe. Nobody could mess with her. However, she did get herself into trouble sometimes."

"My mom?" I asked.

"*Oi, a shkandal.* I remember one time the dean of the school was working with your mother and the synagogue on a project for the underprivileged. Your mother was so involved that she insisted the dean work after hours. The dean forgot to call his wife, and Missy, she was a schoolmate of your mom's—*oy vey*—I try not to make judgments, but she was what do you call *er kricht oyf di gleicheh vent?*"

"*Oy*, a troublemaker like you wouldn't believe," Bubbe said as the rabbi shook his head.

"Anyway, she spread a rumor around the school—which meant the whole neighborhood was notified—that the dean was having an affair with your mother. It was *hekdish.* Your mom found out that Missy was the girl who pulled the prank and cornered her into admitting what she had done. Missy didn't realize that your mom had wired the sound system throughout the halls and every outlet she could find. The whole school heard her confess."

"My mom did that?" I giggled.

"And she wouldn't have had it any other way," Goodblatt answered, crossing his arms and straightening his body. "After all, your mom was a fan of *yetzer re* and *yetzer tov.*"

"What's that?" I asked.

"Ah, my dear girl," Goodblatt said. "It's what you were talking about with your grandmother—the balance your mom always talked about. *Yetzer re* and *yetzer tov* represent the inclination to do good or bad. However, they intertwine."

"*Yetzer re* and *yetzer tov,*" I said. "You know, I think Mom may have mentioned something about that."

"Did you know that most of your mom's philosophies were developed in Hebrew school? She was one of my best pupils if not the best. Her insightfulness was why I not only admired her, but took so much pleasure in befriending her daughter."

"Me?"

The rabbi nodded. "It's similar to karate's *yin* and *yang*, the negative and the positive. They balance each other. The positive centripetal force, the *yin*, which is kind of like the *yetzer re*, can sooth or lighten the *yang* which is comparable to the *yetzer tov.* Or, maybe look at the plagues that occurred when Haman wanted to annihilate the Jews. It was because of Haman's cruelty—the *yang* or *yetzer tov*—that his own people were destroyed by the plagues. However, if Haman hadn't been so evil, the Jews might not have found freedom, which is *yin* or *yetzer re*. It all balances out."

"Who is Haman?" I asked.

"You're going to learn all about Haman in Hebrew school. Your mom used to enjoy creating art pieces for the synagogue. During Hebrew school she carved a sculpture of flies buzzing around a crossed-eyed Haman. It remains in my office. She was able to capture the humor in the horror. I'll show it to you when you are better and come to the *shul*—if you want to?"

"Sure," I said.

"Maybe we can develop our own *Torah* karate," Goodblatt said.

We said our *Shaloms,* and though I was exhausted, I couldn't rest. What did Goodblatt mean by *Torah* Karate?

CHAPTER XI

A Spiritual Connection

Filled with necessities as I made my way towards school, my backpack was decorated with rainbow wings attached to a canvas fabric. I had painted the knapsack with puffy white clouds floating in a pastel blue sky. As I walked down the street in a daze, I reached behind to feel the soft feathers sprouting out of the back. I cherished the time when my mom had awarded me with the silky material to create my new school bag. We'd worked for hours upon hours to make it perfect. At my old school, everyone kept on asking if they could try it on and touch it. The kids at this school didn't even notice it. They just pointed at me with disgusted expressions, like I had pooped in my pants—except for David. He told me that the wings were *totally cool*.

A crunch underneath my sneakers jerked me back to reality. Glass was scattered throughout the sidewalk. When I peered upward, I was faced with a spray-painted and bent gate. *Mazel Tov* was written in graffiti and there were remnants of a fir=e. I couldn't believe my eyes; the Cohen Deli had been ransacked again, and the punks had made it worse by scattering words of blessings all over.

And there was Roni's clique, clustered together like flies on sticky paper. Knowing them, they were gossiping about David's misfortune. I made no attempt to say anything and was hoping that they would, as usual, ignore me.

"I hope David's not hurt. I'm going to give him some apple strudel and cheer him up during recess," Roni announced to the other girls.

Where did she think she was going to get that apple strudel from anyway? If it wasn't made in the Baron Bakery, it couldn't be any good. The corners of my lips began to arc upward.

"My mom said that the police department was working hard to catch the culprits, but it's getting tricky because the witnesses won't testify."

"I don't blame them. Who knows what they'll do next?" another girl said.

"Yeah, Mr. Cohen was scheduled to go to court. It was a secret, but those creeps must have found out," Roni said.

If it was so undercover, how did Roni find out? And, what right did she have to blab?

The side doorway opened, and David stepped out with his face pointed toward the pavement. He headed in my direction, but Roni intercepted him to jabber about how her uncle was a detective and would catch those jerks soon.

David just nodded and continued as the girls followed. While the girls babbled, he turned his head toward me and waved with a shrug.

Was he trying to tell me that he had no other choice but to hang with those gossiping imps? He was a worm wriggling in dirt just like everyone else.

***

During a break after math, I noticed Roni and her group hovered in a circle. Everyone was hanging in the hallways. Some groups were sitting or standing and chatting, and the jocks were kicking a hacky sack. I sat alone in front of my locker on the floor and drew a caricature of Rabbi Goodblatt. Goodblatt's tress was lengthened and wrapped around the picture like a snake, and I made him a *yin* and *yang* ponytail holder like Master Luna's. I wondered what Master Luna's reaction was going to be when he returned from his tour in Asia, then I watched my pen form daisies that sprouted out of a little flower pot on Goodblatt's *yarmulke*. His face was clean-shaven, unlike many other rabbis. I made sure I highlighted his dimples to emphasize his youthful quality, though he must have been at least in his sixties. I included in the bubble to the right of his head the words: "The snake is a dangerous creature, but it can be tamed in time."

I considered the Rabbi's advice. He might have been right, but I was sick of waiting. I drew the snake with an open mouth about to swallow the flowerpot.

From the corner of my eye, I saw David talking to some other kids. Each student had a book called *The Chosen,* and some were pointing to the text.

"Wait til you get to the part... um... better not ruin it, but it's really intense. Got to go," he said as he moved over to kick the hacky sack with the athletic crew.

"How about a lesson or two?" David asked as he stole the beanbag. He dribbled it with his feet by passing it from one ankle to the other in the air and then heaved it upward with the fore-front of his foot, turned, and gave it a back kick. With speed, the pouch of sand was returned to David, and he was kicking it up in the air once again.

Then he tripped over me and fell. As he stood back up, he noticed my drawing.

"You've got the gift. That totally looks like Rabbi Goodblatt." Someone stepped on the picture.

"Oh, I'm sorry. I didn't mean to do that," Roni said.

David gave Roni a dirty look. The bell rang and I said a quick goodbye, grabbed what I needed, flew out of the school, and headed for the synagogue.

Roni was a pipsqueak. Why didn't David just tell her to mind her own business? I needed to focus on something positive or I was going to do a spinning kick into oblivion. Maybe I'd give Rabbi Goodblatt one more chance. If there was anyone in this neighborhood who could help me find some answers, he was the one. If not, at least he had great stories to tell.

CHAPTER XII

Sparkling Insignia

Friday night after the Shabbat meal, Bubbe insisted that I not move an inch from the dinner table. Sitting there as her big bum waggled out of the room, her exhilaration stunned me. Her fingers clenched while she held her arms high in the air as if she had just won an international baking award. Then, as if she were a ripe sugarplum about to burst, she danced back into the dining area holding a purple box with a glittering golden bow wrapped around it. What could it be? The present was huge. A television would change my attitude towards Shabbat in an instant.

"Well, what are you waiting for?" Bubbe said as she wiped off some dust from the box. "It's been cooped up in storage waiting for you to grow up."

I guessed it wasn't a TV set.

"*Mazel tov*, I can't believe the time has come. Your mother was so incredibly clever, and you are just like her. Open it. Open it," Bubbe said as she made big swirling motions with her arms.

"But it's not my birthday or Chris...*Chanukah* or anything."

"Ah, but it's March already, the month for *Purim*," Zeyde said placing his hands on Bubbe's shoulders.

"The kids were chattering about that in school. I never heard of it. Do you get presents on Purim?"

"Just open it. Your mother spent days creating this outfit when she was your age," Bubbe added.

Inside was some sparkling fabric. I lifted it out and spread it across the floor so that I could get a complete picture. It was a blue security outfit, like people who guarded special exhibits at the museum; except that it had soft flowing silver wings and was kind of futuristic.

"My mom made this when she was my age?" I asked.

"Oh yes. In anticipation of her having a daughter like you, I wrapped it long ago, after she outgrew it." She pinched my cheeks. "You may have to adjust it a little, but *mekheieh*, she would be jumping from cloud to cloud singing *halleluiah* if she saw you in it. Since you were born, I've visited this gift every *Purim,* while it sat in storage waiting for the perfect time to give it to you."

"My mom used to celebrate *Purim*?"

"Are you forgetting that your mom was brought up a Jew?" Bubbe said with a smile.

"Yeah, I know, it's just that the idea of her doing all this religious stuff seems weird." I imagined my mom dressed in the outfit. "Actually, it's not so strange. Mom liked angels." We had that in common. "This is the costume for tomorrow's festival, isn't it?"

"*Gloib mir.* The celebration is a hoot. All the young ones dress up like Halloween, but it's even better. Wait til you see what the kids wear. *Sheppen nokhes,* they are so bright and cheery and entertaining like those superheroes that wear underpants. None of those *Kalamutneh* goblins or *Got zol ophiten* ghouls, or throwing eggs, and *oy vey*, pranks, definitely none of those." Bubbe's voice raised, her cheeks became rosy, and if I didn't know better, I'd think she was playing a game of charades with three seconds remaining.

"May I go make the alterations for *Purim*?" I asked.

"*Ziskeit*, this is *Sabbath*. There is no working on *Sabbath*," Bubbe said as she gave my face a squeeze and my cheek a kiss.

I argued that sewing wasn't work, but Bubbe and Zeyde wouldn't listen. They said that my machine was electronic and not appropriate. Figuring out what was and was not acceptable in this religion was totally confusing. I had given up. After kissing Bubbe goodnight, I turned toward Zeyde, who followed up with a wet, sloppy one. Then I swept my gift up from the floor and hid my disappointment as I went to my room.

***

The next morning I felt tickling fingers waking me from a sound sleep. For a second, I thought it was my mom. But it wasn't.

"It's *Purim* time," Bubba and Zeyde sang with bright cheery voices.

I rolled over and covered my head with the blanket, wondering if my mother had inherited her antics from them. Oh no, the festival was today. I sat straight up.

"Oh my, *bubeleh*. You need to be careful of that wall," Bubbe said. "Maybe we shouldn't have placed the bed there."

A sarcastic "brilliant conclusion" is what I felt like saying, but curiosity about my costume persevered. "What about the carnival?"

"That's not until tomorrow. Today's *Shabbat*, and I think you'll like the service," Bubbe said.

"Do I have to listen to that guttural lingo?" I said. "Can't we wait until I understand Hebrew a bit better?"

"Rabbi Goodblatt will be doing most of the service in English. You'll have fun," Zeyde said.

I pulled my covers back over my face.

"What should we do? She doesn't want to go," Zeyde said.

"If she doesn't want to go, I don't want to force her," Bubbe said.

I heard my grandparents feet shuffle towards the door.

"It's a shame. Her mother got lots of ideas for her costume at the *Purim* Family *Shabbat*," Bubbe said.

"And this service is a hoot. The congregation laughs so loud. Oh well, maybe another year," Zeyde said as I heard the turning of the knob and the creaking of door movement.

"All right, you win. I'll meet you downstairs for breakfast," I said with an *hmph*. I knew my grandparents were playing me, but I didn't want to take any chances. Forcing my body out of bed and dressing was torturous. Thinking about listening to Hebrew gibberish stuff was even worse. When my stomach began to grumble, I made my way down the stairs for hash browns and sunny side up eggs.

My eyes focused on anything as long as it wasn't Bubbe or Zeyde. I begged *Hashem* for them not to say anything to me. No, luck, they drowned me with their story of *Purim*.

***

I was still a bit grumpy when it was time for *shul*, but it was too late to put up a fight. So I followed them through the park to their religious castle. Once inside, I collapsed on a bench beside my grandparents. Roni was positioned a few seats down with her mother. Their excruciating glares caused my sunny-side-up eggs to splash and scramble in my stomach. I opened the Bible and stared at the jumbled ink marks of Hebrew and listened to songs I couldn't understand.

"Why does Roni keep looking in our direction? And, why doesn't she mind her own beeswax?" I asked.

"She doesn't mean anything by it," Bubbe said, caressing my back. "Sometimes people's insecurities make them do strange things. When your mom was young, she'd run out into the pouring rain when she thought someone was being mean. Oh, did she drive me nutty, but it made her feel better—not that I want you to do that. No, no, no. Never do that."

We smiled at each other.

I remembered how Mom and I used to love playing in the rain. One time this elderly couple gawked at us.

"People ogle because they are curious, in awe, or ignorant," Mom had explained as they scuffled passed us, their eyes glued to our soaked bodies. "If anyone ever gapes at you, either stare back at them with fire or blow them off like cold wind. Or ..." she jiggled her hips, placed her thumbs in her ears, and waved her fingers as the doddering couple shuffled away. "...ridiculing the ridiculous is always an option."

Bubbe's hand pressed against mine. "Your mother and Rose used to be best friends," she said nodding toward Roni's mother. "The *shcticks* they used to play—teasing and pulling pranks on each other all of the time. Your mom liked hiding and scaring Rose. They used to laugh and giggle like you wouldn't believe."

"The Beakmans would like to know if you're a *lebedicken mensch*, just like your mom," Zeyde added with a chuckle.

"But why does Roni have that grimace on her face?" I asked.

"She's probably wondering how us *meshugeners* can keep up with a *shaineh maidle* like you," Zeyde said, giving my nose a tap.

As I rested my temple on Zeyde's shoulder, he placed his arm around me and gave me a kiss on my forehead. Returning his affection with a kiss on his cheek, I straightened my spine, regaining my composure. However, as comfort soothed my mind, Roni's scowl was in plain sight. So I slouched back in the bench and twiddled my thumbs, waiting for the Rabbi to begin. A weird-shaped toy was handed to me, and an uncontrolled pounding, snapping, and yelling erupted.

"That's called a *grogger.*" Bubbe pointed to the object that clicked as it rotated.

Bewildered, I rose to view the activity. Why were they spinning those clacking gadgets? And why was everyone jumping and dancing in the rows and aisles?

A man peeked out from behind a curtain. He pranced around the stage in a curly yellow wig, twirling one of the clicking thingamabobs.

"*Shabbat Shalom!*" It was Rabbi Goodblatt.

"*Shabbat Shalom!*" everyone hooted in unison.

In English, he started to tell the story of how on the fourteenth of *Adar,* Mordechai and Esther saved the Jews, and every time Goodblatt said, "Haman," the whole congregation whirled their clamor blasters and stomped their feet. Bubbe and Zeyde nudged me to join in. It was too weird for me to do anything but stare.

"It's to stamp out Haman so he can't exist," Zeyde explained, hammering his feet on the ground. Then he grabbed a zebra-striped racket-producer.

"Haman!" Goodblatt roared.

Zeyde started spinning his arms and hopping about. Bubba gave me a small tickle, and I giggled.

"You never told me that a synagogue could be fun."

"You never asked," Bubbe replied.

Caught up in the moment, I started to spin and bounce.

Goodblatt read from the scroll while he acted out each character, changing voices and positions. Everyone laughed.

"That's the *Megillah,* the story of how Esther and Mordechai saved the Jews," Bubbe said.

Two rabbis made-up to look dirty and ragged entered the stage, and Goodblatt placed a phony, sagging mustache over his lip and pretended to whip them.

"Work, work, work—harder, harder, harder!" Goodblatt cackled as he mistakenly thrashed himself. The whole congregation was overflowing with cheer.

Then he switched the wig around, threw on a girlish-type dress and high-heeled shoes, and pranced around the stage like a runway model on steroids. Throwing off his wig, he placed a huge twirled moustache on his lip.

"Together we shall thwart Haman's—" Everyone yelled and spun their *groggers*. "—evil plan."

"The Jews sure have been persecuted a lot." I paused. "*Hashem* means God, but *Adanoi* also means God, right?"

"Yes," Bubbe answered.

"Why do the Jews have a whole bunch of different names for one God?"

"*Yahweh* is supposed to be the ultimate name, but there are many different purposes for using the different names, like *Adanoi* for prayer or *Hashem* in a story. There are many theories, but it is what is in your heart that is important."

"Haman!" Goodblatt shouted, and Bubbe wiggled her butt against me and shook her clatter-thumper.

Listening and watching Goodblatt act out the story of the *Megillah* made me forget about sleep deprivation.

"Tonight, at sundown when *Shabbat* ends, you can work on your costumes, and tomorrow we enjoy a phenomenal festival. *Shabbat Shalom.*" Goodblatt ended the services.

Urging my grandparents to quit socializing so we could leave wasn't easy, but I persisted and finally prevailed.

***

As soon as we reached home, I darted up to my room. With fervor, I worked through the night. Sewing and adjusting the costume to my size was a snap. However, it was important that I didn't mess up anything my mom had done. Making sure the wires were hidden was kind of complicated, but it was totally cool when the flashing light bulbs embellished the shiny stars. My shoulders tingled, and I imagined myself as a real angel searching the clouds. In what felt like no time at all the alterations were finished—at least the major ones. It was still necessary to add the final touches, so I set the alarm, making sure I'd wake up with enough time. After continuous checks and detailing every inch of the costume, I fell into a deep sleep...

The bell chimed, highlighting the celebration.

Swaying back and forth, my mom floated through the air. Her chiffon dress blew in the wind as she leaned back. Her hair flowed gently in the breeze.

Why was my mother soaring through the air, bonging a bell on top of a tower?

The echo was unrelenting.

The bell chimed again.

My eyes widened. The image began to blur. Blinking repeatedly wasn't helping me focus.

More ringing—covering my ears didn't stop the clanging.

The old-fashioned timer from the top of the biblical tower disappeared.

***

My mother's graceful body was replaced with my poster of Bruce Lee. My eyelids fluttered.

My alarm clock bounced on my side table.

Shutting it off, I rubbed my eyes. Today was the *Purim* party.

I prayed that my mom would be overjoyed with my alterations. Then I slyly dodged the sloped wall.

Hopping in the shower and lathering my hair with shampoo invigorated me. My curls had to be squeaky clean after foaming every inch of my body until my skin tingled. Drying my hair afterwards seemed endless, but I wanted my long locks to be exceptionally wavy to magnify the ethereal effect of the outfit. Then I doused my mom's perfume over my whole body to add a soft scent.

My make-up was lined up on the countertop in front of the mirror. As I gazed at my reflection, I could've sworn the image of my mother and father appeared through a mist. Were they watching?

A gust of wind entered, blowing the glitter all over the room— even into my hair. I peeked in the mirror.

Pretty cool touch, except for the massive glitter scattered all over the floor. Each piece was tiny and sticky. Cleaning it up was going to be like trying to pick Scruffy's fur from the sofa after she'd frolicked on it while she was in her shedding heyday. If Bubbe saw this, she'd lose it. I swept whatever sparkles I could gather behind the dresser. I crossed my fingers and hoped that Bubbe wouldn't check until after I had time to pick, scrub and scour. Taking a moment, I inspected my costume, making sure that nothing was forgotten.

I slipped into the midnight blue material. As silver sparkles shimmered in the sunlight, I lifted my translucent chiffon silver wings and connected them carefully to my shoulders.

To show that this angel was a security guard, I connected a box that held the batteries I had recharged the night before and inserted them behind the security badge. The batteries were used to trigger the wires that would light the bulbs outlining the costume, the wings, and badge. Nothing happened. The bulbs didn't flicker or brighten or anything. My heart was beating at space shuttle speed. I turned the lever on and off and on and off and on and off—diddly-squat.

What had happened? Everything worked last night. I lost count of the times I triple checked the connections. As I felt myself hyperventilating, I sat back and caught my breath. Leaning my head back, I closed my eyes.

Please, Dad, help me figure this out. After all, he was the one that had taught me about electrical stuff. Help me make Mom like what I did.

Taking a gulp of air, I lowered my head. A battery lay on the floor by my worktable. My stomach turned a flip. It must've dropped out of the container after I had installed them. It was right in front of my face. I opened the back of the badge and stared into the half-empty case. Flowing through the air was my mother's sweet-scented perfume. After placing the battery back in its box and making sure it clicked for closure, I turned the control on. The costume sparkled like a Christmas tree, or in this case, a *Chanukah* bush—*Halleluiah*.

Oh no, I better not waste the power.

I didn't miss a beat. The switch was off, and my focus turned to cosmetics. After brushing my face with silver, highlighting my cheeks with sunset red, and emphasizing my lips with a dazzling ruby gloss outlined by a rust-brown pencil, I looked into the mirror, did the Baron wiggle, and sang another *halleluiah*.

Not forgetting my mom's secret tip, I thickened my eyelashes with deep black mascara and enhanced my eyes with a midnight-blue liner. Switching the flashing lights back on, I held my breath and peered back into the mirror. Then I ran downstairs to get approval from my grandparents.

They were ready and waiting at the bottom of the steps. Zeyde caught my hand and gave it one of his big drooling kisses. His wet lip smacker was disgusting, but I wouldn't trade it for the world. Bubbe embraced my other hand.

"*Oybershter in himmel*." Bubbe threw up her arms. "I forgot the *hamantoshen*."

She ran into the bakery and grabbed a huge bag, and we strolled to synagogue.

***

At the synagogue, we passed Roni Beakman and her mother and exchanged *Shaloms*.

Roni was wearing a store-bought white princess costume and bright candy-red lipstick to match her blush.

"Your costume is wonderful," Bubbe said to Roni.

"Thank you," she replied with a stupid grin on her face.

"We bought it at Macy's," announced Roni's mother, and then her eyes scanned my outfit. "You're outfit is very...interesting. You must have made it. We'll see you at *shul, shalom*." And the Beakmans went on their way.

Zeyde and I glanced at each other.

"They weren't very impressed," I said.

"I don't think it's that. Rose got kind of *schmulky* when your mother married your father because he wasn't Jewish and I don't think her husband approved. Your *Purim* outfit might bring back memories that she doesn't want to face," Bubbe answered.

"But if she was such great friends with Mom, what did it matter what her husband thought?" I questioned.

"When you marry someone it isn't always so easy." Bubbe said as she led me into the sanctuary.

After a short sermon where Goodblatt was again in his silly outfit and twirling the *groggers*, we entered a room that had been transformed into a festival. Everyone was in colorful, store-bought costumes and consumed with a moon bounce, art projects, ball games and dancing. I got some glances, but I wasn't sure what they meant.

I excused myself so I could go to the bathroom to collect myself.

"I wish you were here, Mom," I said into the reflection. "I didn't mean those things I said to you."

The bell rang from the neighborhood clock.

CHAPTER XIII

The Jewish Method
Turn a Cheek and Never Lose

After class, my Hebrew teacher handed me a note from Rabbi Goodblatt. Instead of meeting him for my tutoring session on the second floor in his office, he wanted me to join him in the basement chapel. I rushed down the stairs wondering what new revelation Goodblatt was about to reveal. When I opened the large double doors, I froze. Taped all over the podium were drawings of symbols from the Torah. Standing next to them were stick-figured karate diagrams. Some were single kicks and punches; others were throws and blocks. A few pictures depicted movements that were strung together with dotted lines representing *hyungs*.

This must've been the *Torah*/Karate thing he was talking about.

He urged me to stand and observe the pulpit. I saw a Bible and a karate book standing side by side.

"These are *zeligs*, blessings," Goodblatt announced.

"Those three-by-five cards or the *Torah*?" I asked.

"Of course the *Torah* is a blessing, but don't you see what is on the cards?" he asked.

"English and Hebrew words. It looks like stories from the *Talmud* and goofy martial-arts sketches drawn by kids." I smiled.

"Hey, I take pride in my artwork," Goodblatt said.

"Actually, that one's not bad," I said, pointing to a man dressed as a warrior giving a peasant some food.

"It's interesting that you are drawn to that. Do you recall when I spoke of the *parsha* about Jacob dreaming about angels climbing the ladder to heaven?"

"I remember that." I studied the drawing. "Oh, I see. Those must be the angels crawling up and down the ladder in the background."

"Exactly. Can you think why this is an important story?"

"His ego didn't get in the way so he could see the vision?"

"Right. Brilliant. Do you know what that word means?" He pointed to the word *Anochi*.

"It's in Hebrew," I said.

"Try sounding it out."

"That's the *aleph* and that dash underneath makes a sound like an A - ah, right?"

The Rabbi nodded. I pronounced the word.

Goodblatt clapped and pointed out the English word *alphabet* on the other side of the card. He explained how specific karate moves could relate to Jewish words and concepts.

"*Anochi* is the first word of the Ten Commandments."

"The stick figure is just standing there," I said.

"That's right. *Anochi* literally means *I am*. Before we do a form or kata—"

"Or *hyung*," I interrupted with a grin.

"Or *hyung*, we need to stand at attention. It's as though you are announcing yourself: I am. You and I can create *The Jewish Method—Turn a Cheek and Never Lose*," he said. "It's perfect, and we can have so much fun. Look here—the idea is to avoid violent contact. Our martial arts form will be related to the dove—the symbol of Israel. You are already a black belt. This will highlight a new dimension."

"So you are going to teach me?" I asked.

"We are going to develop it together—if you'd like that?"

I studied each picture. One drawing was of a man doing a revolving back kick. Formed around his body was the outline of a *shofar*. As he twisted back to kick, his movement upward curved like the shape of a ram's horn.

"Oh, look here," I said as I pointed to a picture with a Star of David above a house and lines representing wind that passed over. Above, it said Passover.

"Maybe *Pesach* should be made into a *hyung* filled with leaping kicks and other karate moves in the air so it will represent God's passage over the houses," I said.

I was overwhelmed with inspiration. In an instant, my body began to form karate moves that related to various passages in the Bible.

"Hey, look at this," I said as I pressed my hands together and bowed.

Goodblatt stood there waiting for me to continue. I just looked at him.

"Don't you get it? This bow represents *shalom*. Peace. Isn't that the greatest? After *anochi*, standing and presenting yourself, there is *shalom*. The translation is 'I am peace.' It's so simple, and there is no fighting. It's peace—hello and goodbye—the beginning and the end of *Turn a Cheek*." I continued to pinpoint what Jewish words and concepts should develop into moves or *hyungs*...or *katas*.

Goodblatt's cheeks were rosy and plump as his smile widened.

"Look, this is the first *parsha* you talked about when you were at *shiva*—where Jacob has to push himself out of the womb because his twin, Esau, was grabbing onto his heel. Remember?" I asked. I couldn't help myself from showing my double-handed block, and then I soared across the room as I kneed and kicked and chopped. Goodblatt lit the room with his cheerful beam inspiring my ideas.

"This is so cool," I said. "You can swoop down and then up as if avoiding a hit, twirl into a roundhouse kick—see how the knee lifts up and the front of your foot propels out. Then the momentum can flow as you lean upward into a back fist. It's like having no choice because of the other person's move. Or maybe because someone pulls you, the velocity causes you to elbow his back."

"I see you've healed from your wounds," Goodblatt said, and I smiled.

"Hiyah." I did a jumping front kick into a roundhouse strike and pirouetted into a knife hand blow. "Hiyah."

"I guess that's a yes," Goodblatt said.

I ran to the Rabbi, wanting to give him a hug, but I stopped myself. Bubbe had told me that the more religious men didn't show women any type of affection through touching. It had something to do with their admiration toward women. I didn't know if I was considered a woman yet, nor did I understand the reasoning, but I didn't want to show Goodblatt any disrespect.

"Rabbi Goodblatt, this is so amazing. This is going to be the neatest most incredible project in the entire universe." I halted and looked at my watch. "Oh no, I didn't realize how late it was getting. We've been at this for three hours. Bubbe's going to kill me."

"I'm sorry, Alexia. I didn't realize the time either."

As I rushed to gather up the cards and give them to Goodblatt, he motioned for me to keep them.

"You tell Lilly that I am to blame. I'm the one who kept you late for your studies!" Goodblatt yelled as I darted out the back exit.

CHAPTER XIV

The Tenements

After helping Bubbe clean the house, I went to my room to practice *The Jewish Method*. The story of creation would make an incredible *hyung*. Each day could have a specific move. *How about a double-handed down-block to represent earth and...*I tried many different blocks and kicks in order to find the perfect fit, but bumping into my bureau and having to duck because of that sloped wall grated my nerves. As I tried to experiment some more, I slammed into the garbage can and junk flew across the floor. I needed more space. Follow-through for some of my moves was impossible. Many times I had to stop and back up so that I could finish my pattern. To top it off, Scruffy wouldn't stop scratching at the door. After trying to ignore the ear-deafening noise, I stomped over and opened it.

"It's all yours," I said, marching out, slamming the door, and running down the stairs. "Oh no." Scruffy might poop all over my room, so I ran back up to leave the door open so Scruffy could get to his litter box.

I needed a large space where I could be totally by myself. After telling Bubbe that I was going out for a breath of fresh air, I headed for the Cohens' deli. A Milky Way bar and Mr. Cohen's silly magic tricks were just the right medicine. Plus, a chat with David wouldn't hurt.

"Hey my little *motek*, what's that?" Mr. Cohen said as he went to tickle my belly.

I grabbed my stomach for protection. From his fingers, a Milky Way bar appeared.

"You read my mind," I said with a smile, remembering my father.

"You only want me for my candy," he replied with a wink.

I tried to be inconspicuous while my eyes wondered through the store searching for David.

"And David," he said.

Feeling my cheeks heat up, I reached in my pocket for some money. Mr. Cohen chased me out of the store.

"Never offer me money for a Milky Way again or I'll tell your Grandmother on you." I turned my head and noticed that Mr. Cohen had the same dimples as David.

Regaining my composure, I moseyed down the street and began to daydream.

Soon I turned an unfamiliar corner. A block of deserted buildings faced me. Though I knew that I should've gotten back to a more populated area, my curiosity got the best of me.

***

I passed through what had once been a doorway and looked upward. The shell of a structure still remained. In the center of the block, behind fallen bricks and rafters, were the remnants of a crumbled fountain. Next to what had once been a grass-filled yard, was a sectioned area that might have been a beautiful garden in its heyday. Weeds now saturated the area.

It was quiet—no people to bother me—I could concentrate. I figured it must be a message from God—my studio to create *hyungs* and moves for *Turn a Cheek*. Taking my jacket off, I thought about the story of creation and how perfect this place was.

I stretched and quickly began my kicks and punches relating them to heaven and earth and how God had separated water and created the sky. The world would be built with a combination of rolls while the blue above would be represented by consecutive front and roundhouse kicks. My mind and body flew throughout the crumbled rocks and stones as I leaped over and across chunks of cement and bricks, envisioning water rising above dry land forming seas.

Then, imagining vegetation popping up, I was forced to twist, allowing my escape from each growing shrub. Then I blocked, pretending to dodge a tree trunk falling and tumbled forward into a flying front twirl in order not to harm baby chimps and other animals. Behind the fountain, I dropped myself down with exhausted bliss. I was on my own, content and creating my new world.

All of a sudden I heard some mumbled voices. It was coming from the one building that had all four walls to it. I moved closer.

"Ow, that's my nose!" a whiny voice cried.

"Yeah, and you're not going to have one if you don't watch out. Someone's gonna pull your ring right through your brain. All of you!" a gruff voice bellowed. "We've gotta be organized and in control."

It was the same voice that had told me not to mess with him when I got bashed over the head. I crept over to the building, making sure not to utter a sound, and searched for a hole in order to see what was happening.

A medium-sized stocky guy with a bird tattooed to his neck was stepping over a bloody-nosed boy he called Norm. He was shouting at a group of about fifteen boys ranging in ages from teens to early twenties. The guy was called Crow, and no matter how horrible or vulgar he sounded, everyone stayed quiet and listened. He must've been the leader.

"I don't want to hear about the cops or nothing. If we plan ahead, we won't get caught, and we can build ourselves an empire. But if we get sloppy, like this pipsqueak here, we are *doomed*. Got it?" He rammed his foot into Norm's stomach. "No Mr. Nice Guy ever, or someone will squeal. We've got to instill fear. Getting kicked in the privies by a little girl don't cut it."

All the guys laughed, and Norm stood up with a scowl. He tore his shirt off, looking as though he had just conquered Alexander the Great. He took out a needle and pierced his nipples, slipping through them large-hooped earrings that dangled.

I winced.

Some guys covered their eyes, and I could see some of them cringing. But then they all patted each other on the back with acceptance. Crow went up to Norm.

"If you had some real *chutzpah,* you'd pierce that," Crow said pointing between Norm's legs.

After Norm looked down, he peered up and seemed to be glancing around. No head moved. Norm unbuckled, unbuttoned, and unzipped his pants, took what looked like rubbing alcohol from his bag and poured it between his legs. Then he gulped down a Budweiser, and popped something in his mouth. As he raised a needle in the air, everyone cheered, swilled beers, and hooted.

I squinted to see what he was about to puncture and gasped.

"Now, this is a way to celebrate our new hide-out," Crow announced as he forced Norm's hands down.

After the dirty deed was done, Norm held himself between his legs, and his face altered as if he had been thrown into a space shuttle at warp speed. Crow slapped Norm on the back and raised Norm's arm in the air. Roars of approval followed.

I moved my gaze upward to avoid the disgusting sight. My eyes focused on a soft orange streak that crossed through the clouds, and I understood: there is a reason for everything. Fervor strengthened my spirit. I vowed that *Turn a Cheek and Never Lose* would be something that every goofball in that pack of sleaze-bags would learn to dread.

The punks stumbled out of their new meeting place, Norm limping behind them. I waited patiently. The synagogue was my destination as soon as the site was cleared. My strategy was ingenious, and I couldn't wait to begin.

CHAPTER XV

The Plan

I entered the synagogue from a side entrance so I wouldn't have to go through the sanctuary and disturb the people who were praying. As I peeked through the door, I did a little hula dance when I saw Rabbi Silverstein bowing and sputtering to a group of about fifteen men. It was safe to assume that Goodblatt was in his office.

The janitor, Mr. Johnson, was vacuuming the rugs and wiping down the tables. "Well, hello, young missus. Per chance are you looking for Rabbi Goodblatt?"

"Has he gone for the day?" I asked.

"Oh no, Missus Alexia, I just saw him downstairs eating corned beef on rye." He smirked. "I thought I saw some karate books by his side."

I thanked Mr. Johnson and pushed the flickering button to a squeaky wooden elevator so I could get to the basement.

The bottom floor had many rooms, including a huge area used for *Shabbat* dinners, and sometimes services were also held there when the congregation was too large for the sanctuary. When I opened the doors, Goodblatt had a whole bunch of Hebrew literature laid out next to a book with a praying karate master on the cover. Goodblatt looked up and his face brightened. "Perfect timing," he said, lifting the books. "But it's a bit late for you to be out and about. Shouldn't you be home for dinner?"

"I'm on my way, but I just wanted to stop by and tell you about a special project I'm working on and see if you could help me out."

"So, tell me about your special project."

"It's a surprise." I prayed he wouldn't ask too many questions.

"I don't know how I can help you if you don't tell me what you need."

"It's easy. Remember those huge *yarmulkes* you showed me? You keep them in that storage place." I pointed towards some doors.

"Yes, you know someone with *kepis* that *groise?*" he asked, widening his arms around his head with a chortle.

"I could put the material to really good use—I mean you said that nobody's used them since you can remember."

"That's true, but that is not my property. It belongs to the synagogue. Why don't you tell me what you need them for and then I can tell my associates why they are missing?"

Oh brother, now what was I going to do? The *yarmulkes* were perfect for my plan, but there was no way I could tell Goodblatt why I needed them. He'd rat on me sooner than a baby bawling because his big brother stole his blanky.

"Could you tell them that it is in honor of my parents and for the good of the neighborhood?" I asked.

"You've got to be kidding. Come on, Alexia, you've got to do better than that."

Now what was I going to do? Nobody else had *yarmulkes* that size. As a matter of fact, I couldn't imagine anyone who would need them *but* me. I'd have to think of another game plan.

"Okay. Thanks anyway."

I was about to leave, but Goodblatt motioned me to follow him. "Alexia, I was just kidding. A four-hundred pound giant doesn't even have a head that size, but it would be nice if you told me what you were planning." A sigh released from Goodblatt when he didn't get a response. "My associates would be glad to get rid of them, but we might have thrown them away. Follow me, and we'll go check."

Goodblatt went over to the supply closet and started removing everything in sight: used candles, broken lights, wires, and tons of miscellaneous objects. The junk was piling up. I began to worry they had been thrown away after all.

"Ah, here they are," the Rabbi said, pulling out some triple-extra-large *yarmulkes*.

"Oh my! Thank you so much."

I refrained from hugging Goodblatt and blew him a myriad of continual kisses as I left. My plan was in motion. Those punks wouldn't even know what piercings had punctured them. But it had to be kept secret. What if Goodblatt figured out what I was up to?

***

I couldn't think about that. I had to begin step two, so the next day after school, I visited Shanty's Vintage Clothes. Mr. Shanty must have been close to a hundred and moved slower than a wounded snail, but he owned the only secondhand shop in the neighborhood.

"You want what?" he asked. "What's a *laggy cloth*? I never heard of that."

"No, no, some really large clothes. You know, that will be too big for me," I explained.

"We don't have parched clothes. Just top-quality used garments. Mmmmm, these are good." He offered me a piece of toffee. "See if you like anything," he said.

I fiddled my fingers around trying to find a brown, chocolate chewy taffy. To my dismay, they were all yellow.

"No, not the candy." He slapped my hands. "Can't you see I only have the banana left," then he pointed to some clothing. "I was talking about my merchandise."

He started to mumble something about nobody liking bananas and kids these days. Then he pulled me close to him explaining how his stock was organized. He reeked of something like garlic mixed with banana fritters.

"Do you want me to find you something specific?" he asked.

"No, thank you. You've been very helpful, but I think I can find what I want."

He insisted that he help me, but I, finally, was able to convince him that it was more important that he stay at the front desk.

I found a bunch of large men's sweat suits and some bulky button-down sweaters and baggy pants that were totally on the mark for my strategy.

Hobo-homeless, here I come, I said to myself. I didn't think even Goodblatt could figure this one out.

The bags weighed a ton, but I didn't want to pull my hair out while waiting for Shanty again so I heaved my goodies and exited.

***

All of the punks were hanging out on the corner drinking beers and smoking cigarettes. In order to avoid contact, I started to cross the street. Norm stumbled my way and stuck his foot out in order to trip me. I used my heavy load to lean on, avoiding his sneaker, and countered his foolish prank. He lost his balance and tumbled into the trash can.

I didn't even touch him. The Jewish Method had worked, but I wasn't about to stick around. My purchase was too precious to jeopardize. Turning my head as I hurried to safety, I saw Norm as he sloppily lifted himself out of the garbage. Some remnants of pizza hung from his cheek. The other gang members mocked him.

"She didn't have anything to do with this. I just tripped. Too much Bud." He crushed an empty beer can from the trash.

A nine-year-old girl could squeeze that cylinder of tin. How those boys got away with all that gangster stuff was beyond me. As I lugged the hefty bags, picturing that nose-ringed dimwit dripping with melted cheese occupied my mind.

***

In no time, I was dragging my heap up the stairs toward my room with tons of ideas whirling in my thoughts.

"Hold on one second, young lady. *Oy vey*, you had a field day at Shanty's," Bubbe said. "Why are you spending your allowance on *shmutsiks* from Shanty's? We give you plenty to buy brand new."

"This is for a project for the synagogue."

"Well, your dinner is cooling on the counter next to the refrigerator."

"Can I eat it a little later? I've got so much I've got to do." I asked. If Bubbe found out what I was planning, I'd be grounded for life.

"Okay, but the *kasha* and bow ties will get cold if you don't eat it soon."

Hurrying to my room, I positioned the *yarmulkes* on the table next to my sewing machine. The black spool to thread the needle was hidden in the back of a drawer. Then I laid out the Shanty clothes on the floor, mixing and matching, and pinpointing where the patches should go. I inserted snaps so that the hobo part of the costume could be removed in an instant. Then I grabbed some black unitards and used some of the excess material to form muscles on the arms, legs, and chest. I added a glittery Jewish star on the back for pizzazz.

By sewing Velcro, set on elastic material, into the bottom of the Jewish caps, the lower part could be lifted to form a *yarmulke* or pulled down to shape a ninja mask with a silver star of David twinkling on the forehead. Black snaps were added to insure the disguise didn't slip around. I threw on one of my costumes, positioning the hat so that it covered my hair, and released one curl on each side of my face. Then I grabbed a pencil holder, pretending it was a bottle of liquor. Gulping my simulated wine, I swayed to and fro, stumbling around my room as if in a drunken stupor.

"Not happening dude." Pulling down my *yarmulke* to form a ninja mask and unsnapping my dowdy outerwear to reveal a muscle-bound ninja, I dashed to the side and spun around, using my knife hand blocks against gang members. Then I rolled in front of the mirror raising my arms in victory.

"Pretty cool," I said to myself.

My tummy rumbled, and an Israeli tune began blaring from downstairs. Quickly changing back into my regular clothes, I ran to the living room where Bubbe and Zeyde were enjoying snifters of cherry Manischewitz.

"So what's our little *kinderlekh* up to?" Zeyde asked as I tumbled into the room. "Whatta glow."

"I got a yearning for some of Bubbe's bow ties," I said as I ran to kiss and hug my grandparents. When I got to the kitchen, Scruffy was nibbling at my dinner.

I sneezed. "Totally gross, you fur ball." I nudged her away. I sat at the kitchen table while my grandparents chatted and I picked away the cat-contaminated parts of my dinner.

"To our *ainikel and chei*," Zeyde cheered.

"She has finally settled in," Bubbe said as their glasses met with a ting.

Listening to my grandparents giggle while they told Yiddish jokes to each other started to make me nervous. I understood bits and pieces of what they were saying and even laughed at one of their jokes.

Could this mean I was becoming a Jew? What would my dad think?

"She's an amazing little girl, and so much like Jude," Zeyde said.

"Thank *Hashem* she doesn't have that mischievous flare. How Jude used to get into trouble."

I peeked through the door.

"To our *bubelehs*," Zeyde said. "I hope you're watching." He lifted his glass to heaven.

Bubbe stood to meet Zeyde's glass.

They were toasting Mom and me.

I peered at a star through the kitchen window as I crept through the alternate exit of the kitchen, up the stairs to my niche in the attic. If my plan didn't work, I'd be doomed.

CHAPTER XVI

Who is That Homeless Person?

The next day after school, I hurried home to finish my schoolwork. Bubbe was sure to check.

"Jude said you were a straight-A student, so I expect nothing less," Bubbe commanded.

When I was finished, I packed a dirty, mangy bag with one of my costumes and ran towards the door.

"Hold it, young lady," Bubbe said as she held out her arm.

I looked up at Bubbe.

"Did you finish your homework?"

"Every bit of it, even the extra credit," I lied. I hadn't even opened my science reading. "Do you want to see it?" My throat tightened. I was pushing it. Crossing my fingers behind my back, I hoped she wouldn't check.

"That's okay. I trust you," Bubbe said. "But such a *shmutsik* sack. You need to throw it out. I've got plenty of nice ones in the closet."

"Oh no, this is my favorite. I just need to jazz it up." The wrinkles on the sides of Bubbe's face formed a frown, but she didn't argue. What a relief.

"Well, you better get started because I'm not going to let my granddaughter walk through the streets like an impoverished imp."

I promised I'd turn the sack into an enchanting designer original as soon as possible and said good-bye.

***

Rushing to the tenements, I found my special nook near the fountain, hid in a closed-in area, and changed into one of my ninja get-ups.

Making sure I was alone, I made my first *Turn a Cheek* move, a sliding step into a side roll. As I tucked, swirling on the ground, I heard a commotion. Grabbing an empty bottle of cherry Manischewitz I'd picked out of my grandparents' trash, washed, and filled with grape juice, I continued my curl ending next to my spy hole. A rat squeaked by, and I squirmed and bumped into some metal debris.

"What's that?" the head punk uttered. "Yo, pip squeak, go check it out." He pointed his finger at Norm.

Norm passed near my hideout. My body froze. Around ten rats scuffled through the rubble. Norm laughed at the sight and moseyed back to the clan. I scrunched my body tightly, holding my own mouth to stop myself from screaming at the dirty creatures.

"Just some feisty mice scrapping for some grub," he said.

Everyone gave a chuckle, and they continued their meeting. I let myself relax a bit and with care crept back to my viewing spot. Crow began setting his plan for their next attack.

"Ya know - that little know-it-all Baron girl was shopping at Shanty's store. Why don't we give that a whirl? That old man's gonna get a big dump in his pants," he said. "We'll meet at eight p.m. on the corner of Cherry and Walnut. He'll be closing up shop. We'll take his money, maybe find some outfits and then really mess with his store. It'll be a snap."

When the meeting was over and the gang left, I changed back into my clothes and rushed back to the alley behind the bakery.

***

How was I going to move that big trash bin? Realizing that I wasn't strong enough but figuring that it wouldn't hurt to give it a whirl, I pushed my back against the metal tub and flattened my feet against the brick wall. Inhaling with all my might, I gave a big heave trying to straighten my legs. Nothing moved.

No way was I going to give up. I used all my strength to push again, and again and again. On my last attempt, Scruffy meowed and jumped in my lap, while I was in a seated position, leaning back on the dumpster and heaving. Then that finicky feline hopped onto the fire escape and climbed below each windowsill bumping against the glass until she found one that was opened.

"Scruffy—give you an inch, you take a mile. You're a menace." As I watched the metal staircase move while the cat scurried up, I noticed some levers on the side. "Hey, Scruffy, sorry. I take that back."

I climbed on top of the trash container, making sure not to fall in, and grabbed the railing in order to leap onto the wobbly steps. Placing my hand on the handle, I tried moving the switch. I placed my palms on the crusted knob, putting my foot on the side railing and using all of my energy. It shifted slightly. My stomach began to gurgle.

Positioning myself above where I had gripped, I clasped my palms around the upper part of the stairwell and jumped on the attachment. It loosened completely. I then turned the piece, moving the bottom portion of the stairs away from the smelly storage vat. After flipping my new escape route, I snatched my bag and rushed out of the alley around the corner to the entrance to our apartment, next to the bakery. After all, Bubbe had probably closed up shop.

***

"Alexia, you look a little flushed. Are you feeling all right?" Bubbe asked.

"I'm fine."

"My goodness, you are filthy. Run upstairs and take a shower, then dinner will be ready. Oh, by the way, did you get the material to fix that *shmutzik* sack?" Bubbe asked with a smile. "How you are going to fix that thing up, I don't know."

"Don't worry; it'll be fit for the new designer fad."

"Okay. Run up," Bubbe said, nudging me.

I whizzed up the stairs and looked in the mirror. I lifted my hand to smell my armpits. After making a silly face in the mirror I rushed to take a quick but thorough shower. Before I ran down the stairs for dinner, I laid out some vibrant-colored patches of cloth that I had in a drawer.

Zeyde said the prayer for dinner, and I wolfed down my meal of chicken and dumplings. Scruffy meowed.

"Your meal is over there," Bubbe pointed to Scruffy's bowl in the kitchen. "And you, young lady, need to slow down or you're going to choke."

"I'm sorry, Bubbe. I just want to get started on that bag before I go to sleep. Can I be excused?"

She nodded her head in approval.

"Enjoy," Zeyde added.

I looked at the clock and ran up to my room. I had an hour to turn the bag inside out and sew patches on it. It kind of had a chic flashy appearance one-way, but if rotated back, it was tattered and worn. I put the cushion and some clothes under the covers in case my grandparents peeked in and then wiggled into my ninja garb—concealing it with my dingy getup. I opened the window and climbed out, closing it just enough, making sure it wouldn't lock.

***

I ran to Shanty's hoping I wouldn't be too late.

Noticing a man walking down the street with a briefcase, I slowed my pace and began to wobble, pretending to be a homeless drunk.

"*Shalom,*" Goodblatt said to me.

I grumbled and spat on the ground. My nerves helped me as I pretended to stumble, lowering my head to the ground while I inwardly prayed that Goodblatt wouldn't recognize me.

"Our synagogue is open to you if you should need anything," Goodblatt said, handing me a bag. "Here's a roast beef on rye. It's fresh from the deli."

I pushed the bag back at the Rabbi. However, Goodblatt was persistent.

"No, no, take it, I insist." Goodblatt said.

The guilt of taking Goodblatt's food was powerful, but I knew that I had to hurry to Shanty's, so I accepted his offer. As soon as he was out of sight, I darted toward the thrift shop. From the corner phone booth, I dialed 911. With a cloth over the receiver, I explained that there was a robbery.

Holding on to my Manischewitz bottle, I slithered out of the booth and rolled onto the sidewalk knowing the earthy colors of my outfit would blend perfectly with my surroundings.

Then I spotted Goodblatt crossing the street. He was headed in my direction. This wasn't part of the plan.

The gang members turned the corner and met Goodblatt. I took a swig from my bottle, trying to contemplate my options while I ran forward to listen.

"*Shalom,*" Goodblatt said.

"Peace?" Crow said. "I don't think so." He laughed.

"Samuel? Aren't you Daniel Danburger's son, Samuel?" Goodblatt asked Crow.

Silence filled the corner. The boys looked at their leader.

"What if I am?"

"Excuse me," the Rabbi continued, eyeing another boy. "Aren't you Josh Barsky's son?"

"Who are ya, the new game show host of *Who's Who?*" Crow advanced toward Goodblatt. "You better get new glasses and forget what you think you see."

Goodblatt calmly nodded and continued down the block. One of the hoodlums raised his chest and positioned himself in front of Goodblatt, but Crow motioned to let him pass.

"We've got more important business to attend to," he said.

As the punks went on their way, I slid to the pavement, trying not to be noticed. However, Goodblatt tripped over me.

"How did you get here?" the Rabbi asked.

Not again! I kept my face to the ground, mumbled, and pretended to be passed out. Goodblatt tried to lift me. My limp body and awkward position made it impossible.

"I'll call the police to help you as soon as I get a chance," Goodblatt said as he covered me up with my blanket. "Who knows what those kids are up to."

Glass from Shanty's windows scattered across the pavement.

Goodblatt ran towards the destruction. I couldn't wait for the police. Too fast for anyone to see, I ducked under the blanket, pulled off my tattered outfit, pulled down my *yarmulke* to cover my face, and became a muscle-bound ninja. My black unitard blended into the darkness except for the silver stars of David that glittered from my back and forehead.

I dashed to the shop. Using Goodblatt as a railing, I lifted myself through the opening in the glass, landing inside the shop.

"*Oy,*" I heard Goodblatt mutter.

Disguising my voice, I pushed Shanty underneath a pile of clothes, apologized for the inconvenience, and warned him not to move.

As one of the troublemakers plunged through the shards, I kicked a bunch of hangers above his head, impeding his move-ment. Each punk attempted to capture me, but escaping their attacks by *turning my cheek and never losing* was like savoring hot chocolate while admiring the first snowfall. Swinging on the ceil-ing rafters and cartwheeling over the tabletops, I countered their blows, causing their strikes to come back at them.

Goodblatt stood there, periodically dodging a flying shoe or using a cart of clothes to block an assault. At one point, he asked me who I was, but his answer was left blowing in the wind.

One boy was about to clobber Goodblatt from behind with a mannequin's leg. I leapt from an upper shelf. The culprit turned to use the weapon on me. Instead, I skipped to the side, and the centripetal force from the strike caused the sucker to smash into the remainder of the plastic model, tangling him between ladies' garments and wire hangers.

A pimple-faced punk dove toward Goodblatt. Gearing up for his rescue was meaningless because Goodblatt raised the big candy bowl, and the bully's face smashed right into it.

"*Oy gevalt!*" Goodblatt said as the delinquent dropped to the ground.

A siren grew louder as it approached, and the punks scattered.

"Yo, Shanty, if you can hear me, you're dead meat if you say anything to the cops!" Crow yelled. "And Rabbi, if you say any-thing, Shanty'll pay for it and so will your synagogue." Crow hurled a bunch of ballet gear to the floor. "Yo, Jewish Ninja, don't even *think* you saw the last of me."

As Crow ran out, I hid up in the shelving and overheard Goodblatt and Shanty explain to the officers what had happened.

"Hey, did you see where that Jewish Ninja went?" Goodblatt asked.

"The Jew did what?" Shanty asked. "That black boy pushed me under some *chatchkas,* and all I heard was my life's work crashing and smashing. Where'd he come from?"

Goodblatt explained to the officers that everything had happened so fast that he wasn't able to see any faces. Wincing at the lie, I had to hold myself back from climbing down and telling the officers the truth. After all, revealing my identity would destroy everything.

After Goodblatt consoled Shanty and promised to come over with some helpers in the morning, he left, and Shanty climbed to his apartment above the store. Making sure the coast was clear, I gathered my bag and clothes and rushed home.

CHAPTER XVII

The Surprise

On the front page of the *Torah Tribune*, was a blurred picture of a black muscular figure running down a street. Thank God for that *yarmulke* mask. In bold above the photograph the caption read "Who Is This Jewish Ninja?" Discussions about the mysterious Jewish Ninja were all over the streets, in the bakery and in the shops.

Nerves trembled throughout my system. No way could I ever be caught. On the other hand, it was kind of cool to publicly be called a ninja, and the newspaper article said that I was a hero.

Spying in the tenements and spoiling every ploy those numbskulls plotted became routine. Each time they planned destruction, I called the police. Sometimes the officers obstructed the scene of the crime before it started. But when timeliness was not on the storeowner's side, I became the Jewish Ninja and foiled their ploy. However, when one of those dimwits was caught, there was not enough evidence collected and the captured crook was released. Though the robberies lessened, they still continued.

"This Jewish Ninja is something else. Where did he come from?" Bubbe asked as she poured Zeyde and me some fresh-squeezed orange juice.

"Can you imagine? Every other day there is an article about him and nobody has a clue as to his background," Zeyde said, holding up a newspaper showing a picture of a Jewish star blending into the night.

"I'd think it was Goodblatt, except that the Jewish Ninja was seen with him that first night he showed," Bubbe said. "And Rabbi Goodblatt is skin and bones compared to the muscles they say that ninja's got."

"Hey, you never know. Maybe I'm the Jewish Ninja." Zeyde flexed his chubby arms.

"Not with this *matzah ball* gut," Bubbe said as she elbowed his belly. Zeyde crossed his arms over his stomach, pretending to be in pain.

"You don't know anything about this, do you?" Bubbe asked me. "After all, you are the star martial artist in this family."

"Hiyah, hiyah, hiyah," Zeyde karate-chopped the air and then tickled me.

"I wouldn't mind giving those *meshugeners* a big karate chop in their gut. Hiyah!" I said, laughing and playing along with my grandparents, but when I yawned, Bubbe lectured me about not getting enough sleep. She sent me off to the synagogue to study—but not before giving me some Baron bagels for Goodblatt.

***

"*Tsegait zich in moyl*—my favorite," Goodblatt said when I handed them to him. "After Hebrew classes, will you meet me in my office to share this treat?"

I agreed, and after classes we split the bagels and smothered them with cream cheese.

"It's very interesting how the Jewish Ninja never touched any of those knuckleheads when they were fighting," Goodblatt said.

"Yeah, it's pretty cool," I said, licking the tasty spread from the side of my bagel.

"Oh, so you know how that Jewish Ninja operates?"

"Uh, not really." Goodblatt was making me feel weird.

"You know, she had some of the same moves we've been developing," Goodblatt continued.

I wiped a smudge from my mouth. "You mean *he*, don't you? You don't know the Jewish Ninja, do you?" I asked.

"I think I might," Goodblatt said staring straight at me.

"Who is he?" I tried to avoid his gaze.

"He is not a he."

"He's not?"

Goodblatt raised his eyebrows. I knew the gig was up. "So, this is your special project?" Goodblatt said.

"Do you think anybody else knows?"

"I hope not, for *your* sake. You're going to get hurt. Those boys are *meshuguner mamzers*. They'd eat you alive if they had the chance."

"How did you know?"

"Come on, Alexia. Your costume was great. The muscles you made in that getup are deceiving, but when you leaned against me to leap through that glass, your muscles squished together. It took me a while to figure it out, but I know your moves. We've been working at *Turn a Cheek* diligently for a couple of months. You're a champion. Nobody else has your talent. You should be lucky your grandparents don't turn *your* cheek."

"Please don't tell."

Goodblatt stood in silence, his hand to his chin.

"Those punks will hurt Bubbe and Zeyde, and who knows what they'll do to the bakery if they find out I'm the Jewish Ninja."

"And who is to say that there won't be a slip up and they'll find out anyway? Then you're really going to be in quicksand," he replied.

We discussed the situation, weighing the pros and cons. Then Goodblatt added in the argument of guns.

"I'm sorry, Alexia, but a series of kicks and punches won't block a bullet."

"But they're scared of guns."

"Those hoodlums have no fear."

I told the Rabbi about their hideout in the tenement and how I spied on their every move. They knew the police were watching them because Crow's father had something to do with the force. He had heard his father say something about their gang not being as much of a threat as the other criminals since they didn't have guns. Plus, I had called the police every time a crime was planned, and I only jumped in to deter the gang until the police came.

"If I hear or see a gun, I promise I won't become the Jewish Ninja."

"You are a young girl, not a superhero. I'm not saying your martial arts techniques aren't phenomenal, but I'd have a *harts vatik* if something happened to you. It would be *all* my fault."

I continued arguing the positives of the Jewish Ninja, and finally Goodblatt's voice softened.

"If I let you continue, when you call the police, you must beep me three times on this," he said as he handed me an electronic device. "After all, I was a karate champion in Israel, and I *am* your mentor."

I argued that it might get more dangerous if someone else was involved. "Plus, what if they connected us?" I reasoned. "And what if they attack while you're giving a sermon on *Sabbath*?"

"We'll cross those paths when we get to them."

Agreeing to Goodblatt's instructions, I placed the mechanism in my pocket and began my Hebrew lesson in his office instead of the basement.

CHAPTER XVIII

Wild Bull

During my next spying spree at the tenements, Crow behaved like a wild bull burrowing through thousands of crimson blankets.

"One of you is a traitor, and whoever you are, you are dead meat!" he roared. "We are raiding the Baron Bakery right *now*, with no time to spare. None of you ain't gonna go outa my sight."

I rushed home and called 911. Too rattled to think, beeping Goodblatt didn't even enter my mind.

The lights to the bakery were turned off, which meant that my grandparents had closed the gates and were upstairs at their apartment. Entering the alley to change into my ninja outfit, I hid behind a large metal mail dispenser. It started to rain, then pour. It would have been great if the showers had deterred the punks, but sun was not going to shine through that thundercloud. They rounded the corner pounding sticks and bats against their hands.

"Come on, come on." I looked to the skies, hoping the police would arrive.

A lightning bolt hit a tree. My stomach performed its usual anxiety-ridden acrobatics routine.

A flash of light pierced through a bulb on a street lamp. The mob didn't flinch as they marched toward the bakery. Skipping into a round-off followed by as many back handsprings as I could muster, I whizzed right through the center of the mob and flipped into the dark. Crow halted the gang.

"Get him *now!*" he yelled.

Hidden behind a car, I observed as the group stopped. Flustered, they scattered and searched the streets, but could not find me.

"Get him now! What are you, deaf?" Crow roared.

The crew rummaged through trash, investigated little lanes and crevices, and checked behind signs and wherever you could imagine. They slipped in sludge as the downpour increased. I swung across a light and vaulted over a motorcycle sliding behind it. A bunch of hoodlums headed in my direction. Holding on to the sides of the cycle, they studied every corner, finding nothing.

Little did they know, I had shimmied up a pole. When I swirled down, escaping behind some cars, the post was hit by lightening. My heart thumped as a thunderous crash pummeled the street. Some heads peered out of windows, but not one innocent bystander ventured into the storm. Sirens sounded in the background, and the hoodlums scattered. I noticed Crow kicking and pounding on some cars as he ran for safety. Racing home, I relished the thought of sipping Bubbe's warm *matzah ball* soup and curling up in my bed.

CHAPTER XIX

The Report Card

I felt like a bowling ball was bouncing on my head and sandpaper was rubbing against my throat as I woke up the following morning. Sneezing and coughing didn't help matters. I forced myself out of bed to the mirror. After glancing at my puffy red eyes and trying to breathe from my stuffed-up nose, I went to the bathroom, blew into a tissue, brushed my teeth, and washed my face. Peeking into the mirror once more, I closed my eyes and sighed. Triple sneezes followed.

Opening Bill's letter sometimes comforted me. When I lived with my parents, he visited all of the time and always worked on some kind of project with my mom and dad. He'd even show up at my birthday parties. Since I left Spring Falls he's written and sent me a beautiful silk kamono from Japan and other exotic presents from his travels, but he hasn't come to visit. Maybe he's afraid to see me because he missed Dad so much. They were best friends. I opened a drawer and slowly straightened out a carefully folded piece of paper.

Dear Alexia,

I am so sorry about what has happened. Your parents were very dear to me and so are you. I'm sorry I did not make it to the funeral, but I had urgent business in Europe and did not find out until it was too late. Bob and I are dedicating the mall in your parent's name and we have been working diligently on your father's patents. The proceeds will be held in trust for when you reach the appropriate age. I will keep you and your grandparents up to date.

Love,
Bill

Bill's note didn't make me feel better. Scanning my room, I searched for my book bag. Sighting its wings under the dirty clothes I had thrown to the floor the night before, I unzipped it and felt for an envelope. I pulled it out and placed it on my table. I had almost forgotten. Gazing at it for a few moments, I opened it and peered at the paper inside.

This was going to be one of those days. Bubbe and Zeyde had to sign my report card. I got dressed and made my way to the breakfast table.

***

"Oh *bubeleh*, you look as though that horrible storm rumbled right through your window. Drink some of this," Bubbe said as she handed me some pulpy orange juice and felt my forehead with the back of her hand. "*Mazel tov*, no fever. I'll make you some more Jewish medicine after school. Someone ate the last batch and left the empty container in the refrigerator." Bubbe glared at Zeyde.

"It wasn't me, but it should've been." Zeyde's eyes sideswiped toward me and motioned me to sit by him. He grabbed both my cheeks and squashed them together. "Oh, you remind me so much of your mother. Whenever she got sick, Bubbe's special soup was all she asked for. Bubbe makes the best. There's good in the bad, and Bubbe's *matzah ball* soup is the good. The bad is feeling like a truck rammed into your head." He leaned over to hand me a tissue. "*Yetzer re, yetzer tov.*" Then he gave me a kiss and lifted his newspaper. "Oh, look at this. Thank *Hashem* nobody got hurt." He pointed to a picture of the pole that had fallen the night before. "And another article about the Jewish Ninja—he's a true *mensch*. The neighborhood has calmed down a lot since he showed up."

"Here, have a potato *latke* with your eggs. You've got to feed that cold." Bubbe dropped two onto my plate.

"You think I can stay home from school today?"

"Come on, *bubeleh*, everyone gets the sniffles this time of year," Bubbe said.

"In that case, you need to sign this. I got mostly A's." I handed my grandparents the report card, figuring that I had no choice but to confront the situation.

"Ah, our little brainy-buns. Your parents always bragged about your grades—never getting less than an A." As Zeyde smiled, I winced.

"What's this?" Bubbe exclaimed.

"Figures it would be in science class," Zeyde said.

"It's the first class in the morning and that teacher is so boring," I said. "Plus, that Roni is always pulling some prank to distract me and get me in trouble."

"When it comes to grades, you don't let people distract you, young lady," Bubbe said.

Zeyde took Bubbe aside, and they began to argue. Bubbe kept on repeating the letter D.

"This is atrocious. You don't want our granddaughter to become a *groisser gornicht,* do you? We need to limit her time out so she studies more." Bubbe's face turned red.

Oh no! I needed time to practice and spy in the tenements.

"She is not a blow-off," Zeyde said. "You are overreacting. This will be Alexia's first summer here. Give her a little break."

I was relieved that Zeyde was sticking-up for me, but Bubbe remained furious.

"Grades are important. That's why Jude was so successful."

"That is true. But it's just one class. She got A's in every other subject. She's just adjusting and needs to work a little harder," Zeyde argued. "Lighten up."

I zoned into my own thoughts. It was so hard to focus on science class. Dissecting was disgusting, and reciting big complicated words that were meaningless was mind numbing. To top that off the textbook was cumbersome and just got on my nerves.

"Alexia? Alexia?" Bubbe tapped my shoulder. "You're lucky your Zeyde has a soft spot in his heart for you. You've got to promise to work harder—no distractions. You are to study a chapter from science class, and we will test you every weekday on each section." Bubbe wasn't buying my excuse.

"Your Bubbe just wants the best for you. It's important these days to get a good education. Your parents were very successful because they were top of their classes and got scholarships to Yale, but if you get lazy, it's going to be tough. Bubbe and I don't have a lot of money, and when you get older, we might not be around." Zeyde always agreed with Bubbe.

"It's okay. I should've done better. I won't get anymore Ds." There was nothing else I could say.

CHAPTER XX

Revenge

Resentful, I threw my textbook into my bedroom closet. I'd return it at the beginning of the next school year. It wasn't that I hated the subject. In fact, science used to be my favorite class. My previous teacher was so cool. We chose our own projects and I even painted the whole circulatory system of our body with an essay about how the veins and arteries worked. Some people made maps and graphs and built replicas. Then we had discussions and everyone was psyched.

But this class was horse dung. As a matter of fact, I dreaded school every day. I had no close friends. Tutti wasn't nearby. David was cool, and we were starting to build a relationship, but Roni always interfered. She was making my life miserable. No matter how much I avoided her, she was always up in my face. She made me red-hot like the fiery lava spewing out of the volcano on the cover of my book. I grudgingly dragged it from my closet.

Oh, pig's feet.

It would have been very easy to return my earth science hardback and get some money back from the school. But no, Bubbe made me save it so I could study from it every day. I glared at it, picked it up, and then with venom brushed it off. Opening it and sifting through the pages wasn't so bad. The pictures showed the world's mountains and caverns along with the earth's varying atmospheres. The colors were stunning shades of auburn, forest greens, and ivory, highlighted by glorious oranges and reds from sunsets. Mr. Hames always picked the boring, ugly pictures and topics, and studying those convoluted words, that had no purpose, was just stupid. With a heavy sigh, I turned to the table of contents.

Bubbe had written in bright red magic marker *June 16* beside the chapter entitled "Sedimentary Rocks." How tedious. Who cared about volcanic eruptions, magma and whatever kind of boulders they formed? But I memorized basalt, pumice, and obsidian and prepared myself for Bubbe's exam, grateful at least that I wasn't in a confined classroom anticipating Roni's wicked pranks and Mr. Hames's mind-numbing lectures.

I raised my eyes to the skylight. "Whatever dimension you're in—I'm not going to disappoint you," I whispered as I envisioned Mom floating inside a cloud.

Forcing myself to memorize the erosion of sediment, dead plants, animals, and how they were deposited into the strata and squeezed together to form minerals and whatnots was my only alternative.

Bubbe's annoying screech bellowed from below. I grabbed the volcano book, pen, pad and my bright-patched bag and hurried down the stairs, ready to take my daily quiz. Plopping myself down, I handed Bubbe the book.

"Don't be so excited," Bubbe said. "You'll thank me one day."

Thanking Bubbe for the knowledge of sediment was not on my future to-do list, but it was a necessary function to get on with my life, so I conformed to her wishes and finished her exam.

"Not bad. This is a cake-walk for you—no pun intended," Bubbe said with a giggle. "Why didn't you do this at school?" Bubbe tried to rub away my milk moustache. "Don't move, you'll make me get it on your shirt."

"Bubbe, I'm sorry I didn't do well in school. Mr. Hames's lectures just put me to sleep. I slipped up. Can't you cut me some slack?"

"Oh, I'm sorry. What's a grandmother to do? How about, I'll lighten my grip, when you show me you're not going to fall? It's my responsibility to make sure you stand sturdy. Would you expect anything less of me?" Bubbe said as she raised her arms.

"Okay, I get it. Do you want me to do the deli shopping after my visit to the park?"

"No thank you, my *bubeleh*, but you can pass by the Cohen's Deli if you like. That cute boy David is turning out to be such a *mensch*. You'll have a perfect excuse to drop in on him," Bubbe said with a roguish smile. "Here, let me fix your top."

Who did she think she was insinuating that I liked David? I mean I like him, but that didn't mean I liked him, liked him. And, even if I did, it was none of her business.

"I can do that myself," I said as Bubbe tried to fix my buttons, then, of all things, spit on a napkin and pointed it at my mouth.

Why do grown-ups think they have a right to wipe their slobber on you?

"Yuck." I pushed Bubbe's hand away and rubbed my sleeve over my mouth. "I can clean myself. Plus, I don't need an excuse to visit David. I mean, he's my friend and in my Hebrew class. Sometimes you just say things from left field." I snatched my stuff and with my head held high strutted out the door and toward Steinbeck Square.

Thinking about Bubbe's snide remarks made my lips perk and ears steam. I wasn't a kid anymore, and I could say hi to David whenever I wanted. No way was I going to let her sneak into my private life.

***

To spite Bubbe, I decided to peek in the Cohens' window anyhow. If I had any kind of crush on David anyway, it was none of her beeswax.

Glancing and finding that no one was around calmed my nerves. Roni would just make things worse. She always popped up when David was near—what a pain. Plus, my stomach couldn't handle any more conflict. With no one to aggravate me, my sidewalk game became my focus. Following the cracked patterns with no interference was heaven.

However, as one of the crevices veered into a curving cobra pattern, it wrapped around a Mary Jane shoe. Following the pink tights upward, I was accosted by Roni's face.

Crossing the street was the easiest way to avoid confrontation. My wave to David would have to wait.

It was better that I escaped to my private retreat and used my *Turn a Cheek* to get out my aggressions. Rushing to my special spot, I rested my bag by the fountain and listened for any sounds coming from the punks' hideout. Pigeons cooed by some rubble, but that was it. Just to make sure, I crept over and peeked into the hole that allowed me to spy on the muttonheads' meetings. Freedom—the coast was clear.

After taking in a mouthful of air, my chest lifted and I was rejuvenated. Speeding back to my little alcove made me feel as though I was flying with the angels. The sun glistened, and daisies intermingled with a mixture of weeds that flooded what must've been a colorful array of flowers and plants at one time. I stretched my neck, arms, and body and began forming *hyungs*—new and old.

Thoughts of Bubbe's irritating comments and poking disappeared as my body flowed smoothly through the ruins. The constant repeated reminders from Bubbe sifted away into the blue, and irksome Bubbe-tugs and gross saliva were kicked over rooftops. Instead, I circled and punched, drifting with the breeze. Remembering my Sunday karate performances for my parents, I wondered if they were watching from above.

A thud boomed from the lair. I hurried to my secret nook and peered into my spy hole. The punks were gathered, but their normal rowdiness was subdued. An unexpected quiet filled the hideaway.

With his fists clenched, Crow stomped on a block of cement in front of one of his followers. The boy cowered in a corner. Then Crow, like the creature from the black lagoon, advanced toward another minion. Crow's hovering caused his lackey to stumble backward, and Crow moved on to terrorize one more. A guttural sound of hostility emerged from his throat. Drool dripped down his chin. For an instant he stood as if he were a statue. Then he moved forward, screeching like a rabid gorilla. Other than Crow's incoherent screams, silence filled the room.

With a flushed faced, Crow kicked some disintegrated brick barriers. Thrashing and whirling his arms, he waved around the refuge and stuck out his stubby neck so that each punk could experience his bug-eyed outrage.

"The next attack is the Beakman Boutique, and if any of you mess up I'm going to pound your skulls until they become mashed potatoes and devour them during dinner!" Crow roared as he cursed his crew.

When he was done with his profanities, a frail voice asked, "What about the Jewish Ninja?"

I flinched as I anticipated a biting answer from Crow. Instead, he clapped like a wild freak and raced over to pat the boy on the back.

Where did that change of attitude come from? I was starting to feel a little queasy. Maybe Crow was crazier than I had anticipated.

"The Beakman Store is just a ploy. We're going to deface that Jewish Ninja and destroy him for good." Crow howled like a hyena. "It's clue time. Get that Jew's identity and then, pow!" He slammed his fist against his hand. "He's a goner. All we have to do is grab that mask and uncover his face, and he ain't got nowhere to hide."

"How about if I distract the Jewish Ninja? Then you can pull off that thing that covers his face," Norm called out.

"Right on your *schnozzle*, Norm." Crow went over and flicked Norm's nose ring with his finger.

"Here's the plan. Everyone focuses on the ninja. You've got to surround him, and I'm going to start strangling him. If for some reason I can't get to him, one of you better be on the ball and clutch his throat."

"But that Jewish Ninja can't be held down. He's too quick," one of the bullies retorted.

"You imbecile," Crow roared. "All we need to do is take off his mask. He's going to be so busy defending himself from being choked that he's not going to even think about protecting his disguise." Dribble spurted from the sides of Crow's mouth as he grabbed the guy's neck and slapped off his glasses. "See?" Then he dropped the kid and pointed his finger toward the guy Goodblatt called Josh Barsky. "I want you to snatch his head gear and tear it off."

"What about me? I'm the one who suggested it," Norm argued.

"If you screwed this up, your ass would be tattooed in grass, so just feel lucky I'm giving you this break," Crow replied. "Not only that, you're lucky I picked that gaudy Beakman place, and you don't have to steal nothing from there. The hand-me-downs at Shanty's have more style."

Crow was right about one thing—the Beakmans' taste had the flare of a wet firecracker, but I wished he hadn't picked them, even if Roni wasn't exactly my favorite person in the neighborhood.

That Crow was living in a fantasy world if he ever thought I was about to let him uncover my identity; although a shiver did pass through my spine when I thought of those bullies trying to rip my muscles off. I could imagine Roni dancing the *hora* or something if she knew the predicament I had gotten myself into.

I rubbed my fingers in my hair, held in a yelp, and waited. After many deep breaths of air and recovering my composure, my mind hummed in order to bring on a meditative state. My breathing and composure stabilized.

If Crow's gang wasn't going to harm the store or anyone in it, there was no need for me to show up after I called the cops. On the other hand, what if one of the Beakmans got caught up with the gang and got hurt? Just because I didn't like the Beakmans didn't mean I wanted any harm to come to them. Plus, I'd had a long conversation with Goodblatt during *Rosh Hashanah* about Roni's obnoxious behavior towards me, and he insisted that the Beakmans were "wonderful people with extraordinary souls." Then he told me that *Rosh Hashanah* was a great time to forgive and make an effort to understand those that we have discrepancies with.

There was no way I would ever be Roni's friend, but I respected Goodblatt. Plus, if my mom had been best friend with Roni's mom at one point, then Roni had to have some kind of redeeming quality.

I went home and prepared myself in case the police didn't show up on time. I wore a double mask and made triple sure that the binding was secure. After slinking into my muscle get-up, I skimmed my way into two extra unitards. In case one of the sleaze-bags ripped an outer layer, I had inner material for protection. I twirled my arms in circles and bent my knees, checking my agility. Everything seemed to be intact. I was about to punch the keys for Goodblatt's beeper but got sidetracked when my outfit got caught on the windowsill. I had to slither and slink in order not to rip the fabric. Caught off balance, I slid down the railing of the fire escape and landed flat on my bum. Luckily, the extra muscle padding protected my non-existent Baron butt, and the pain didn't last. I found a pay phone, called the police and hurried to the Beakmans'. I'd almost forgotten—I punched in the numbers to Goodblatt's beeper and left a message where I would be.

***

While hiding across the street behind an old station wagon, my eyes followed the punks as they marched on their rampage.

"Halt!" yelled Commander Crow as he saluted his men.

They gestured back in formation. His eyes searched the streets. Crow whispered to the guy that Rabbi Goodblatt had called Josh. Josh ran behind a Volkswagen and ducked his head. Meanwhile, Crow motioned for two skinny guys to squeeze behind the gates to the store.

I prayed for the police to hurry, but there were no flashing lights in sight or sounds of sirens heard.

"We'll wait two minutes. Then this gate gets obliterated!" Crow screamed, his neck craning in every direction. He paused for a moment. "Plan change—destruction starts now. If the Ninja don't show, we wipe out the whole store." He lifted a huge bat and began to pound at the gate.

I flew into action, springing to the top of the Volkswagen and flipping over Crow so that I could kick the bat from him. Then I disappeared above the ledge to the right of a window above the gate.

"Josh, you idiot, you were supposed to grab him," Crow said with clenched teeth. "Get me another bat!" he yelled. "Now!"

Five large clubs pointed in his direction. Crow grabbed a bat, lifted his hand above his head, and ordered the dim-witted dorks to get back to their positions. He hauled his weapon and began clobbering the metal protective gate with vengeance. I leaned against a bar connected to the sign and swung in a circle, catching the bat between my knees, raising it to my arms through a hole in the cloth. Then I tossed it behind the building. I rolled onto the neighbor's awning in order to escape view.

Crow held out his open hand, and one of his goons put another weapon in it.

"Don't even think about winning this one. I've got it covered, you karate turd!" he yelled as he took a long chain from his bag and hooked one end to a loop at the bottom of the pole. Then he fastened the other hook to his belt.

I needed to buy time until the police arrived. What was taking them so long? The chain was hooked tight, and the rod it was connected to was surrounded by cement. Then I noticed a crack in the concrete.

If I raced across the awning, I could build up speed and plunge into the rod Crow had locked himself to. The pole would shake, throwing Crow off balance, and I could tangle him up in shackles. Then flip-flopping into the alleyway out of sight would not only frustrate them into more beer can mashing, but also delay their break-in to the boutique.

As my adrenaline surged and I made a jumping leap to gain power, the canopy ripped and I fell to the ground. Crow grabbed me from behind.

"Gotta do everything myself," Crow said as he began to strangle me.

Raising my wrists, causing pressure against Crow's thumbs, I twisted from his hold. Josh, however, had done his duty and pulled off my mask.

Crow seized the cap. Holding it up in the air as though he had marked his bull in triumph, he faced me as I placed my hands on the trunk of a Chrysler, giving me leverage for my feet to follow. Then I climbed to the top. Luckily, black polyester still covered my face.

"Hiyah!" I said with glee, though I lowered my voice for effect.

Crow yelled in frustration.

Sirens sounded in the background, and I noticed Goodblatt running down the street. I bowed and did a back flip off the car, running into the night. Then I diverted to a side corner so I could eavesdrop.

Crow was cursing up a storm. He motioned for his goons to disperse and then he ran down an alley. Norm followed and I tracked them from the rooftop. Though the lane was dark, the light from side windows allowed me to observe them.

Crow threw down my ninja mask and began to stomp on it. With the top of his foot he heaved the mask to his hands and tried to pull it apart. He stopped. The covering was inside out and there was a symbol. Crow joggled Norm with excitement. Norm began to scream.

"Shut up, you dick-wad," Crow said as he slapped Norm. "Look, look." Crow squished the material in Norm's face. Norm halted, not moving a bone.

"The insignia! Don't you see? We've got him. That's the symbol used for Goodblatt's synagogue. I knew that Rabbi Goodblatt had something to do with this. He's gonna pay. We just got to figure out where the Ninja came from."

I felt heat flush throughout my body.

"What does that mean?" Norm's voice quivered. "I mean, lots of Jews have *yarmulkes* with that sign."

"Don't you get it? It's a start. Remember, Goodblatt was at Shanty's. That Rabbi must be putting the Ninja up to all this. Didn't you see him just show up at the Beakmans'?"

Fear flashed up my spine. I was in luck that Crow didn't suspect me, but Goodblatt was in danger. If Goodblatt got hurt, it would be my fault. I needed to think of something, and quick.

CHAPTER XXI

The Gun

I searched the stars for guidance. Nothing was offered, not a flicker in the sky except for a passing plane. I fell asleep tossing and turning. My parents used to preach that every problem could be solved, but this situation was hopeless. After a restless night, glaring light beamed through the skylight to wake me. I raised my sweaty hands to remove my sticky hair from my perspiring face.

My parents were gone. Bubbe and Zeyde could never replace them. They'd start talking about something that had nothing to do with what I'd gone to them about in the first place. Trying to discuss problems with them was like being trapped in a foreign film with no subtitles.

Tutti spoke my language and understood me inside and out. But Tutti lived too far away, and her parents were always snooping. If they overheard what was going on over the telephone or read her mail, things would get really messy.

Goodblatt was another alternative, but he had already warned me about guns. He was bound to go straight to the police. That would jeopardize my grandparents. So many times I thought of contacting Master Luna, but I didn't want him to think I'd replaced him with Goodblatt. Or, what if Master Luna went into cahoots with Goodblatt? I'd be double doomed. If I didn't decide what to do immediately, Goodblatt and the synagogue would be in danger. My pillow was soaked with tears.

If I could figure out what Crow had planned that might make matters easier. Now that school was over, I had a little more time. I gathered my funky, patched-up bag, and readied myself for Bubbe's earth science exam as plodded down the stairs.

***

As I entered the breakfast area, I dropped my stuff, got out a pen and pad, and waited for Bubbe to bombard me with questions about the earth's atmosphere.

"Where are you off to today?" Bubbe asked, pouring the oranges that had just been juiced into my glass.

"Thank you," I said taking a sip. "I thought I'd go to the park and do a little yoga."

Bubbe handed me a cinnamon raisin bagel with cream cheese. "I put some raspberry in the spread. You know, a little added spark for my special *punim*." Bubbe gave my cheeks a pinch. "I could just eat you up." She leaned over and gave me a kiss on my forehead. "Zeyde and I have been missing you for dinner lately. Why don't you come home by six and I'll make *kasha* and bow ties with double-stuffed cherry cheese for dessert?"

Why was Bubbe being so nice? Should I remind her about the daily quiz? Why not? I had studied. Besides, I got a kick out of showing Bubbe that I wasn't the dimwit she thought I was.

"No, not today. You've been doing so well, you get a day off."

After expressing gratitude for dinner, I hurried off.

***

Running as fast as I could and hoping no one would see me, I darted down the abandoned street and into the tenements. After setting my bag under a bush, I practiced *Turn A Cheek*, but I couldn't focus. Dumping myself down near a nook next to my special spy-hole, I dropped my face on top of my palms and stared at the daisies that sprung up between the vines. I picked one.

"It's going to work. It's not going to work," I said as I plucked the petals one after the other. When the flower was bare, I threw it away and reached for another and another. As the empty stems piled by my side, I heard an obnoxious crooning rumbling in the background.

Crow, with zest, led his crew into the hideout. His head bopped and arms swooped. It was mid-morning, but these guys were gulping beers and wallowing all over the place. They carried boom boxes and sang in a raucous manner. Crow hurdled on to a hunk of cement and acted as though he was conducting an orchestra. He motioned two boys to carry a box and place it near him. Then, with a frantic gesture, he began flailing his arms again. I think he was trying to sing, but he rapped like a bear with phlegm stuck in his throat:

Ninja shows up here, shows up there;
Showin' up everwhere.
Watcha gonna do? Watcha gonna do?
Crow's got the wings—Gots the know how;
What do ya know? We're goin' on a pow wow.
Watcha gonna do? Watcha gonna do?
Flyin' High—with a cap. Pulled it off;
Now the ninja is zapped.

Crow pushed his arms straight out and spread his fingers wide, halting the chorus. He hopped on a large sturdy box some of the gang had brought behind him. Crow simulated a tap dance and chanted, "Ba, ba, ba, ba, ba, ba boom." Then he bound into a barrel that made a loud whack and everyone cheered.

Meanwhile, in between peeping at the travesty and covering my face, I held my head in dismay.

"It seems as though that pip-squeak ninja might be connected to that scatter-brained Rabbi. Maybe Goodblatt's his uncle or something. Everyone knows that Schwartz guy, right?" Crow asked.

The whole clan whooped and hollered.

"We're not going to put up with nothing no more."

The pack got wilder.

"Schwartz is our next target."

Everyone raised their cans of Bud and howled with approval.

What did Schwartz have to do with this? Just because he was good friends with Goodblatt didn't mean they were in cahoots. I had seen Schwartz at my parents' *shiva*, and I often saw him leaving Goodblatt's office, but it was ridiculous that Crow could even presume he was involved.

Crow halted the howling and signaled two of the boys to move the box to the center of his stage.

"Open it!" Crow demanded.

His flunkeys unbolted the latches and pushed the cover upward. As if a hurricane had ended, its damage leaving nothing to be salvaged, silence engulfed the room.

I froze in horror. My eyes followed Crow's arms as they boosted a rifle high above his head. More were in the container.

He twirled the gun like a baton. He placed it under his arm and pretended to shoot. "Bam, bam, bam!" he snapped. "What's a ninja ta do," he sang and then snickered.

I could see that some of the punks were no longer in a jovial mood. The overall excitement had ceased and many of them just stood there facing the guns.

"You said we were just having fun. We didn't need guns," Josh said.

"I had no choice, so I changed my mind. That ninja freak is messing up everything. You think we should just give in?"

Josh slowly shook his head.

"Do any of you think we should give in?" Crow yelled. "Do you?" He jabbed a finger at a gang member, causing him to fall backward. "How about you, or you, or you?" He pointed in rapid fire as he moved across the room.

A chill cooled the heated hideaway.

"Hey guys, we just gotta show them we mean business. We don't gotta shoot them." Crow took out some revolvers and twirled them as if he were a sheriff in a cowboy movie. Then he juggled them and began handing some out.

"They're not loaded. It's just like having a toy."

I didn't wait for the meeting to finish. I rolled from my position, crawled to grab my bag and darted to Mr. Schwartz's newly opened convenient store.

***

While running, my hand felt around my pocket for the beeper to call Goodblatt. However, the telephone on the corner distracted me from continuing my search. Grabbing the receiver, I punched in the numbers 911. I pulled up the bottom of my shirt and covered the phone receiver, muffling my voice.

"Mr. Schwartz at 511 Snyder Avenue is about to be robbed. They have an arsenal of firearms."

"What? I can't hear you," the voice on the other end said.

"Five eleven Snyder Avenue is being robbed. They have guns." I repeated, trying to articulate my words with the shirt still covering the phone.

"Five eleven Snyder is being robbed? Is this the Jewish Ninja?"

"Yes, please hurry." I hung up, found an alley, threw on my indigent wear and entered Schwartz's store. Making sure my voice was raspy and holding my stomach as if I were in pain, I asked for some Metamucil.

"If you look on the back shelf in aisle two, you should see it. Would you like me to get it for you?" Mr. Schwartz asked.

"Thank you. I can get it," I answered, covering my voice with coughs.

As I pretended to search for my medicine, the half-wits entered the store one by one. Bending down and switching into my ninja outfit, I pulled down my cap and crept to the back corner in order to hide my bag. The only plausible place was a pile of toilet tissue packages piled near a door in the rear, so I tucked it behind the mound. My heart skipped a beat when I saw Crow lift a pistol from his pocket.

The pea-brains needed to be distracted. I inhaled, taking in all the breath I could muster, and as the air escaped I climbed up a stepladder and flipped over a rack of Hallmark cards. Not wanting to be seen, I rolled down the aisle into the next, until I reached the center.

"Hiyah!" I yelled, springing to my feet.

The goons gaped at me. Avoiding an attack, I sprang to safety behind a rack of nacho chips. Crow's eyes crossed and his disciples stumbled. My heartbeat was racing faster than a mouse escaping Scruffy's wrath.

All of a sudden, Crow grabbed Mr. Schwartz by the hair and pointed a revolver at his throat. The sound of my pulse stopped.

"You don't want him! You want me!" I shouted from behind the rack.

"Then come out, come out, wherever you are!" Crow chanted. "Or he gets it." Crow pulled Schwartz's skull back.

"I'm coming out. Just let him go."

"Get your smelly tush out here—now!" Crow demanded.

There was no choice but to move out from behind the Doritos. Crow threw Mr. Schwartz to the ground and pointed the weapon at me, his grin growing with every minute. He pulled back the hammer of the gun.

"Yo, Jewish Ninja, you got nowhere to hide. Take off that mask—now!"

"Why don't you get one of your footmen to do it?" I said, feeling the creepy crawlies gnaw at my stomach even though I placed my hands on my hips to flex my fake muscles and display utter confidence.

It was a chance, but what else could I do? If I could either stall him until the cops came or find an opening and *Turn a Cheek* when and if Crow's sidekick went for my mask, I might escape this fix.

"How about I just do it myself?" Crow said, pointing the gun at me while he strolled in my direction, adding a hop step as if he were already doing a victory strut.

As he reached to uncover my face, I heard sirens. I grabbed Crow's hand, placing pressure on his wrist, then turned and lifted my leg to knee the gun from his grip. The pistol went off when it hit the tiles. But, they weren't supposed to be loaded. Feeling a sharp pain pierce my rib, I grabbed my side and dropped. Crow was gone before he'd had a chance to remove my mask. As I straightened my disguise, crimson liquid dripped from my hands.

"You poor boy! Here, let me help you!" Mr. Schwartz said as he reached over to inspect my wound. "You shouldn't move until the police get here." He wrapped a towel around my side. "I'll call an ambulance."

He tried to remove my mask, but I blocked his attempt.

"That material over your mouth will make it harder for you to breathe," Schwartz said.

"No, I can't reveal my face."

No matter how caring and persuasive Schwartz tried to be, there was no way I was going to give in.

"Fine, fine. Who am I to pester a boy who has just been shot? What are you, sixteen or seventeen?"

I didn't answer.

"I guarantee when the ambulance comes, they are going to take off your whole outfit. Your health is more important than some costume. I'm going to call emergency."

I begged Schwartz not to let any authorities get a hold of me, but he wouldn't give in.

"You don't want Rabbi Goodblatt to go to jail, do you?" The words just popped out of my mouth.

"Rabbi Goodblatt? What does he have to do with this?"

"You have to take me to the basement of Rabbi Goodblatt's synagogue or he will get into a lot of trouble. He'll explain." Though I was in a great deal of pain, I didn't forget to use my husky voice. "I promise, it's just a scratch. It's not serious."

"*Oy vey*, what has Mort gotten himself into? I love that man, but ugh."

"You know the Rabbi is a doctor," I said feigning a foreign accent. "He got his doctorate in Israel." The more I tried to wriggle my way out of my situation, like quicksand, the deeper I sunk.

"I know the Rabbi like the back of my hand and the only doctorate he's got is in religion."

I couldn't figure out what to do, so I allowed my mouth to jabber on. When Schwartz hesitated and started shaking his head, I got nervous that he wasn't going to fall for anything so I tried the Jewish strategy called guilt.

"I didn't mean to lie," I began. "It's just that I didn't want any harm to come to Rabbi Goodblatt. I'm an immigrant and if they find out that I am a foreigner, they are going to deport me and the Rabbi will go to jail. Please, he was just trying to help my aunt. My dad was beating me and would have killed me if he found me. The Rabbi was trying to help me get my citizenship so my dad wouldn't capture me and do who knows what." I wasn't sure if Schwartz was buying my story. I showed him that the bleeding has stopped. "I'm fine."

"How is it, we are best friends, I know him for forty years, and he doesn't tell me these things?" Schwartz muttered to himself in Hebrew, and then sighed. He checked my injury. "All right, whether you are making this up, I am not sure. But, better safe than sorry. Let me get you to the back. I'll go and talk to the police and then get you to the synagogue. The wound doesn't look that bad. It's not good, but it's just a flesh wound. You'll survive."

Schwartz carried me up the stairs to his apartment and began cleaning my wound. As he pulled back extra material and then more, he laughed. "That's an interesting way to build muscles, young man."

Not knowing what to say, I avoided the issue by feigning sleepiness.

Schwartz left a message on Goodblatt's answering machine and carried me to his guest room.

"I'm going back to the store to deal with the police and we'll decide what to do when I get back."

When he came back I was awake, but I kept my lids closed. He gently covered me with a blanket.

"Maybe I should let you rest and wait for the Rabbi to get back to me," he whispered. "If he doesn't call tonight, I'll bring you to him in the morning." He checked my temperature and pulse while I let my body ease. My face tingled when I felt fingers try to lift my mask, so I shifted position to make it impossible for Schwartz to lift it without waking me. There was quiet. Then I heard the door close.

CHAPTER XXII

Where is Alexia?

Early the next morning, though my ribs ached, I searched for a telephone to call Bubbe and Zeyde. They must've been having conniption fits. When I heard the knob on the door shake, I scurried back to where I was sleeping.

"It's time we got to the synagogue," Schwartz said. He wrapped me in the blanket and lifted me. "You're a lot lighter than I thought you'd be."

"I can walk. The wound is not that bad," I said. Schwartz was not a big man, and I weighed more than a hundred pounds.

"If you stand horizontally, you may bleed some more. I'd rather not take any chances." He stood sturdy as a rock and with speed hurried me to the synagogue.

***

He entered through the back where the wheelchairs are able to gain access. I winced as Schwartz bumped down the stairway to the basement.

"Sorry about that. Are you sure your okay." He held me with one arm and lifted my blanket to check my wound. I wasn't sure what he said, but the words he mumbled in Yiddish or Hebrew sounded like a prayer. Schwartz looked scrawny. I had no idea he was so buff. "You're going to be fine," he said as he gently laid me on a chair. "We are more likely to find a private spot down here so we can figure out what to do."

The large hall used for Shabbat dinners was a turn to the left at the end of a long stairway. A clatter came from the kitchen that was located straight ahead. Schwartz tried the door to a large darkened room used for seminars and lectures located across from the dining area, but it was locked. Then he approached a long hallway.

"Why don't we go down there? Nobody ever uses those rooms," I suggested.

As if I were only a feather, Schwartz lifted me and carried me through the vestibule that led to the kitchen, and then down a long foyer. At the end, were two medium-sized rooms that were rarely used.

"Your choice," Schwartz said.

One was a powder room filled with hardwood chairs and a table. It was used as a resting area for getting ready for bar mitzvahs and shows and stuff. The other room was a bit cozier.

"I guess that flowered sofa will be okay, plus those oversized seats might be kind of cozy."

"I'm glad you approve. You're willing to speak your mind. Could be a good sign." Schwartz laid me on the sofa and told me to stay put while he searched for Goodblatt.

"Like I'm going anywhere," I said with a grin.

I made sure Schwartz was gone before lifting my mask. As I adjusted my position, I heard chanting. I realized the sound was coming from a vent in the wall. From a higher vent came the distant sound of a telephone ringing soon replaced with Goodblatt's voice.

"Hello, Rabbi Goodblatt speaking. Oh, if the note reads urgent could you bring it up to me." There was a pause. "I'm sure Roy won't mind if you leave your post for a second, and it could be important. Thank you."

That must have been Sylvie. She was the secretary during the week. She was extremely lazy but loveable.

Schwartz came back to check on me. I pulled down my mask and lifted my head.

"I left a note with Sylvie and checked the congregation. He's not there. Are you okay? Let me check your side."

"Don't worry about me. I'm fine. I heard the Rabbi through that vent. He's in his office." The pain in my rib had intensified, but there was no way I wanted Schwartz to find out, nor was I in the mood for another hospital.

"If you're okay, I'm going to get Rabbi Goodblatt."

"Who is in the sanctuary?" I asked, causing Schwartz to halt as he started to leave.

"Not many people. Why? Who do you know?"

"Oh, I don't know anybody. The Rabbi talks about the Barons a lot. I was just wondering."

"He's close to the Barons, but they aren't there, but the Beakmans are. I'm going to check his office."

What was it with those Beakmans? They were haunting me. I heard a knocking noise from the opening above as Schwartz ran out. It sounded as though Goodblatt's door was creaking open from above. I wanted to move closer to the vent, but when I moved the pang in my side felt like a sharp thick needle twisting.

"Thank you, Sylvie," Goodblatt said.

"You are quite welcome. May I just tell you a story, Rabbi?"

There was a pause, and I prayed that the Rabbi didn't nod his head in approval. Once Sylvie got going, she was impossible to stop. She was the kind of person who was nosy and asked too many questions, and I wanted her out of the Rabbi's office as soon as possible.

What if Sylvie read the note? My intestinal tract tightened and my heart tumbled to my belly as if it was spinning full speed in the washing machine.

"How about later? It says this note is urgent."

"Okay, but don't forget. This is a good one." Sylvie snorted and left.

Goodblatt chuckled and I heard the door close. There was some movement, and for a moment, I began to breathe with more ease.

"*Oy vey*, that child will be the death of me." I froze. Goodblatt mumbled a Hebrew prayer. Then I heard him talking to Bubbe on the phone. "Calm down, Lilly. Shlomo just left me a note that he's with her downstairs in the synagogue." I hadn't read exactly what Mr. Schwartz had written, but it was probably about the Jewish Ninja being injured by the punks. And though Goodblatt might have been confused about any immigration problems that might have been mentioned, it was evident he knew Schwartz was talking about me. "I'm about to go check. I don't know why she didn't come home last night, but I'm sure there is a good explanation. She stayed at Shlomo's. She must have hurt her ankle or something. Don't worry, you stay there and I'll bring her back to the bakery."

In the pause that followed, I pictured Bubbe ranting and raving and Zeyde rubbing her shoulders. He was always trying to calm Bubbe down.

"She should've called. I know. Well, the police usually have to wait forty-eight hours before they investigate a missing person's claim. I'll speak to Shlomo and then call you as soon as I know."

As soon as the phone conversation was over, I heard Schwartz entering Goodblatt's office. He sounded as though he was hyperventilating as he interspersed words about a wounded boy in the basement. "Get your first aid kit and follow me," Schwartz said.

"Is he okay?" Goodblatt sounded worried.

"He'll be fine, but Mort, you've got a lot of explaining."

"I'm coming, I'm coming. You don't have to pull me."

The door slammed. I made sure my mask was secure as I heard them race down the hallway. When I lifted my legs so that I could hop up to greet Goodblatt, the sting in my side made me decide otherwise. Lying back on the sofa would have to do. I don't know whether they used the steps or elevator but they arrived in my waiting room in a flash. Goodblatt rushed over and checked under my bandage. Then he listened to my pulse and heart rate.

"You guys are just like the hospital doctors," I said.

"I'm calling an ambulance," Goodblatt said, and as he rushed over to a telephone hanging on the wall, Schwartz stopped him.

"The boy told me about his family in Israel and you protecting him. Are you ready for what's ahead?" Schwartz said, with his eyebrows furrowed low.

Goodblatt gritted his teeth and glared at me. I could feel my bottom lip tense.

"I told him how you saved me from my father in Israel," I said, feigning an accent.

I saw Goodblatt's jaw loosen. I couldn't tell if the puzzled look on his face was a good sign or not.

"Mort?" Mr. Schwartz was contorting his face like he was holding back a laugh.

"I also told Mr. Schwartz that you wouldn't want anybody to know anything about me because it might be *dangerous* if anybody were to find out," I said, hoping that Goodblatt would get that I didn't want Schwartz to know who I was.

Goodblatt went over and bent to check my wound one more time. "You are one lucky little boy. It's just a nick." The Rabbi gave me a gentle poke in my side, and I winced. "However, his rib might have been damaged, so we might need to take him to the hospital to get an x-ray," he said to Schwartz with a wink—as if I didn't see it.

Something crashed on the other side of the basement and feet were scampering about. Then banging and clashing erupted. Goodblatt and Schwartz ran out the door. I moved my legs across the sofa. I felt a burn in my side, but the sting numbed and I decided to bear it. Still dressed in my ninja gear—lacking some of the stuffing (my muscles)—I pressed my hand against my wound for support as I followed the men out of the door and through the hallway. The punks were knocking down tables and throwing chairs into doors.

Crow shot me the night before. You'd think he'd want to stay out of sight. They were stupid idiots, mentally deranged, or both. Out of control, like rabid raccoons, some of the punks were covering the walls with graffiti and the others were just throwing things wherever. They shattered stained glass windows and tore curtains on the stage.

"It sounds like a war down here. Why don't the congregants rush down?" I asked Goodblatt.

"When they built this place, they made sure that the sanctuary would be a sturdy, well-protected haven, sheltered from any noise that would disturb services. Though it's filled with congregants, they can't hear a thing."

"There he is. Get him!" The punks pointed at Goodblatt.

Goodblatt began blocking with his arms and whatever he could find for defense, including the scattered furniture. He asked Crow why he was doing this.

"What, do you think I'm a numbskull? You didn't think I'd figure out that you two are partners?" Crow answered. "I'm no fool. It's because of you he's harassing us, and you are going to pay!" Crow spit at Goodblatt's feet.

I rolled on the ground, tripping Crow, too keyed up to notice any soreness.

"Are you okay?" Goodblatt asked me as he held Crow down.

"Yeah." I threw Goodblatt some rope that had fallen from one of the closets.

Crow cursed and howled at us while we wrapped a rope around his wrists. He then thrust his elbow into where I was injured, and blood began to stain my top. Goodblatt caught Crow's upper arm, bent it backward, and gave it an extra turn.

"Are you sure you're okay?" Goodblatt asked me.

"I'm fine. It looks worse than it is."

"I thought you got shot. What, did ya raise from the dead, you bumble-faced, snot-head?" Crow bellowed as Goodblatt bound him against a column.

"*Hashem* works in mysterious ways," Goodblatt said as he patted Crow's head. He winked at me.

Schwartz threw Goodblatt a long cable that he had grabbed from another closet. Goodblatt clutched one end and threw me the other. As an onset of gang members chased Schwartz, we tightened the cable to trip the fleet. Schwartz stood stunned and turned. Then, as one bully passed, Schwartz grabbed the sculpture of a family and let him crash right into it.

"I'm getting the hang of this," Schwartz said.

I threw over some twine and Schwartz tied him up. "Be careful, they have guns," I shouted, though no weapons were in sight.

Norm came running behind Goodblatt, ready to clobber him on the head. Goodblatt simply leaned forward, moved his hips to the side, grabbed Norm's nose ring with his pinky, and twirled him around like a revolving wheel, leading him to fall on his face. I hopped back, allowing space for Norm to fall. Schwartz threw the cord, and Goodblatt held Norm while Schwartz and I tied him to a pillar near the elevator.

"Just like the old days," Schwartz said to Goodblatt.

"The old days?" I asked Goodblatt.

"Shlomo and I were in the army together—another story," Goodblatt said.

Crow inched his way out of the binding and bolted to the elevator. But Goodblatt had used a switch behind one of the closet doors to turn it off. Crow punched the button over and over and then headed for the stairs. Just in time, I shut the heavy metal door and turned the lever to lock it.

"Help me, you dumb twits. Get the guns from the bag!" Crow yelled to his hidden henchmen.

A duffle bag was in the center of the corridor. One of the hoods with a tarantula tattooed on his forehead scooted from behind a turned table and stretched for the sack. Holding my side, I hopped across some chairs and jumped, heaving my heel into the bag, which knocked into the spider. The punk dropped the firearms. I scooped up the pack and lugged it over to Goodblatt.

Goodblatt and Schwartz tied the hoodlums up one by one. "These guys went too far." Sirens sounded in the background. "Follow me. We'll go up the back way."

As we passed the door to the kitchen, I heard a noise and peeked in. Mr. Johnson had a gag in his mouth and was tied to a counter.

"You stay here," Goodblatt said to Schwartz and me as he rushed to release Johnson.

"Are you okay?" Goodblatt asked him.

"I'm fine, sir, but those thugs got bugs in their brains."

"Why don't you go upstairs and direct the police down here?"

As soon as Goodblatt released him, Johnson thanked Goodblatt and ran upstairs.

"Alexia. Let me check your wound." Goodblatt headed in my direction.

"Alexia?" Schwartz shook his head. "That explains everything, the strange accent, the phony muscles and when I checked his heart...never mind. Your grandparents are going to kill me."

"Oh no. They must be looking for us," Goodblatt said. "Let's go. The police will take care of these characters."

Goodblatt left a note explaining that the punks were the culprits that had been terrorizing the town and the guns in the bag were theirs. I unlatched the door. Police sirens sounded. Goodblatt, Schwartz and I hid to make sure the police read the note. However, not only did the officers make their way to the basement, but the entire congregation followed. I relished every moment as I watched the crowd's relieved stares and comments as the punks were handcuffed and led away.

"Now, there is plenty of evidence to lock them up. You need to go change into some regular clothes and get to your grandparents before they have coronary failure," Goodblatt said.

"You're not going to tell them everything?" I pleaded.

"They're your grandparents, Alexia, but it might be better if the Jewish Ninja stays a myth to others. We'll discuss it, but we don't need the Jewish Ninja anymore. We've got enough evidence for those guys to be locked up for a long time."

Goodblatt then told the whole Jewish Ninja story to Schwartz, who promised to not reveal my identity. They contemplated my gunshot wound and the Rabbi was confident that because all of the congregants observed the gang's egregious conduct together, more than enough witnesses would reveal themselves and convict those criminals.

"You're moving around just fine. If your ribs were seriously damaged, you wouldn't be as active as you are, but we'll pass by Shalom Medics after we see your grandparents just to make sure. You are one lucky kid."

"I'll just tell Bubbe and Zeyde that I fell on a sharp, metal object," I said.

"Do you have normal clothes? It would be too much for them to handle you as the Jewish Ninja when they first see you. As it is, they are worried sick. That doesn't mean we shouldn't tell them."

"They are in my big patched bag. It's underneath the toilet paper in Mr. Schwartz's store."

My side began to throb. I bent over to caress the tender area. Every time I took a breath my ribs tightened with tenderness.

"*Oy vey*, that rib might be worse than we thought," Goodblatt exclaimed, lifting me in his arms. "To your grandparents, we'll take care of your injury, and then your only focus is school and your *bat mitzvah*."

I started to tell Goodblatt that I had no arguments, but he placed his hand over my mouth and interrupted.

"Nothing else said."

CHAPTER XXIII

School Again

When Bubbe and Zeyde saw me they ran to me hugging, kissing and making a huge fuss.

"We've been up all night, calling the police. We didn't know what happened to you. Those *meshugener* delinquents might've done something horrible." Bubbe was frantic.

"Why didn't you call?" Zeyde exclaimed.

"I'm sorry, I was at Mr. Schwartz's and..."

Goodblatt and Schwartz's threw intense warning signals toward me.

"Why don't we have a seat in the living room?"

"*Oy Vey*, what happenned to you?" Zeyde exclaimed.

"It is just a graze, but we should go to the hospital and double check," Goodblatt announced. "First, Alexia needs to explain the circumstances and as your Rabbi and long time friend, I am praying that you stay calm and try to understand."

Bubbe was fanning her hand in front of her face, and Zeyde, his jaw tense, held her.

The television was on in the background and we all heard the breaking news about the arrest of the mob that had been plaguing the town.

"We need to give our thanks to Rabbi Goodblatt, Mr. Schwartz and The Jewish Ninja, whomever he may be," the newscaster announced.

Bubbe and Zeyde turned toward Goodblatt and Schwartz and then they slowly twisted in my direction. They figured it out and I was about to turn into chopped liver.

"We should be thankful that nobody is hurt and collect ourselves. Why don't we take Alexia to the hospital and we'll discuss what has occurred on the way," the Rabbi carefully stated.

My grandparents were surprisingly serene when our account of the Jewish Ninja unraveled. And, they agreed that nobody should be told, but made me promise never to become the Jewish Ninja again. I thought I would be punished for life, but my grandparents said that they felt blessed that I was in their lives.

***

A new school year meant a new homeroom, and I hoped Roni wasn't in mine—7A. There she was, on the first day of school, strolling down the street with her clan. I couldn't believe my eyes. They were wearing those shiny denim outfits—the kind that looked like it had plastic covering the material. And the lace attached to the bottom of the skirts looked like doilies made from rubber bands or licorice stuck on cardboard. I figured nobody had wanted to buy those want-to-be fashion eye soars at her family's store.

As I entered the school area and waved to David, I waited for the bell. The students in 7A were called to enter their line, and, sure enough, that's where Roni strutted. Trying to ignore her presence, I took my place in line as far away from her as possible, in the back.

David bumped beside me. "We got put in the same class this year. Guess what? We get Mrs. Barsky for science. She's the coolest. And we get to create amazing projects about the galaxy and stars." David handed me a Milky Way bar. "My dad said to give this to you."

Roni moved to the back, by us. "By the way, do you want one of these neat new outfits for your bat mitzvah?" Roni paused waiting for an answer. "My mom RSVP'd, didn't she?"

I looked around to see if there was someone else she might've been talking to, but she was looking at me. What evil scheme was she planning?

"I'm not sure," I replied.

At first the thought that she was trying to get rid of unwanted stock hit my mind, but she was wearing that satire of style with pride. My mom used to tell me that being judgmental wasn't fair because people had different tastes and who was to say who was right, but come on. I didn't get it. I cuddled in my cozy aqua sweater to warm myself while we were led to our classroom.

Later that day, Roni cornered me by my locker.

"Um, did you want something?" I said.

"Sort of," Roni replied and then blurted out, "I'm sorry. I'm sorry for being such a dimwit. It's just that I thought your mom was mean to my mom and did something awful and then when we got the invitation to your *bat mitzvah* my mom explained everything. And I feel *really* rotten."

I couldn't believe what I was hearing.

"Do you want me to come to your *bat mitzvah*? I mean, I'd understand if you didn't."

"That would be great if you came," I said, but I wasn't sure if I was being totally honest.

"My mom told me how much she loved your mom and how they were best friends. No one ever told me. I thought they just hated each other. Look, see these earrings I'm wearing? Your mom made them for my mom. I haven't taken them off since my mom gave them to me."

"They are really pretty," I said as the dangling dewdrops swung from Roni's ears.

"My mom was just upset because your mom left, and then my dad didn't like what your mom sent because he thought they were sacrilegious, and then your mom stopped sending things and that upset my mom. Dad can be overbearing sometimes, but it's not because he's mean. He's just got his ways. He didn't even want my mom to have this cool stuff in the same building as the religious stuff," Roni said as she flaunted her outfit.

Her father may have been a little rigid, but he had a point.

"It's just that he's so conservative. For that matter, can you imagine, he actually forbade me to wear this?" She wiggled her skirt. "Even getting my ears pierced was taboo. Mom got mad and he lightened up." She rubbed the earrings between her fingers. "He says he wants to change with the times but its kind of tough. Anyway, my mom said that your mom was really liberal and tons of fun. She really loved your mom a lot. She misses her."

I smiled. A hacky sack hit me in my side, and I flinched. David came over and grabbed it.

"Sorry about that. Hey, you guys look kind of chummy—totally cool." He grabbed the toy and went back to his buddies.

"You know, David and I have been friends since we were babies. He's like a brother," Roni said. "I was kind of feeling slighted when he was paying so much attention to you. I really didn't mean anything."

"It's okay."

"My mom thought it would be kind of cool if you and I were friendly. I'd kind of like that too. I mean, if you wouldn't mind."

I nodded my head and smiled as Roni pranced back to her clique. Her silly denim outfit was kind of cute in a weird way. I wasn't sure if I really wanted to be friends with someone who treated me the way she had, but on account of her and my mom being best friends, I thought that my mom might've wanted me to give it a try.

CHAPTER XXIV

The White Dove

"Let's take a little hiatus. We've got time," Zeyde said as we headed toward the synagogue.

He skidded a pebble across the otherwise peaceful pond in Steinbeck Square. Bubbe relaxed on a bench. Biting into some challah bread, I lost my balance, and it fell to the ground. A ruby red bird flew by, swooping down to steal the sweet dough away.

"Look at that, do you think that cardinal will fly away with our sins?" Zeyde asked. "I've never seen one dive to get bread like that. Or maybe it's a sign foretelling a song and dance we'll never forget." Zeyde slid his feet on the ground like Michael Jackson's moonwalk and spun in a circle.

"The birdie's prediction has just come true," I said, laughing and handing Zeyde the bag he had dropped.

"Did you know that unlike other birds, the males sing as well as the females?" Zeyde dipped his hand in the sack and handed me some more bread.

"No, I thought women always sang better—la, la, laaaaa," I sang while I cracked an operatic voice.

"I meant that the male birds don't usually sing, smarty pants," Zeyde tossed a piece of bread at me.

I found a smooth flat rock and bounced it across the water. "Whenever I used to get out of sorts, Mom would take me down to the river by town, and we'd skip rocks. She told me that you two used to have contests for hours sliding the rocks across this pond. She said that it was the best way to get rid of evil spirits."

"Evil spirits? She must have gotten that from *Rosh Hashanah*." Zeyde winked at Bubbe, who was resting on a bench beside us.

"What's that thing?" I asked Zeyde, pointing to an object hanging out of Bubbe's pocketbook.

"It's a *Shofar*—a horn. You blow it to bring on the New Year. It's not as large as the one at the synagogue, but it will do," he said.

"That's not for a few months."

"*Rosh Hashanah* is the Jewish New Year—the first of the high holidays in the Torah."

Bubbe handed him the horn. He lifted the instrument to his mouth and puffed out a loud scratchy noise. I covered my ears.

"It's beautiful once you get used to it. There is a feel to it. You've got to understand it." Zeyde said as he held it before me.

"Can I try?" There was no doubt in my mind that I would have better success when I took it and ran my hand across the smooth texture. "Is it made from a shell?"

"A ram's horn," Zeyde replied.

The elegant device reminded me of one of those sculptures at this cool contemporary museum Mom used to take me to. She used to show me lots of fun artsy places.

I puckered my lips and let out some air. Nothing happened. Zeyde gave a sly look. I used all my might to blow again. No way did I want Zeyde to get the best of me so I struggled until I felt my cheeks burn. I scrunched my face toward Zeyde and then I plopped myself down beside Bubbe.

"Enough is enough. We're going to be late." Bubbe nudged us along. With a huge grin, Zeyde raised his eyebrows. My head shook as I tried not to crack a smile.

***

We entered the Jewish chapel as services started. Rabbi Silverstein was launching the sermon. His voice was monotone except when he cleared his throat. While I was nodding off, Bubbe elbowed me in my side.

"It's Rabbi Goodblatt—you'll like this part."

Opening my eyes, I was still a bit woozy when Goodblatt's chipper voice said something about Jews wiping the slate clean and having a fresh beginning.

"It is the day, where you can put your pride aside and forgive everyone and everything. Brothers and sisters can excuse and forget arguments. It is a time when foes become friends."

Goodblatt went on and on and on and on. As I looked around the sanctuary, I considered making a run for it. Maybe, I could excuse Roni, but I could never forgive those punks for what they did. They tried to kill me and destroy this synagogue. No way, should they be excused? Those goons demolished my grandparents' bakery and bloodied my head with a rolling pin and shot me. Never in a million years would those slime buggers ever be my friends.

"One must pray for their aggressors to change their ways," Goodblatt continued.

They needed to go to jail and stay there forever. Goodblatt said that himself. This made no sense. My brain felt like it was going to explode.

No way did I want to stay after services. Talking to these people was like running into a locked door. But, Bubbe insisted that we stay and chat, pulling me over to the apples and honey. Fine, if I was going to be forced to sustain these bruising concepts, then I was going to confront the Rabbi face to face. I couldn't believe that Goodblatt didn't grasp the aggravated stress we had to endure in order to be freed from the torture those scumbags inflicted. I marched over to him.

"What about people who are immoral and wicked? Those punks wanted to obliterate this community," I said with vehemence. "Look at *Hashem*. He destroyed the Egyptians because they were cruel and evil to the Jews. He didn't forgive them."

Goodblatt nodded his head. "I understand what you are saying, but if you examine what happened, *Hashem* gave the Egyptians many chances before He laid down the law. Remember, *Hashem* kept on sending plagues every time the pharaoh went back on his word. It wasn't until Pharaoh's soldiers chased Moses and his people across the Red Sea, which had been parted for their escape, that *Hashem* drew the line. When the Hebrews finished crossing, *Hashem* allowed the chasm to refill, in order to protect the Jews from their attackers. The Jews never once raised their arms in hate. The Pharaoh brought about his own destruction."

"So what you're saying is that we should forgive everyone, even though they are despicable, like the punks, because God will take care of everything?"

"Well, it is good to avoid unpleasantness in a way that will protect your well-being. And, that is what we did. We distanced ourselves from evil. But, sometimes our emotions overrule our logic and what we feel is horrific might need a second look."

"What do you mean?" I was perplexed.

"Think about your own life. You've done things that you regret, am I right?"

"Well, yeah, I guess." The heat of Goodblatt's stare made me rephrase my statement. "Okay, sure. Everyone has."

"Maybe you have had arguments with your mother or father or grandparents or even a friend, like Tutti?"

I nodded, remembering when I didn't speak to Tutti for a whole week.

"You forgave each other...right?"

"Yeah."

Then I remembered my mom.

"What if you never got a chance to work things out?" I asked. A knot tightened in my throat.

"It can be something that you will always regret." He softened his voice. "But it is also something you can learn from."

That made sense, but then I thought of that egotistical maniac Crow.

"But, what about those barbarians? They threatened every shop owner in this town. Forgiving them seems ludicrous."

"The point is, that when people do something that hurts your feelings or is really despicable, that doesn't necessarily mean they are horrible people."

"You can't tell me those punks weren't horrendous despicable products of scum? And, what about Hitler? He wasn't a heinous, appalling, sickening beast?"

"When it comes to Hitler, the evil pharaohs, and Crow's gang, it is difficult to understand, but *Hashem* has his reasons. There are many debates on these issues, and I don't have the answer. But, in most instances it is the action that is harmful, not the person. Your parents and Tutti are not wicked animals are they?"

"No." What else could I say?

"Most people just need to be given a chance to learn and grow from their mistakes. Violence spurs anger, and nothing is accomplished." Goodblatt leaned towards me. "If you are kicked, it is natural to hit back. Then the attacker wants revenge, and a fight begins. But, what does the aggressor do when he punches someone and instead of battling back the person avoids his contact and moves away?"

"If they are anything like those punks, they keep on coming at you. Look at what they did to the synagogue."

"Exactly, they kept on attacking and got themselves locked up."

I said nothing.

"Remember when we talked about Moses?"

I nodded.

"Eventually, the *punks* dug their own hole, and retreated back into it."

I just stared at the Rabbi.

He paused and then grinned with a sigh. "Okay, let's look at this differently. You have learned about Noah's Ark, am I right?"

I nodded.

"Which was the chosen bird to find land?"

"The dove."

"Right. The dove is the most inoffensive of birds. Though attacked by other birds, the dove never attacks in return. That's why the dove was chosen by *Hashem*."

"That's a tale. This is reality."

"The story comes from truth. *Hashem* created good in everything. Therefore, anything that is bad is good, but there has to be balance. Remember *yetzer re, yetzer tov*. It is how you look at it and what you see into it. A whole nation, Israel, reveals its essence by announcing to the world that a dove is its symbol. It is a country that opens its arms to peace and serenity."

"What if someone has to fight in order to defend herself? Like what happened when that gang ransacked downstairs?"

"Protecting yourself is different from attacking another. In history the Hebrews avoided their attackers, preferring never to evoke war. This is what made them a strong community," Goodblatt explained.

"Yes, but they were being threatened by another race. What happens when your own people batter and harass you?" I questioned with fervor. "This neighborhood is mostly Jewish. These guys were Jewish. You knew who they were. They attacked their own people. Do you forgive them and let them get away with it? What if it happens again?"

"Nobody gets away with anything. *Hashem* balances the world in his own time and way. He has His reasons and we have to accept them." Goodblatt's eyes met with mine. "The actions of those punks were callous and nasty. They needed to be stopped. That's why we have a police force."

"But since I've been here and I don't know how long before, the evil behavior of these lunatics was despicable. The cops weren't doing anything. As a matter of fact, nobody did anything until I got here."

"Maybe, *Hashem* brought you here for that very reason. Sometimes it takes more time than we prefer, but there is a purpose. *Hashem* works in mysterious ways." Goodblatt placed his palm under my chin. "Your mom was a caring soul and a true believer in balance. *Rosh Hashanah* is a time to correct the imbalance, and I know your mom used to cherish this holiday."

I contemplated Goodblatt's words. His eyes met mine.

He said, "*Shalom.*"

And, I said, "*Shalom.*"

CHAPTER XXV

Thank You, Hashem

A few months had passed, and I was disappointed Christmas was crossed off the calendar. *Chanukah* sort of replaced it. Bubbe lit candles for eight days and said prayers, giving me little gifts for eight days. It was more religious though. Christmas was more like a fairy tale and Dad dressed like Santa Clause. Then it was my birthday, and Bubbe and Zeyde explained that I would have no party because they were still mourning for my parents.

"We'll celebrate after the New Year when you have your *bat mitzvah*."

"Aren't I supposed to have a *bat mitzvah* on my birthday?"

"We decided to celebrate your *bat mitzvah* after we finished mourning your parents, which ends after a year has passed."

"Does that mean we shouldn't party on New Year's Eve?"

Mom and Dad used to drink champagne and we'd dance all night long while we watched New Yorkers reveling in Time Square.

"Your mom was everything to us. It is our tradition that we pay respect to your parents and the joy their life has given us for a full year, giving us the time to adjust."

"I thought I was supposed to have my *bat mitvah* when I was thirteen," I asked.

"Twelve, thirteen, or whenever deemed appropriate." My grandparents agreed.

"Why did you choose to have it after New Years?"

"Because we wanted to finish paying the respect to your parents that they deserved, and having a huge celebration for you was something we know your parents would have wanted."

I didn't want to haggle with my grandparents, but I was excited that the Jewish community was going to think of me as a woman and I'd have more responsibilities. I knew my parents would be watching from wherever they were and I wanted to make them proud.

***

"Where are you going? There's plenty of time," Bubbe said, holding a platter of sunny side up eggs, a buttered blueberry bagel, and some hash browns.

"Gotta go—I told Goodblatt I'd meet him at *shul* early. I'll see you there."

I didn't wait for an answer. There was a slight wobble as I tried walking in my high-heeled shoes. They were my first pair. My mom had given them to me a while back. I wondered if she could see me from heaven or wherever she was. They were a little roomy, but it was the perfect occasion. Plus, they matched my favorite party dress. I threw on my down jacket, switched into furry boots, placed my heels into my bag, and was out the door.

While passing through the square, I halted to view the glimmer that glistened above the pond. I absorbed the chill, breathing in the air. A flat rock lay by my foot. No ice covered the water yet, so I scooped the stone in my hand, twisted my wrist, and skipped it across the water. It bounced three times, making small waves.

As I gazed, a reflection of my mom and dad dressed in outfits I had created for their last anniversary, appeared in my mind. My father was wearing a white tuxedo shirt with a bright rainbow design, and down the center it read DAD in pearl blue puffy paints. My mom spun around in a matching dress. Down the center was written MOM. There was no doubt that my parents would have chosen these outfits to wear to my *bat mitzvah*.

Allowing my imagination to fly, excitement filled my body. My mind drifted some more. My mom was wearing her pilot's helmet. She used to take me to the fields. We'd put on our helmets and pretend to travel to a fantastic world of imaginary bliss.

"Mom, I don't know where my goggles are." Thank *Hashem* nobody was in the park. They would have thought I was crazy.

I envisioned my mom pointing to her head.

"I know, Mom. Our minds take us where we want to go." She always used to tell me that.

Mom raised her high-powered Canon camera. My heart filled with soothing warmth as I watched Mom take Dad's hand. The shadow of a pine tree framed them.

"Here, take our picture. It's yours forever." I heard Mom say as she lifted her graceful arm. "Don't let Bubbe sell it or give it away."

Where was my mom's camera? I'd ask Bubbe after the ceremony.

"Oh no." Having lost track of time, I rushed to the synagogue and ran to Goodblatt's office.

"It's too late for last-minute studying, but no matter. Everything you need is right up here," He pointed to the middle of my forehead. "Here, wear this."

Goodblatt gave me the most beautiful *yarmulke* I had ever seen. Colorful angels floated around it.

"You know that *yarmulke* I wear on special occasions—the one I wore to your parents' *shiva*?"

I nodded.

"Well, when your mother moved away and offered it as a gift, she also gave me this and said that if she wasn't around, she wanted someone I loved to know about our special friendship. I want to give it to you."

"It's beautiful. Thank you." I was about to place the gift on top of my head but stopped. "Aren't *yarmulkes* just for boys?"

"No, they are worn out of respect for *Hashem*—for anyone."

"And I can wear it today up on the podium?"

"It would be an honor. Now hurry up and go take your seat."

Goodblatt handed me some clips for the *yarmulke*, I switched into my dressy shoes and, carefully, hurried down the stairs to the sanctuary. Bubbe and Zeyde had already arrived and were sitting in the front row. They slid over in order to give me room. I nuzzled close to my grandparents as they pressed their palms against mine.

Rabbi Goodblatt called me to the pulpit.

"Alexia has recently had her thirteenth birthday, a day when she is considered a woman. Much has transpired in the past year, and I know her parents would be proud."

Goodblatt talked about my parents and grandparents, and then said that it was destiny that my portion of the *Torah* was called *Vayeshev*, a section that emphasized the importance of family.

I carefully climbed the stairs that lead to the podium keeping my back straight and my head balanced. Even though I had my *yarmulke* clipped, I wanted to make sure it didn't go cockeyed. Plus, I couldn't let my ankle twist. Taking a nosedive in front of the whole congregation wasn't befitting of a girl about to become a woman.

I introduced myself and read my portion of the *Torah*, explaining that this special segment was about the sale of Joseph and the hardships he endured.

"My brothers didn't sell me. I don't even have brothers. But like Joseph, when I arrived here, I felt as though a pit of snakes and scorpions were threatening to eat me up alive. My question to Rabbi Goodblatt was why did I have to suffer so much? Why did my parents leave me?"

As I peeked at my grandparents I noticed Bubbe wiping her eyes with Zeyde's handkerchief. Then I realized that everyone's eyes were set on me.

Mom, I said in my mind, *you've got to know I never meant any harm to you. I've always been in awe of your talent and grace. You and Dad were the most incredible people that I ever knew.*

Though pride and honor streamed through my body, the softness of a teardrop dampened my cheek.

"Rabbi Goodblatt, Bubbe, Zeyde and everyone have shown me that my parents never left me. In fact, they gave me a brand new beginning."

I continued. A breeze kissed my face. My eyes followed across the rows of congregants. As I sang my *Torah* portion, my heart pattered. There was Bill Sanchez and his cousin Bob...José. Bill had a huge bag from Paulie's and was trying to get my attention with a thumbs-up. He must've been referring to that deal with the company producing Timmy. Master Luna was in the congregation and his presence was as bright as sunshine at noon. I couldn't wait to show him *Turn a Cheek*. There was Roni with her clique of girlfriends. She was still wearing her new earrings. Next to her sat

David, with a big smile on his face and a present in his lap. The redheaded boy Tutti'd thought was cute at *shiva* sat next to David, and then at the end of the row sat my best friend, Tutti. She waved her fingers as I finished.

Could you imagine if I told her what happened this year? Her red hair would turn purple and she'd spin til her pigtails stood up—not really—but she'd go haywire. Goodblatt wouldn't mind. She was my best friend.

As Goodblatt bumped beside me in fun and congratulated me, he took control of the pulpit. I chuckled and then listened. He spoke of the endearing creativity my mother evoked, and the brilliance my parents extended throughout their communities. Then he ended the ceremony.

I noticed the sunlight glowing through a stained glass window. Picturing the violets, dandelions, and roses flowering in our garden by our meadow, I imagined my parents sitting on my mom's cardboard furniture eating spaghetti and meatballs and my dad's flying fertilizing machine nourishing the grass. They lifted glasses of wine in a toast.

Love is not love, which alters when it alteration finds, or bends with the remover to remove. O no! It is an ever-fixed mark that looks on tempests and is never shaken. I imagined my mom reciting her favorite Shakespearean sonnet.

I heard clapping and saw Bubbe and Zeyde rise to their feet, cheering. Above them I envisioned my parents holding hands in their tuxedo attire beside the stained glass window. All four beamed brighter than I had ever seen.

Taking a moment to close my moist eyes, I knew my family would always be with me.

Thank you, *Hashem*.

THE END

JEWISH NINJA GLOSSARY

Because these words are translated from other languages with varying alphabets, spelling alters with interpretation. I have done my best to clarify the various words and phrases.

Hebrew and Yiddish are two different languages spoken by the Jewish people. The main difference between the two languages is that Hebrew is the official language of the people residing in Israel, whereas, Yiddish is the second most prominent language spoken by the Jewish people in different parts of the world

PHRASES

A bisseleh chain iz shoin nit gemain - Yiddish - A little charm and you are not ordinary.

A klug - Yiddish - Darn it.

A klug tzu mir! - Yiddish - Woe is me

A magaifeh zol dich trefen - Yiddish - A plague should befall upon you.

A shod - Yiddish - A devil or demon.

A shreklekheh zakh - Yiddish - A terrible thing.

Bon Appétit - French - The translation from french is *bon* which means good, and *appétit* is translated as appetite. Good Appetite.

Er drait zich vi a fortz in rossel - Yiddish - He's going in circles.

Er kricht oyf di gleicheh vent - Yiddish - Literally he climbs up straight walls, however, it refers to a troublemaker.

Gloib mir - Hebrew or Yiddish - Believe me!

Gooteh neshumeh - Hebrew or Yiddish - Soul, spirit; divine element in man, a person who cannot hate; also refers to a child.

Gornisht helfen - Yiddish – Nothing.

Got in himmel - Yiddish - God in heaven! Said in agony, fear, frustration, grief.

Got zol ophiten - Yiddish - God forbid!

Groisser gornicht - Yiddish - Big good for nothing.

Harts vatik - Yiddish - Heart ache.

Meshuguner mamzers - Yiddish - Crazy bastard!

Oi, a shkandal - Yiddish - Oi is taken from oy, an exclamation of chagrin, dismay, exasperation or pain. *Shkandal* is a scandal which is an action that is regarded as morally wrong and causes social resentment and disapproval.

Okh un vay - Yiddish - One of the expressions, like *oy, oy fey*, and *oy vey*, spoken in chagrin and to be conveyed as "woe is me" or "alas."

Oybershter in himmel - Yiddish - God in heaven or literally "The one above in heaven."

Oy feh - Yiddish - Similar to *"oy," "oi," "oy fey,"* and *"oy vey,"* and means disappointment or displeasure.

Oy gevalt - Yiddish - Is an expression and similar to *"oy," "oi," "oy feh,"* and *"oy vey,"* meaning dismay. *Gevalt* is translated as "force" or "violence." However, it is used as having the sense of expressing, "Oh my God!" or "Good Grief!" and is spoken when something that is unfortunate or unlucky happens.

Oy vey - Yiddish - Similar to *"oy," "oi," "oy fey,"* etc..., meaning disappointment or displeasure.

Oy vey gevalt - Yiddish - *Oy vey gevalt*, I think there are enough yiddish *oy* expressions to drive anyone receiving them batty. This one tops them all. Oh my God, I can't take this anymore, this is too much.

Shaineh maidel - Yiddish - A pretty girl. *Shana, shaina* is pretty and *maidel* is a young girl.

Shana punim - Yiddish - A lovely face. *Shana, shaina* is pretty and *punim* is face.

Sheppen nokhes - Yiddish - To enjoy or gather pleasure, especially from children.

Shreklecheh zakh - Yiddish - A terrible thing.

Tsegait zich in moyl - Yiddish - Literally it means melt in the mouth. Like in English it means delicious.

Vos iz mit dir - Yiddish - What is wrong with you?

Yeong-Wonan Phong Ahn - Korean - Name of Black Belt Form.

WORDS

Adar - Hebrew or Yiddish - Exalted, adar, connected to the word strength, is the twelfth month of the Jewish calendar and is the month of good fortune.

Adonoi - Yiddish or Hebrew - Traditionally in Judaism this means master or lord and refers to God. The word *Adonoi* is used during prayer whereas the word *Hashem* is used at other times. The reasoning comes from the reluctance to pronounce the name anyplace other than the temple in Jerusalem in respect for *Hashem*. *Yahweh*, is meant as the true name as opposed to a pronoun, and is not meant to be spoken because of its purity.

Ainikel - Yiddish - Grandchild.

Aleph - Hebrew - In Hebrew this is similar to the first letter in the alphabet, A. It can represent a glottal stop or take the sound of the vowel that is next to it.

Anochi - Hebrew or Yiddish - The opening word in the ten commandments is "*Anochi*," meaning I am and continues to say, "the Lord your God." Being the first word of the First Commandment itself, *Anochi* encompasses the entire Torah and refers to God's very essence.

Bar Mitzvah - Hebrew or Yiddish - Along with bat *mitzvah*, this is a coming of age ritual. Literally, *bar* means son and the translation of *mitzvah* is a commandment of law, which in more modern terms means a good deed. In the Jewish religion, at the age of thirteen, a boy becomes a man, thus accountable for his actions. A huge celebration ensues to mark this monumental event.

Bat (Bas) Mitzvah - Hebrew or Yiddish - Literally *bat (bas)* means daughter and mitzvah (mitzveh) is a commandment of law. However, *mitzveh* is commonly used to mean a good deed. This is similar to a *bar mitzvah*, but refers to a girl becoming a woman. At the age between twelve and thirteen, a girl becomes a woman and is required to fulfil certain *mitzvehs*. There is a big celebration with friends and family.

Bobkes - Yiddish - Literally excretion of sheep or goat, but used when someone is worthless, inferior, has nothing to offer.

Bon Appetit - French - Bon is translated as good and appetité is appetite. Good appetite. In this book it is the name of a magazine Bubbe is reading that is based on food and recipes.

Bubbe - Hebrew or Yiddish - Grandmother: many Jewish children call their grandmothers Bubbe. Though this is a Hebrew word, Bubbe is not italicized in the story because it is a proper name.

Bubeleh - Yiddish - Term of endearment, darling.

Challah - Hebrew or Yiddish - A rich sweet doughy egg bread that is twisted or braided and is eaten on *Sabbath* and holidays.

Chanukah - Hebrew or Yiddish - This is a Jewish holiday celebrating the successful rebellion of the Maccabees when they rebelled against Antiochus IV Epiphanes. According to the Talmud, a late text, the Temple was purified and the wicks of the *menorah* (nine branched candelabra used to celebrate *Chanukah*) miraculously burned for eight days, even though there was only enough sacred oil for one day's lighting which is why the use of the *menorah* to light candles is part of the *Chanukah* tradition. This holiday begins on the 25th day of *Kislev* according to the Hebrew calendar, which may occur any time during late November to late December, and is observed for eight nights and days and is also known as the Festival of Lights or the Feast of Dedication.

Charoset - Hebrew or Yiddish - *Charoset, haroset,* or *charoses* is a sweet, dark-colored, paste made of fruits and nuts eaten during the Passover Seder. Its color and texture are meant to represent mortar (or mud used to make adobe bricks) which the Israelites used when they were enslaved in Egypt. *Charoset* comes from the word clay and after reciting the blessing it tastes great spreading it on some *matzah.*

Chatchkas - Yiddish - A trinket or something decorative to put around the house. Knick knacks.

Chei - Yiddish - Hebrew - Life.

Chutzpah - Hebrew or Yiddish - Nerve, audacity, gall, cheekiness. Used more to intonate humor rather than anger.

Dobohk - Korean - *Gi* - Japanese - *Do bohk* (*Do* - translated as way of life) (*Bohk* is translated as training clothes). This is the uniform worn in the *dojang* (gym or studio) by the practitioners of the korean martial arts. The *do bohk* was designed to replicate the *gi.*

Dojang - Korean - Like the term *dojo*, *dojang* is a term used in Korean martial arts that refers to a formal training hall used to conduct training, examinations and other related encounters.

Dojo - Japanese - This is a Western concept and literally means a "place of the way." Initially, *dojos* were adjunct to temples. The term can refer to a formal training place for any of the Japanese *do* arts but typically it is considered the formal gathering place for students of any Japanese style such as karate, judo, or samurai, to conduct training, examinations and other related encounters.

Drek - Hebrew or Yiddish - Human dung, poop, manure or excrement; inferior merchandise or work; insincere talk or excessive flattery.

Elohim - Hebrew or Yiddish - God, usually used in prayer.

Fardeiget - Yiddish - Distressed, worried, anxiety ridden, anguish, misery.

Gi - Japanese - *Dobohk* - Korean - *Do* is translated as way of life. *Bohk* is translated as training clothes. This is the uniform worn in the *dojang* by the practitioners of the korean martial arts. The *dobohk* was designed to replicate the *gi*.

Grogger - Yiddish - Noisemaker or instrument derived from the Judaic holiday of Purim.

Groise - Yiddish – Big.

The Haggadah – Hebrew or Yiddish – This is a Jewish book that guides the Passover Seder. It tells the story of the Jewish liberation from slavery in Egypt as described in the book of Exodus in the Torah.

Halal – Hebrew – A shortened version of *Halleluiah* described below. It means splendid, emitting light or shining.

Halleluiah - Hebrew or Yiddish - Praise be to God.

Hamantoshen - Hebrew or Yiddish - This is a filled-pocket cookie or pastry in Ashkenazi Jewish cuisine recognizable for its three-cornered shape. The shape is achieved by folding in the sides of a circular piece of dough, with a filling placed in the center. It is traditionally eaten during the Jewish holiday of Purim. *Hamantoshen* are made with many different fillings, including poppy seed (the oldest and most traditional), prunes, nut, date, apricot, apple, fruit preserves, cherry, chocolate, cheese. and other sweet delectables.

Hashem - Hebrew or Yiddish - Name of God. *Hashem* is used in the general sense when talking about God. However, see *Adanoi* and *Yahweh* which also refer to God.

Hassidic - Hebrew or Yiddish - Hasidic Judaism comes from the word piety and is a branch of Orthodox Judaism that promotes spirituality through the popularization and internalization of Jewish mysticism as a fundamental aspect of faith. It was founded in 18th-century Eastern Europe by Rabbi Israel Baal Shem Tovas.

Hekdish - Yiddish - Slumhouse or poorhouse. A mess.

Hora - Yiddish - Romanian - Hora is a traditional Romanian folk dance where the dancers hold each other's hands and the circle spins, usually counterclockwise, as each participant follows a sequence of three steps forward and one step back. It is a popular dance during Shabbat and other holiday celebrations during Jewish holidays.

Hyung - Korean - Can mean big brother but in the martial arts such as *Tae Kwon Do* and *Tang Soo Do* it means "form" or "pattern." It is a sequence of martial arts techniques and can be performed with or without a weapon.

Judaism - Hebrew or Yiddish - Judaism is a monotheistic religion and is the philosophy and way of life that Jewish people follow. The *Torah* is the foundation and part of the *Tanakh* or Hebrew Bible.

Kalamutneh - Yiddish - Dreary, gloomy, troubled.

Kasha - Hebrew - Yiddish - English - Grits or wholegrain buckwheat, mushed cereal, porridge; can also mean a messed up confusion. It is popular to mix kasha with pasta shaped in bow ties.

Kata - Japanese - In the martial arts, katas are choreographed patterns of combative movements. Katas were used in training methods so that fighting techniques would be preserved and passed on. By practicing in a repetitive manner the student develops the instinct to use these techniques in varying circumstances.

Kepis - Yiddish - Head, another word for *yarmulke*.

Kinderlekh - Yiddish - Term of endearment.

Kiyap - Korean - A loud yell to emphasize a movement in the martial arts.

Klug - Yiddish - Smart or clever.

Klutz - Yiddish – Clumsy.

Knish - Hebrew or Yiddish -A knish is an Eastern European snack food that consists of a dough that is either baked, grilled or fried and usually has a filling of either mashed potatoes, ground meat, sauerkraut, onions, *kasha*, or cheese though there are other varieties.

Kopvaitik - Yiddish - Headache.

Koved - Yiddish - Respect, honor, reverence, esteem.

Knishes - Hebrew or Yiddish - Made popular in North America by Eastern European immigrants mainly in Poland, this snack food is a popular Jewish delight. A filling of either mashed potatoes, ground meat, sauerkraut, onions, kasha, or cheese is covered with dough and baked, grilled or deep fried.

Kugle - Hebrew or Yiddish - A noodle and bread pudding that is frequently sweetened with raisens.

Kvelled - Hebrew - Glow with pride or beam with delight.

Kvetching - Yiddish - Complaining.

Latke - Hebrew or Yiddish - A potato pancake.

Lebedicken - Hebrew or Yiddish - A lively person.

Levayah - Hebrew or Yiddish – Funeral.

Matzah - Hebrew or Yiddish -*Matzo, Matza or matzah* is an unleavened bread traditionally eaten by Jewish people during Passover (*Pesach*).

Matzah ball - Hebrew or Yiddish - Jewish dumpling usually found in chicken soup made from a mixture of *matzah* meal. *Matzah* is unleavened bread that looks like a big square cracker, and the meal is when it is crumbled up. *Matzah* is a traditional food used on Passover. *Matzah* meal is made by finely grinding *matzah* crackers into a breadcrumb-like consistency. Combined with ingredients it is rolled into a ball and makes the delicious *matzah balls*.

Megillah - Hebrew or Yiddish - The book of Esther that tells the story of Purim.

Mekheieh - Yiddish - A great pleasure. Something that is amazingly delicious, wonderful, and incredible.

Mensch - Yiddish - A special person that deserves worth and dignity.

Meshugener - Yiddish - Mad, crazy, insane man. It can also refer to someone who is eccentric.

Mitzveh - Hebrew or Yiddish - Literally this is translated as a commandment, but is usually meant as a good deed. According to Orthodox Judaic belief there are 613 *mitzvehs* that Moses handed down. 365 were prohibitions and 248 were positive commands or *mitzvehs*.

Motek - Hebrew - Sweetheart or sweetie.

Mazel tov - Hebrew or Yiddish - A Jewish phrase used to convey congratulations.

Neshomelah - Yiddish - Sweetheart, sweet soul.

Nudnik - Yiddish - A nagging, irritating, pestering, annoying person.

Oisvurf - Yiddish - Bad person, outcast, layabout, ne'er-do-well.

Ongehblozzen - Yiddish - Self-centered, bad-tempered, grumpy, and pouty.

Oy - Yiddish - An exclamation of chagrin, dissatisfaction, dismay, exasperation, irritation, or pain. Similar to *"oi," "oy feh," "oy vey"* and *"oy gevalt."*

Parekh - Yiddish - Medically speaking it is a disease of the scalp caused by fungus triggering the loss of hair and the formation of lesions. When many Jews were afflicted with this illness, folklore developed and "parekh or "parkh" came to connote "wicked man," "filthy person," "stingy person," or "a rat." So this word can mean the disease, a person who has the disease, or a person that is held in complete contempt.

Parsha - Hebrew or Yiddish - The translation is "portion," and formally means a section of a biblical book in the Hebrew Bible. Each week a new *parsha* is discussed and studied from the Bible.

Pesach - Hebrew or Yiddish - Passover in English. This is an important Jewish holiday derived from the celebration of their liberation over 3,300 years ago by God from slavery in ancient Egypt. They escaped from the rulers of ancient Egypt called Pharaohs. Under the leadership of Moses, this became the birth of their nation and honors the Exodus described in the Hebrew Bible where the Jewish people were freed from slavery.

Punim - Yiddish - Face - Often referring to a little girl's pretty face.

Purim - Hebrew - This is a Jewish holiday that commemorates the recordings in The Book of Esther (called *Megillah*) where a plot by the Persian Empire (ruled by Haman) to destroy the Jewish people was thwarted by a plan developed by Mordechai, and Esther who had risen to become Queen of Persia. The day of deliverance became a day of feasting and rejoicing. It is a day of happiness where the Jews send food and drink to one another and donate to charity while the kids dress up in costumes and they celebrate. The book of Esther is read.

Rosh Hashanah – Hebrew or Yiddish - The Jewish New Year celebrating the anniversary of the creation of Adam and Eve and their first actions towards the realization of the human role in God's world. The sound of the shofar and eating apples dipped in honey symbolize the sweet robust New Year.

Rugellah - Hebrew or Yiddish - Traditionally this Jewish pastry was made in the form of a crescent by rolling a triangle of dough around a filling and can be translated to something like a twist. Chocolate, raspberry, apricot and other fillings make it a sweet pastry, sometimes referred to as a cookie. It is similar to *shnecken* but its dough is made with cream cheese, while rugellah is made with sour cream. Also, *shnecken* is rolled and sliced, whereas rugellah is formed from a triangle of dough.

Sabbath - Hebrew or Yiddish - The Jewish people celebrate their week with a day of rest or a time of worship. *Sabbath* begins on Friday at sundown with the lighting of two candles and ends Saturday at sundown. See *Shabbat*.

Schmucks - Yiddish - Literally this means penis, but is used in a pejorative sense to refer to someone as being a horrible, deplorable and obnoxious person. Because of its vulgarity, "schmo" is a term that might be considered less crude.

Schmulky - Yiddish - A sad sack!

Schnozzle - Yiddish - A nose.

Shctick - Yiddish - A gimmick or attention getting thatrical device or routine.

Sensai - Japanese - Literally *Sensai* is translated as "person born before another." It is used as a title to address teachers, professors, and professionals of authority such as lawyers or doctors and to show respect to someone who has achieved a certain level of mastery, in the martial arts.

Shabbat - Hebrew - This is the Jewish day of rest and seventh day of the week when religious Jews remember the Biblical creation of heaven and earth which occurred in six days, the exodus of the Hebrews and look forward to a future Messianic Age. It is a holiday observed every week. Observance falls between sunset on Friday evening with the lighting of candles, until either the sundown the next night on Saturday or the appearance of three stars in the sky. According to Jewish tradition, the Messianic Era will be one of global peace and harmony, an era free of strife and hardship, and one conducive to furthering the knowledge of the Creator. The theme of the Jewish Messiah is the ushering of global peace.

Shalom - Hebrew or Yiddish - This word can be translated as "peace," or wishing someone completeness, or prosperity. It can also be used idiomatically to mean both hello and goodbye.

Shiva - Yiddish or Hebrew - Mourning period of seven days observed by family and friends at a the home of the deceased or someone close to them.

Shmutsik - Yiddish - Anything that is worthless like a scummy rag.

Shnecken - Yiddish or Hebrew or German - In German this means snails and refers to the shape of the sweet bun. It is similar to *rugellah* but its dough is made with sour cream, while *rugellah* is made with cream cheese. Also, *shnecken* are rolled and sliced, whereas *rugellah* are formed from triangles of dough.

Shofar - A horn that is blown to celebrate the Jewish new year.

Shpilkes - Yiddish or Hebrew - Pins and needles.

Shul - Yiddish - Colloquial for synagogue or place of worship. It is said that this word stems from Germans who saw Jews studying in the synagogue, mistook the synagogue for a *shul*, which also means school. However, another view points *shul* as deriving from the Latin term *schola'*. Italian Jews use this term to represent community.

Tae Kwon Do - Korean -A form of martial arts emphasizing kicking and punching.

Tallit - Hebrew or Yiddish - A tallit is a Jewish prayer shawl and is worn over the outer clothes during services. It has special twined and knotted fringes known as *tzitzit* attached to its four corners. Most traditional tallits are made of wool. Often, children wear them for the first time on their *Bar Mitzvahs*.

Talmud - Hebrew - The root *lmd* means to teach or study and the *Talmud* itself is a central text of Rabbinic Judaism. The Talmud has two components. The first part is written, the *Mishnah* and the second is the *Gamara*, an explanations and clarifications along with related writings.

Torah - Hebrew or Yiddish - "Instruction" or "Teaching" is the focal point of the Jewish religion. There are many meanings: one being the first five books of the *Tenakh*. The *Torah* consists of the foundation narrative of the Jewish people, their beliefs, way of life and religious obligations along with their civil laws.

Tzitzit - Hebrew or Yiddish - The name for specially knotted ritual fringes worn by observant Jews. *Tzitzit* are attached to the four corners of the *tallit* (prayer shawl) and *tallit katan* which is an undergarment worn everyday.

Vayeshev - Hebrew - This is the ninth weekly portion or *parsha* of the *Torah* and emphasizes the importance of family. In Hebrew the translation is "and he lived."

Yahweh - Hebrew - Traditionally in Judaism this word is too holy to be spoken and is meant to be the only true name of God. The word *Adanoi* is used during prayer whereas the word *Hashem* is used at other times.

Yarmulke - Hebrew - Also, known as a *kippa*, this is the traditional Jewish skull cap and is usually worn at synagogue though more conservative Jewish people wear their *yarmulkes* throughout the day. It represents respect and honor for *Hashem* and His/Her work above and traditionally was worn by men.

Yetzer re/Yetzer tov - Hebrew - These terms refers to the inclination to do good or evil and are intertwined for *Hashem* created only good, so what is evil is good.

Yin/Yang - Chinese - In Chinese philosophy, the concept of *yin/yang* is used to describe how opposite forces are interconnected and interdependent in the world, as we know it; and how they relate to each other. For instance, light and dark, hot and cold, war and peace, are demonstrations of the concept of *yin/yang*. *Yin/yang* does not necessarily mean that forces are opposing. They can also compliment each other, forming a dynamic system in which the whole is greater than its parts. In other words everything has *yin/yang* aspects. Note: *Yin/yang* is similar to *yetzer re/yetzer tov*.

Yosher - Yiddish - Justice, fairness, integrity.

Yungatsh - Yiddish - Street-urchin, scamp, young rogue.

Zeligs - Yiddish - Blessings, or blessed.

Zeyde - Yiddish - Grandfather: many Jewish children call their grandfathers Zeyde. Though this is a Hebrew word, Zeyde, like Bubbe, is not italicized in the story because it is a proper name.

Ziskeit - Yiddish - Endearing term for a child, sweetness or sweet thing.

About the Author

ALLEGRA SAENS COLEMAN

Allegra Saens Coleman, like Alexia Bonet, the heroine of *The Jewish Ninja*, was drawn to the world of art and imagination at an early age. Her involvement in the creative realm never ceased, and in fourth grade she was awarded a special fine arts scholarship to attend The Moore College of Art. In middle school, she was chosen to narrate an ABC educational series for children. By the time she was a teenager she delved into poetry and acted in many productions at The Society Hill Playhouse. Her summers were joyfully consumed acting in productions with Villanova Summer Shakespeare from the age of fourteen to seventeen (1978–1982) while she became an icon in Philadelphia nightlife based on the aerial acrobatic dance routine she'd developed and performed from thirty-foot rafters at the most popular nightspot in Philadelphia called The London Victory Club.

After graduating from Friends Select in Philadelphia, she earned her BFA in drama from USC in LA. She then embarked on a career as an actress throughout the US and in Europe. When she returned to LA, she was accepted into the Magic Mirror Theater Co., a troupe that featured improvisational theater for children. While Magic Mirror traveled the LA School District performing, they also conducted seminars afterwards teaching the children about performance. After playing the lead in a film called *Philosophy*, she returned to Philadelphia for a holiday visit.

After her visit, however, she was forced to stay in Philadelphia because of a life-threatening brain tumor. While convalescing under the care of her parents, she found that writing relieved her precarious physical, mental, spiritual and emotional distress. It was ironic that while she was bedridden and weak, she discovered an inner voice that enabled her to express herself through the written word, with power that had not been previously realized.

While recovering she wrote a play entitled *Gorilla Dance*, for which she received The Florida State Grant for Emerging Playwrights, and her second play entitled *Fire of The Earth* was given an award from Stageworks Production that included a staged reading at the Tampa Theatre.

In addition to these writing successes, she pursued and received her JD from Temple University in June 1999. In July of 1999 she was offered a business opportunity to create and develop TPDS Club, and under her management, TPDS evolved into a highly successful event space.

Allegra married William T. Coleman III and was blessed with William IV (nicknamed B-4), born in 2003, and Amadeus, born in 2006. Diego, their Havanese puppy, became a part of the family during the 2011 holiday season. Despite the heavy demands of work and family, Allegra has always made time to pursue her writing interests, whether an article, poem, or *The Jewish Ninja*.

In 2010, Allegra was diagnosed with MS, causing her energy and ability to work on an employer's schedule impossible. Therefore, she and her partner, Dolores Browne, created DesignReasons. com, a high-end furniture, art, and accessories business on the Internet. Choosing the most innovative and eye-catching items was the concept for this site, enabling Allegra to fulfill her desire to express her individuality through artistry and creative thinking at her own pace.

In a very real and tangible way, the story of Alexia portrays Allegra's hope, faith and belief that though it is possible that she may not be physically able to shepherd her children's development at a time of severe importance, the foundation she has provided in conjunction with the pillars of family, cultural and religious support will mystically converge in a way that will enable her children to evolve to their full intellectual, spiritual, moral and physical potential and emerge into the understanding of their own self-identity.

20643821R00121